ACT OF
AGGRESSION

Also by John Bishop

ACT OF MURDER

ACT OF DECEPTION

ACT OF REVENGE

ACT OF NEGLIGENCE

ACT OF FATE

ACT OF ATONEMENT

ACT OF MERCY

ACT OF AVARICE

ACT OF AGGRESSION

A DOC BRADY MYSTERY

John Bishop, MD

MANTID PRESS

Act of Aggression

A Doc Brady Mystery

Copyright © 2024 by John Bishop. All rights reserved.
ISBN: 979-8-9906634-1-1 (paperback)
ISBN: 979-8-9906634-2-8 (ebook)
ISBN: 979-8-9906634-3-5 (hardback)
Published by Mantid Press

For information about this title, contact:
Attention: Permissions Department
legalquestions@codedenver.com

CONTENTS

CHAPTER 1

LA CAVA

"**D**r. Brady, I'm sorry to keep you waiting. What a hectic morning. It seems that many of the residents here as well as folks from outside the area have a strong interest in our new club. We are proud of our facilities as well as our new golf course. Do you have any questions prior to the tour?"

I wondered again what I was doing there. We were members at the Horseshoe Bay Golf Club, which was an outstanding facility with four eighteen-hole golf courses. What else could one possibly need? There were facilities at each course for breakfast and lunch, plus a massive new restaurant for evening events that also serviced all four courses for breakfast, lunch, and dinner, with outstanding Hill Country views at the top of the rock. The services at HBGC were over the top, incomparable in this part of Texas.

Some of my friends, however, had played the new La Cava Golf Club and raved about the artful layout with streams, waterfalls, lush zoysia grass fairways, and bentgrass greens. The clubhouse was under construction, but with enough completed to allow members to appreciate the beautiful limestone exteriors and vast decks with panoramic views of Hill Country and Lake LBJ.

I had been told that the club originally was to be called La Casa Golf Club, signifying a sort of home away from home. Then, when the dredging began, and the developer found old limestone caves on the property, the estimated cost of building the course skyrocketed. Golf course architects say it is much more expensive to move limestone around than it is to move plain old Texas soil. Thus, the joke became the name changed from La Casa, home, to La Cava, wine cellar, as in "I need a drink." The limestone was of high quality, so a great deal of it was sold off to pay for golf course construction, with the rest saved for the clubhouse and the two restrooms that were to be built on the course, one on the front nine and one on the back nine. Still, in spite of being able to put the limestone to good use, the cost of breaking it down, moving it, and hauling it away took the project off budget significantly, or so my golf buddies said.

"When do you expect the clubhouse to be completed?"

"Within the next twelve months, for sure. I have paperwork for you to review," she said, and went about copying documents on a high-speed printer in her office. Her name was Patricia Simmons, but she went by Patsy, according to her name tag. She was attractive and could probably sell ice to residents of the frozen north. She was close to six feet tall, with auburn hair, fair skin, and a shapely figure.

Her office was in a temporary building outside the future main entrance of La Cava. Most of us would call her building a trailer. She had called it a temporary building when I made the appointment for the tour. "Meet me at the temporary building outside the new entrance," she had said during our phone conversation. Perhaps the club did not allow the word "trailer" to be uttered on the premises, but "Airstream" was clearly engraved on the aluminum frame adjacent to the entry door.

My wife Mary Louise should have accompanied me for the tour. She was a golfer as well—not to the extent I was, but she played, and loved to dine out, and was a much better judge of how things worked in life than me. She was in Austin for the day for a board meeting. She did a great deal of charity work when we lived in Houston and had slowly resumed that passion over the last few years since we had moved to the lovely little town of Granite Falls.

I had been a high-profile and hard-working orthopedic surgeon in Houston for many years, but as is usual with jobs like that, burnout is always simmering just beneath the surface. I had given up my academic position and the stress of sixty- to seventy-hour work weeks, and moved out to this community west of Austin where I was now an orthopedic surgeon working a reasonable schedule, four days a week. Friday and Saturday were now golf days with my friends, and Sundays were couples golf days with my wife. I was a much happier man and was enjoying my practice and my patients again.

It did not hurt that I had been named a beneficiary in the will of a former grateful patient of mine, an old-time wildcatter who left me 100 acres in an oil-rich area of south Texas. His family was mostly horrified and immediately set about buying me out of the bequest. By the time the legal fees and taxes were settled, I received a nest egg of close to $20 million. That kind of money bought Mary Louise and I a great deal of security and allowed us to move to a beautiful home on Lake LBJ in the Hill Country and allowed me to have a much smaller practice and to play golf two or three days per week.

On the other hand, my schedule also allowed me to get into trouble, as illustrated by my investigation a while back into murders tied to Mourning Doves, a residential haven for abused and battered women, and most recently, my quest to discover the cause of the mysterious death of Sandy Lowell, whom I had met in a grocery store parking lot the day of his death.

"If you have no more questions, Doctor, let me give you a tour of the facilities. Have you played the course yet?"

"No, I was hoping to do that with my wife, Mary Louise. She wasn't able to make the appointment today. She's in Austin for the day on business. We would like to schedule a round of golf soon, if that's possible."

"Of course, not a problem. Shall we?"

Patsy handed me a white hard hat and donned one herself. We exited the Airstream, walked around to the future entrance of La Cava Golf Club, and stepped onto a plywood walkway into the building under construction.

"Are you going to be all right walking in those high heels? It looks like there's ample opportunity to sprain or break your ankle," I said.

"It's not a problem. I've become adept at dodging potholes. Besides, hiking boots really would not do much for this dress, do you think?" she said, turned, and gave me a come-hither look.

Patsy had a point there. She had on a bright-red leather skirt, with a white silk blouse and red heels. She was dressed for a cocktail party, and with that look she had given me, well, I felt the sudden need to burst out of there and run home safely to mama.

I stayed well behind her as she gave me the tour, far enough back that she had to yell her explanations of various dining areas and party rooms. We walked to what would be the grand patio when completed, and I had to admit that the views of the Hill Country were spectacular.

"Pretty special, huh?" Patsy stated.

"Yes. How many people will the outdoor deck hold when completed?"

"Around two hundred."

"Nice party space. I like that overhang they're building. Looks like it will be adequate to buffer the sun as well as the rain."

"Oh, absolutely. Our architect had specific instructions to design the outdoor space such that the elements could be avoided as much as possible. Let me walk you to the golf shop area, which is partially completed. Then I'll have to leave you. I have another appointment," she said, checking the time on her gold Rolex with a diamond bezel.

The check-in area of the La Cava golf shop was complete, but the large area where men's and women's golf clothes would be displayed was behind plastic sheeting and obviously not ready for unveiling. Patsy introduced me to Jason, the young pro staffing the most important area of the shop, which would be where credit cards are used by guests to pay for a round of golf.

"Will the club be fully private?" I asked.

"That is the developers' long-range plan. Of course, the club will need revenue right away, so we will be allowing guest play, both member-accompanied as well as play available to the general public on a daily-fee basis. Our accountants estimate that it will take at least two years for the club to become totally private. But it could be shorter."

"Or longer," I said, playing devil's advocate.

She gave me another look, this one not quite so friendly.

"Here is all the paperwork you'll need to complete to become eligible to join La Cava, Doctor. Please call me and I'll arrange a gratis practice round for you and Mrs. Brady. If you don't mind showing yourself out . . ." she said, then extended her hand, gave me a limp finger shake, and sashayed away.

I wandered around for a bit and found a great deal of empty space. I did discover the future men's and women's locker rooms. It was hard for me to tell how ornate they would be when completed, but the ceilings were high and there were huge windows in place with, again, outstanding Hill Country views.

I was very thirsty by then and stopped back in the pro shop and asked Jason where I could find a cold beverage. He directed me to a temporary dining facility one level down, adjacent to the starter area where the golf carts were parked. I found the facility easily. It was the only food truck on the property. I ordered a cola on ice and a ground beef taco. It has been my experience in life that you can tell a great deal about a restaurant from a taco. That may sound simplistic, but for me, the quality of the taco shell, the amount of lettuce, and the thickness and spiciness of the pico de gallo all enter into play in allowing me to decide whether I want to return to the eating establishment or not. The taco was out of sight. That was a good start for an upscale golf club with an Airstream trailer for a clubhouse and a food truck for a restaurant.

As I finished my impromptu meal, I heard raised voices. The food truck sat on a level piece of ground above the practice range, which was at a lower level, and reached most directly by a series of concrete steps. The voices were coming from a man and a woman, both well dressed and carrying a few golf clubs back from the practice range. They reached a high-end private golf cart with a Mercedes Benz hood ornament, put the clubs in their respective golf bags, and sat in the cart. I was sitting at a small table with an umbrella, on the other side of the food truck, out of their line of sight, which meant I could not see their faces.

"How in the world do you think you can get by with that? You don't think the principals are smart enough to figure out what you're doing?"

"I've worked my ass off, and I deserve compensation. I may have to cut some corners, and slightly falsify the records, but I WILL be paid what's owed me."

"Hon, you've been to jail. You know what that's like. And remember what you've told me about those federal institutions, those so-called prison country clubs."

"Yes, that's bullshit, those white-collar-crime units. I was knifed twice in the last one, up in Colorado. That's why I paid all that money to the forger to get new IDs and a name change. I'm clean as a whistle as far as anyone around here knows. New social security number, new driver's license, the works. You need to work on keeping a low profile and keeping your mouth shut. This will be my big score. We'll be on Easy Street from then on. You just wait and see."

I stood up and walked in the direction of the voices, taking care so as not to be seen. If the male speaker had been to prison and had been knifed twice, he probably wouldn't think twice about doing-in yours truly. By the time I reached the other side of the food truck, all I could see was the back of their heads. I did note the license plate on the golf cart, however. It read HIGHROLLER.

CHAPTER 2

DINNER

"**H**ow was the tour, husband?"

Mary Louise was back from her day trip to Austin. She had stopped at Trader Joe's on the way home and selected fresh shrimp, scallops, mussels, and calamari, and was in the process of making her version of Pontchartrain stew. I was busy mixing the Caesar salad, stirring in just the right amount of lemon, anchovy paste, and Parmesan cheese, as instructed by the chef.

"Interesting. Want more wine?"

"Love some. Rombauer chardonnay tonight?"

"Yep. It's perfect for what you're preparing there, which smells delicious, by the way."

Our dog Tip, an aging golden retriever, was standing at attention in the kitchen, and slobbering shamelessly. Seafood was not on his diet, but I prepared his kibble and added some diced chicken breast I had grilled the day before. He ate the entire bowl in seconds and was awaiting his post-prandial treat from the pantry, tail thumping.

"I didn't play the course. I'll call back and schedule a round for you and me. The clubhouse and facilities are not finished by any means, but the bones of construction look good. I want to get your take on the property before we move forward."

"You know, we have a perfectly good club with four golf courses. Do we really need to have another club?"

"La Cava would not come under the heading of 'need'; it'd be more like in the 'desperately want' category."

Mary Louise was a beauty. Tall, well-endowed in all the right places, and a natural blonde. I say that with some reservation, because lately I had noticed the trappings of hair follicular chemistry in her bathroom and wondered if perhaps the natural part of the blonde had faded somewhat. I was not the kind to inquire, however. Let sleeping dogs lie was my motto, along with Never ask your wife about her hair color, and Try to never answer the question, "Do I look fat in this outfit?"

"Did you play golf today?"

"No. I opted for the La Cava tour. It was abbreviated, so I could have played."

"Why do you say 'abbreviated'?"

"The woman who showed me around, Patsy Simmons, had another obligation, so she gave me the paperwork, showed me the golf shop and the future dining hall, and left me to wander alone. I went down to the staging area, and found their current dining and food service sector, which was a food truck. I had a great taco, though, so I predict the food long-term will be excellent. Something weird happened, though," and I relayed the conversation I overheard between the two people in the HIGHROLLER golf cart.

"Oh my. I wonder if they were discussing something to do with La Cava or another business venture."

"Not a clue, Mary Louise. I have a penchant for getting involved in matters that don't concern me, as you know, so best I just leave their problems to themselves, do you not agree?"

"I agree, Jim, but if they were discussing matters involving La Cava, I think we should steer clear of investing in that venture if there is any possibility of foul play."

"I totally agree."

"Dinner is ready. I have the table set outside on the terrace. Please take the wine and glasses and I'll bring out the food."

Our home was one of only four in a small cul-de-sac, gated for security. The lot was in a V-shape, narrow in the front but quite wide in the rear. We had a beautiful view of Lake LBJ as well as the Hill Country Resort and the marina. We were up the hill high enough to avoid the dreaded infestation of mosquitoes that permeated the lower levels of the lake area, especially in the warmer months. The mosquitoes thrived around the low-lying water but became less interested the higher up the hill they had to fly. I was no expert on mosquito habitation, but we were safer up high than those below.

We had a large terrace, and thanks to Mary Louise's artful planting of palm trees, yuccas, and oleanders, we could not see our neighbors on either side. We had our own private retreat, including a hot tub/spa near the primary-bedroom side of the house, which we used often for soothing our worn, tired muscles, especially those in the erogenous zones.

We toasted our glasses of Rombauer and enjoyed a wonderful meal of fresh seafood. The salad was a nice complement to the fish. I gave Tip a little more of the chicken I had set aside so he would not feel neglected.

"Why don't you walk the boy while I clean up?"

"I can't do that. You worked so hard on the meal, I feel like I should be the one to clean up, not you."

"Of course, you can. I might have a treat for you when you return from the hinterlands."

"Would the treat involve food, or perhaps the hot tub? That way I'll know how long of a walk Tip will get."

"I would say abbreviate the walk. Seafood is an aphrodisiac for me. How about you?"

"You're my aphrodisiac."

Tip got his walk, shorter than he wanted, most likely. I got what I wanted, which was Mary Louise's undivided attention. After hot-tub time was over, we lay on dry towels on top of the bed and sleepily watched Jennifer Garner chase bad guys in Alias, a terrific television series created by the talented J. J. Abrams.

"Why don't we check out La Cava on Sunday, maybe play nine holes? I'll buy you a ground beef taco from the food truck. Only paper napkins, though. Cloth is probably reserved for indoor dining once the place opens."

"I'm not really a paper-napkin sort of girl, but if you insist. I would like to see the golf course. I've heard it's unique and beautiful."

"I as well. I wasn't able to see much of it during my tour, so we can view it together. In fact, we could play nine holes and have lunch, and drive the golf cart around the back nine so we can at least see what sort of torture the golf architect has designed for those of us with lesser talents."

"Plan on the tour, and we'll do lunch or breakfast, depending on what time we wake up Sunday morning. Did you forget we have Buck's party tomorrow night? How does that sound, man of mine?"

"Perfect. Tomorrow is Saturday, and I have my regular game with my bandit friends. I can come home, take a nap, and be ready for the shindig Saturday night."

"I'm sleeping in. The trip to Austin wore me out. As did you," she said, as she got out of bed, pulled the covers down, and crawled in. She patted me as she nestled down into the covers and fell asleep instantly. Falling asleep that quickly is reserved for those who are clear of conscience, I am told. I thought I was a decent fellow, but rarely did I fall asleep as quickly as Mary Louise, and when I did, it was usually due to an overabundance of single-malt scotch whiskey.

I did fall asleep, though, and last remembered Sydney Bristow downing her male opponent, twice her size, with a karate chop of some sort to his thick neck, saving the day for the CIA. Oh, if life were only that simple.

CHAPTER 3

SOIREE

Dr. Buck Owens was the chair of the board of Hill Country Medical Center. He, with a few of his oil and gas buddies, created HCMC to provide outstanding medical care to the residents of our area. Between Llano County, Burnet County, and other counties in between, the hospital had a drawing area of well over 100,000 people. The hospital served quite a few small towns, including Horseshoe Bay, Marble Falls, Granite Falls, Granite Shoals, Kingsland, Burnet, Llano, and Johnson City. While these counties and towns were only an hour's drive west of Austin, the state capital, and several medical centers of some renown, Hill Country Medical Center was attracting a large population of residents who wanted to stay at home for medical and surgical diagnosis and treatment. Austin was becoming the referral city for medical and surgical problems that could not be taken care of at HCMC, rather than the primary care center for those of us in the Hill Country. This was good for the cities, and good for Dr. Buck Owens.

Buck grew up in Texas and started his career in medicine as an old-fashioned general practitioner, treating a variety of maladies while doing minor surgical procedures as well as OB-GYN. He invested in the oil and gas wells his friends were drilling, and he eventually became a wealthy man from royalties and production income. He eventually retired from medical practice, deciding he could do more for patients by investing in their care than he could by seeing them on an individual basis. Thus, the development of the Hill Country Medical Center, Buck's child. I was on the board, as was Mary Louise, as were a variety of businesspeople, department chairs at the hospital, Sister Mads of Mourning Doves, and Del Anderson, publisher of the Highlander, the local paper.

Buck threw a soiree yearly to celebrate the hospital's success. He invited board members, local business leaders, and representatives of HCMC who worked in the outlying clinics in other towns and counties in the Hill Country. His home was huge and sat only about two feet above the waters of Lake LBJ. His lot was designed in a V-shape also, but much larger than ours. His boat dock housed a couple of speedboats and a pontoon boat. I estimated there were 100 people at the party, all outside under groupings of umbrellas over tables laden with citronella candles and bombs to ward off those pesky mosquitoes.

"How is the golf game, Brady?" asked Buck, as we entered the large backyard and deck, spacious enough for all invited.

"Pretty good day today, Buck, but I try to never get cocky."

He hugged Mary Louise and told her, as usual, "If you ever get tired of this guy, don't forget I'm your go-to man."

And as usual, she said, "That will never happen," and bussed him on the cheek.

We wandered, greeting friends old and new. Sister Mads was there, director of Mourning Doves, a residential retreat for abused women. She gave me a big hug, still grateful for my helping some of her residents a few years back during a trying time for all concerned.

Lucinda Williams, Buck's administrative assistant and keeper of all secrets, greeted us upon arrival. She was still devastated over the loss of her daughter, my patient, to violence on the part of a chronic abuser during the Mourning Doves debacle.

Mary Louise and I visited the bar, took wine in plastic cups, and wandered the food stations and sampled Texas delights such as fried rattlesnake—tastes like chicken—barbecued pork ribs, chicken, brisket, jalapeño sausage, corn on the cob, fried okra, and Texas caviar, a mix of beans, corn, tomatoes, and spices that could melt one's tongue if enough jalapeño pepper seeds were added.

After greeting our friends, Mary Louise and I slipped over to a corner of the vast deck, stood by the marina, and watched the last of the sun melt below the waters of Lake LBJ. We kissed, a tradition at sunset, and silently thanked each other for . . . well, each other.

"I hate to disturb you lovebirds, but I need to speak with you," said Buck, as he came up behind us.

"By you, do you mean me, or Mary Louise, or both of us?"

"I mean both of you. I don't know if we have a problem or not, but I'd like you two to help me out regarding a business venture."

Mary Louise and I looked at each other and shrugged.

"What's the scoop?" I asked.

"Are you familiar with the new golf course and real estate development, La Cava?"

"As a matter of fact, I went over there yesterday, got a membership packet, and had a tour from Patsy Simmons, although an abbreviated one. Mary Louise and I plan to go there tomorrow, play nine holes, and get the lay of the land. Why, are you interested in La Cava?"

"Let's just say my friends and I have agreed to invest in the project."

"Buck, I don't know about your friends, but you are a member of Horseshoe Bay Golf Club. Wouldn't that be some sort of conflict of interest?"

"We would be providing an investment in the project, but as silent partners, not as principals. Investing in a project is not a conflict of interest."

"Well, let me think, Buck. Both projects involve golf courses. Both involve residential real estate. How is that not a conflict?"

"My friends and I are not owners of Horseshoe Bay. There is an outfit in San Antonio that built the place, a hotel management company than runs the resort, and a golf course management company than runs the four courses. We are not a part of that. I am simply a member and pay to enjoy the golf and dining experience. If I were an investor, or part of one of the management companies, there probably would be a conflict, since the two entities will be competing against each other for golf revenue dollars. As it stands, there is no conflict."

"Buck, you're the businessperson, I'm just an orthopedic surgeon at your hospital. Mary Louise is a fundraiser. What could we possibly do to help you?"

"Sort of undercover work, which you claim to be good at. Here it is in a nutshell. The original company that started the La Cava development went bankrupt. The project was years in the making. Those folks were primarily in commercial real estate development and bought all that land with the intent to have partners who would handle the golf course construction, the clubhouse construction, and the development of casitas, townhomes, and single-family homes. The original developers were hoping to turn a relatively quick buck by buying up the land and bringing in partners to do the real work while the developers sat back and watched it all come together, especially once the housing projects began.

"What they didn't expect was for one of the principals on the commercial side to loot the escrow account and disappear into Canada somewhere. Each of the investors had to put up personal money and guarantee the loan with a personal signature. Some of them were on the edge already, and the project went under quickly. The looter got away with millions of dollars and was not heard from again. The project had been in bankruptcy for years and just now got started again due to an infusion of money from some of the Permian Basin boys. If you're not in the know, those are Midland and Odessa oil barons with lots of money from production and with very deep pockets."

"So why do they need you and your buddies to invest?"

"To spread the risk."

"So, I do not see what the problem is, Buck."

"The Permian Basin boys are in danger of losing their investment due to discovery of those limestone caves. It cost them millions from the project to unearth those caves and move the limestone. They need an infusion of capital to complete the clubhouse and begin the housing development. Otherwise, they'll have a golf course in the middle of nowhere with no food and beverage service and no housing. I don't care how many daily fees they collect from tee times; you can't make money on a project like that without a superior clubhouse selling lots of food and booze, and healthy real estate development."

"Again, what would we do?"

"What you're best at. Snooping. We want you to join the club, play golf, meet and greet people, see what the membership is thinking. The principals tell me they only have about fifty or sixty members signed on, and they need at least 200 to make it work. I want you to keep your nose to the ground and see if you think this will be a viable opportunity or if it's a snakebite and a no go.

We'll even pay your entry fee and the monthly dues until you can make a recommendation to us about the viability of the project."

"What if they won't let us join? I've heard about that happening with some of the legacy golf clubs in the large cities like Dallas and Houston."

"Jim Bob, trust me. You could tie your membership entry check to a brick and throw it over the wall by the front gate, and you would be accepted into the club. That's how desperate they are for revenue."

CHAPTER 4

THE BODY

Buck's party ran late. He brought in a local country-western swing band, not unlike Ray Benson and Asleep at the Wheel, just not as well known. The more I danced, the more I drank, and so forth. I do not remember when we got into bed but were awakened at 9 a.m. to the intense barking of Tip, who desperately needed to go outside. I did the honors, fed him, and returned to bed at 9:30 for a little extra shuteye, which I needed. Mary Louise slept through the routine but woke me up at 10:30, said she was starving, and suggested we have a cup of coffee, put on our golf clothes, and have breakfast at the food truck at La Cava. That meant she was desperate for carbs, since my girl is not the type to frequent food trucks for dining.

We arrived at 11:30 and checked in with Jason, still staffing the pro shop desk, who said our rounds were complimentary since we were prospective members. He had assigned us a 12:30 time, so we sought out the food truck and ordered an inordinate amount of somewhat unhealthy breakfast food. I ordered scrambled eggs with chorizo and flour tortillas, and a side of hash browns. Mary Louise ordered an egg-white omelet with crispy bacon, pepper jack cheese, tomatoes, and black olives, with a side of hash browns. The vendor had just made a fresh pot of coffee from South American beans, which was thick and heavy and chock-full of caffeine, and we washed our respective concoctions down with the hot brew.

We were tempted to return home for naps, but the caffeine kept us going. We drove down another level to the practice range, found our clubs that we had dropped off at the valet, and hit a few balls. The impact of iron against the ground prompted me to down two ibuprofen tabs with an entire bottle of spring water, followed by a return to the golf cart. Mary Louise seemed to be faring much better than me, but then her consumption of alcohol the night before measured nothing like mine.

We were sent to the number-one tee, a beautiful par five with an elevated tee box. A stream was strategically placed along the right side of the hole and ran from the right side of the fairway to the left, culminating in a small pond directly in front of the green. In my condition, I should not have been surprised to lose three golf balls on that hole—two in the stream en route to the green, and one into what Mary Louise called that cute little pond. I made a nice long putt to score a nine on the first hole.

Golf courses in Texas tend not to be marked all that well. I do not know if the designers expect us golfers to have a good sense of direction, or if they think that a small sign indicating the direction of the next tee trashes up the place. Whatever the reason, I drove the cart down the wrong path, because we ended up not on the second tee box, but in what looked like an extension of a driveway leading from a huge chalet under construction. Since it was Sunday, and no workers were seen, I decided the easiest route was to continue up the drive, make a U-turn, and go back the way we came, in order to find the cart path. That was the moment we heard what sounded like a weapon discharging.

"Was that a gunshot, Jim Bob?"

"I think so. Sounded like it came from the house. Should we check it out, see if someone is hurt?"

"I think we should call 911 and let the professionals evaluate the situation. This is how you get yourself into trouble, young man."

"Thanks for the 'young man' compliment," I said, as I steered the cart up the hill toward the house.

"I guess that was a 'NO' on your part?"

"I just want to make sure no one is injured. Hippocratic oath, and all that."

Mary Louise glared at me, but I kept on course just the same. There was a driveway extension from the house that appeared to intersect the golf-cart path I had been seeking. The path appeared to originate from a lower-level golf-cart garage. The garage was partially completed, with the sheetrock taped and floated but without paint. A door was ajar that looked like it led into the house.

"Jim Bob, I have a bad feeling about this. Call 911. I insist."

I did as Mary Louise asked, then left the golf cart and approached the open door. "I want to make sure help is not required here. Are you coming?"

She sighed deeply, got out of the cart, and came my way. "I hope I don't regret this."

The lower level in the house had incomplete storage closets in what appeared to be a large garage-to-be, but the golf-cart garage was the only functional space. An unfinished staircase led up to another level. We climbed carefully, since no railings had been installed yet. The steps seemed sturdy enough, however, so we pressed on. The first steps led to a landing, then a change of direction to another set of incomplete steps. We exited the stairway into a huge open space.

"Man, what a place," I said. "Think this is all just one big room?"

"Well, we're standing adjacent to what looks like an open kitchen. See where the appliances are supposed to fit? Then it blends into what is probably a dining space, then over toward that other wall, an open entertainment area. Very modern design. Note the sliding glass doors facing the view corridor. Those doors disappear into the walls. Beautiful."

"Do you hear anything?"

"Nothing."

We wandered across the massive open space and looked in nooks and crannies and unfinished rooms for signs or sounds of an injured person but found nothing. As we walked through the space, we carefully dodged carpenters' tools, sawhorses, and stacked lumber. We encountered another set of stairs on the opposite side of the entry, also incomplete and free of banisters. Not a fan of open heights, I supported myself against the wall and reluctantly trod upward. The design was the same as the other side of the house, a landing followed by more steps leading upward. With all the money required to build a house of this size, I thought there should be an elevator somewhere, but we didn't find one.

We reached the top of the stairs and systematically went through five unfinished rooms, which in Mary Louise's opinion were bedrooms with private baths. All spaces were devoid of people, save us two. When we reached the largest of the rooms, I smelled the distinct odor of gunpowder. I put my arm out in front of Mary Louise, and we listened carefully but heard nothing.

We gingerly walked through what we thought was a massive primary bedroom, saw nothing in the main space, then entered a bathroom suite. We found a woman there who looked like she had been shot in the chest, blood still oozing from the wound and pooling below her. I felt for a carotid pulse, but none was present and she was not breathing.

"I just heard a siren. We need to get back downstairs and explain our presence here before they arrest us for murder."

"You're right, Mary Louise. How old would you say she is—was?"

"Early fifties. She is very pretty and is dressed for golf. She has only one sock on. Imagine, Jim, the last thing the poor woman did in her life was put on a sock. That is just too sad."

"I see her purse on that ledge there. Think we should . . .?"

"Jim Bob Brady, don't you touch that purse. We need to get out of here, NOW!"

We exited through what Mary Louise assured me was the front door after coming downstairs, and we stood on the front porch as the two patrol officers that responded to the 911 call arrived. They looked fresh out of the police academy in Austin. We would learn they both had family in the area and claimed fishing for a hobby, so their assignment to the Marble Falls Police Department could not have been more ideal. The taller of the two, Officer David Jenkins, was thin and of fair complexion. His partner, Officer Justin Garcia, was more reserved. He was of medium height, stocky, and with a dark complexion.

We introduced ourselves politely and held up our hands to make sure the officers saw we had nothing to hide. We directed them upstairs to the body.

"So where were you when you heard the gunshots?" asked Jenkins, once he and his partner had confirmed the victim's death and rejoined us in the great room.

"We were on the golf course at La Cava, on the first hole. I got lost leaving the first green, made a right when I should have made a left, and ended up on this driveway extension that leads to a golf-cart garage on the lower level. We heard the shot as we were driving up to make a U-turn," I said.

"You entered the premises after you called 911?"

"Yes. I am a doctor, an orthopedic surgeon at Hill Country Medical Center. I felt I should check the house and see if someone was injured and needed assistance."

"And you roamed through the house, and found the deceased upstairs in what you thought to be the primary bedroom?"

"That's correct. Neither of us touched anything, although I did brush up against the wall going up that second flight of stairs. It's a little disconcerting if you have any sort of height issue."

Jenkins looked at Garcia, and both smiled. They seemed to understand.

"Did you touch the purse?"

"No. I felt her carotid pulse and put my hand on her chest lightly to see if she was breathing. I felt no breath movement, and she had no pulse. We came downstairs and waited for you."

"The medical examiner and the crime-scene techs are on their way. I also had to call in a detective from Marble Falls. We don't get to handle the crime itself. Too low on the organization chart. We usually get assigned to handle the drunk-and-disorderly calls from the public marina at Cottonwood Shores, or the public-intoxication calls from the lake, and sometimes a DUI out on Highway 71. But we'll get there one day, huh, Justin?"

"You bet, David. We'll be big dogs one day, mark my words, brother."

"Well, if you fellows don't need us for anything else, I'd like to go and finish that front nine. We gave you our contact information, so if the detective needs any other information, they can contact us. OK?"

"Yes, sir and ma'am. Appreciate your help. Have a good day," Jenkins said.

Although we played the rest of the front nine, it was somewhat anticlimactic after having discovered a dead body in an unfinished mansion on the first hole of La Cava. The course was, as advertised, a work of art. It was also a ball-eater, what with all the streams and ponds and the narrow fairways. I lost eleven golf balls, a tragedy for me. Mary Louise did not lose a single ball. She bunted the golf ball down the fairways with a rescue club as was her technique, and never got into trouble. She does not usually score that well, but neither does she enjoy hunting for golf balls in the weeds, home of snakes, scorpions, and nasty chiggers. Her golf balls generally died of old age.

We stopped by the pro shop and told Jason about the gunshot and the dead woman. He turned white as a sheet.

"You don't mean Mrs. Devlin? Christine?"

"Jason, we don't know her name. We heard the shot, called 911, explored the house to try and render aid if necessary, and found her upstairs."

"Mr. and Mrs. Devlin are building a home on the first fairway, close to the green. Mr. Devlin is our CEO. He's in charge of the construction of the clubhouse and is part of the real estate company that's developing the property."

"We didn't encounter anyone else in the house, Jason, so we can't help you there. You might want to notify Patsy Simmons of what we discovered. I expect someone from La Cava needs to go over and identify the deceased if possible. Two police officers responded to our 911 call, with a detective and crime-scene personnel on the way."

"Yes, sir. I'll call Patsy right away."

Mary Louise and I headed home for a stiff drink.

CHAPTER 5

SURGERY

In the old days, back in Houston, I would go into my office on Sunday nights and review my cases for Monday. But in my defense, I often did six or eight surgeries on my operating days of Monday, Wednesday, and Friday, and I did not want to get confused about what I was doing where. My specialty of hip and knee surgery involved primarily the insertion of total joints, some virgin, some revision. In my current world at HCMC, I limited myself to four replacements on Monday and four on Wednesday. I would occasionally have to add on a case for emergency reasons—a fractured hip, a knee dislocation, a broken tibia—but while for a time I only had two partners in the group performing the same type of surgery as I did, I had found two new partners, creating a group of five within a larger group of orthopedic surgeons. It was rare that one of the two new guys would not take an emergency case. They were building up their practices. They had children to feed, clothe, and educate. I was going in the opposite direction, headed for the discard pile of old bone doctors.

I arrived at the hospital at 5:30 a.m.. A new parking garage had been constructed recently adjacent to the office-building portion of the complex. The doctors and staff parked on the ground floor, guests and visitors on the second floor, accessible by elevator. The parking garage had been connected to both the office building and the hospital via covered walkways, such that all three structures had become weather impervious. In addition, Buck had enlarged the entries to both the hospital and the office building and had established valet parking during regular business hours. Access was neater and cleaner and much improved for docs, staff, and patients. Patients in wheelchairs or on walkers or crutches now had a direct shot into the office building, the hospital, and the parking garage without any steps, rendering all structures truly accessible for people with mobility issues.

In the past I used an RN and a nurse practitioner, one in each operating room, to facilitate wound closures, dressing application, and room turnover. My nurse Shelly Wood had left for greener pastures in San Antonio, and I was disappointed because, while she was an excellent surgical assistant, she was even better on the phone dealing with patient problems. The nurse practitioner I had previously used at HCMC, Charlotte Stone, was married to a man in veterinary school, and once he completed his training, they also left for the big city life. That left me with only Maya Stern, who functioned as the primary phone answerer, appointment maker, and general problem solver. I was training a new nurse practitioner to work in the operating room Monday and Wednesday, and to work in the office the other three days of the week, handling patient problems. Her name was Belinda Brooks.

I cleaned off my desk, and by that I mean I actually dictated charts and signed documents, rather than swept the entire mess into a large trash can by my desk, which I had been known to do for many years. I missed Fran, my former secretary, and Rae, my former nurse, from my time at University Orthopedics in Houston. Both had been with me over twenty years. We had an unspoken communication, and patient matters were handled swiftly and gracefully by both women. They both had homes in the country, fifty miles from Houston, in completely the wrong direction to be able to strike out with me on my new adventure in Marble Falls.

I had only been working at HCMC for a few years, and already I had been through three administrative assistants and five—yes, five—nurses or nurse practitioners. I really was not that hard to please; I simply had high standards. I believed that a job in the medical field deserved your best effort, whether you were a doctor or a nurse or in an administrative position. There was no room for mistakes in our business. When dealing with patients' lives and limbs, there were no second chances. There were no do-overs. You had to get it right every time. That was too much pressure for most people.

I stopped in the small cafeteria adjacent to the physician's lounge and had a light breakfast of eggs, bacon, toast, and coffee. I needed to keep up my strength for my four cases.

Belinda met me in the identification area of the surgical floor, where all patients were checked in and identified by a wristband and date of birth, and their surgical site marked with an indelible ink pen. IVs were started, myriad reams of paperwork completed, and identity reconfirmed several times. Only after that process was completed was the doctor allowed to see the patient and answer any last-minute questions. My first case was a virgin total hip replacement on a friend of mine, Del Anderson, owner and publisher of the Highlander, our local paper.

"Well, are you ready to get rid of that nasty old hip pain, friend?"

"Jim Bob, I am so ready. I was miserable all weekend. I hurt so bad, I couldn't even get a story together about Christine Devlin, the woman who was shot and killed at her home under construction at La Cava. Did you know her?"

I was speechless for a moment and wondered if I should spill the beans about who discovered the body. I decided against it. "No, I did not, Del. Do you know what happened?"

"Only that a couple was playing golf and heard a gunshot on the first green, went to investigate, and found her dead upstairs. The police were called, along with the coroner and the crime-scene techs, but I have no further info."

"How did you find out about the murder?"

"Newspaper people have their sources, Jim Bob."

"Any last-minute questions or worries, Del?"

"No. You're the man, as far as I am concerned. I know you'll fix me up and do a good job. Of that, I am certain."

Del Anderson's surgery went without a hitch. I watched Belinda sew the deep layers of muscle and fascia around the hip joint. She had good hands. Her skin stitching was equally good. I left the room to go identify the next patient, a man for a total knee replacement. Once that was accomplished, they wheeled him into a second room adjacent to the first and anesthetized him, and after the prepping and draping process, I went to work.

Belinda joined me after she had closed and dressed Del's surgical wound. I performed the total knee procedure, then again watched Belinda close the deep tissues around the knee, and left her to close the skin and apply the dressing, and went back to the identification area to meet and greet my third case. And the routine continued for the rest of the day. We completed the last case around 3 p.m., and thankfully, all went smoothly.

The beauty of utilizing a second room was that we were able to get all four cases done before shift change, which reduced overtime pay and saved the hospital and the patient money, and patients did not have to wait so long for their operation because they were all NPO from midnight the night before and were starving. I had read articles suggesting the payors—formerly known as insurance companies—were considering disallowing surgeons' use of a second room. I did not understand that logic, but I knew it would reduce efficiency, increase costs, and impede patient care. It sounded like a typical move from the payor sector. I pondered for a moment how the former insurance companies could manipulate the new standard to increase their stockholders' dividends, then gave up.

I had a bite to eat before going upstairs to the office. Maya greeted me with a frightened look on her face. Maya was a small woman, a little over five feet, with dark hair and olive skin. She was the single mother of two teenage girls who, as a credit to Maya, were kind, caring, and excellent students.

"What's wrong, Maya? Did someone die?"

"No, but the Marble Falls police have been calling here, wanting to speak to you about a murder. You are supposed to call a Detective Randall Mims as soon as you arrive. He sounded pissed."

"I don't know why. I promise I did not kill anyone."

"Ha, ha, Mr. Funny. Please call this guy," and she handed me a note with the number scribbled on it.

I dutifully called the Marble Falls PD and asked to speak to Detective Mims.

He answered shortly thereafter with, "Are you trying to avoid me, Doctor?"

"Not at all, sir. I thought I should finish the surgeries on those folks that were asleep in the operating room before I called you, though," I said, with perhaps just a touch of a belligerent attitude.

"I am not in the mood for a smart-ass conversation with you, Doctor. I need to discuss the murder of Christine Devlin with you and your wife. I understand you two found the woman while playing golf."

"That is correct, sir."

"I want to sit down with both of you. When is a good time?"

"You mean today?"

"Yes, today."

"I have to complete some paperwork and make rounds on my post-operative patients. Would you like to come by the house around 6 p.m.? Mary Louise will probably fix you a plate if you're hungry. Our address is—"

"I know your address, Doctor. We're the police, you know."

CHAPTER 6

DINNER

"**W**hat do we call you? Detective Mims?" I asked.

"My rank is lieutenant, and I head up the Detective Bureau in the Marble Falls PD. If you want to be accurate, Lieutenant Mims is my official title."

He had arrived promptly at 6 p.m. I barely had time to get home and clean up after our brief phone conversation. I offered him a drink, but he declined, saying he was technically on duty by virtue of the interview he intended to conduct. Mims was tall, around six foot four, weighed over 200 pounds, and looked to be about forty years old. He wore a sport coat over a golf shirt with an open collar, and tan western boots with ostrich skin. Tip, our old golden retriever, liked him immediately, first smelling his boots, then extending his fat head for a pat, which Mims obliged. Dogs are good judges of character, so Lt. Mims scored a few points with Mary Louise and me.

I poured myself an eighteen-year Macallan single-malt scotch. Mims looked longingly at the dark amber liquid in my crystal glass but sipped his bottled water in silence. I poured Mary Louise a Newton unfiltered chardonnay, and we three moved to the terrace.

"Let me start by saying I'm going to record this conversation. Any problem with that?" he asked.

We shook our heads. Tip went over and laid down on top of Lt. Mims's boots.

"Tell me in detail how you came to discover the body of Christine Devlin yesterday."

I told the story in as much detail as I could. Mary Louise interjected a fact or two that I had forgotten, but there was not that much to tell.

"You heard only the one gunshot?"

We both nodded.

"And you saw no one else at the property, either outside or inside?"

"No," I answered.

"Once you entered the house from the lower basement, did you hear anything that sounded like footsteps, or someone running?"

I looked at Mary Louise, and she shook her head. "No," I said.

"When you found the body, did you notice anything that could have represented a struggle of some sort?"

Mary Louise answered. "No, but she appeared to be dressed for golf, or maybe tennis. I thought it odd that she had one sock on and one sock off. It looked to me like she could have just laid down on the floor, except for the bullet hole in her chest and all the blood."

"After discovering the body, did you walk around the bathroom or look in the unfinished closets either there or in the future primary bedroom?"

"No. I saw a purse on a ledge in the bathroom. My wife told me to leave it be, however, and we returned to the great room downstairs to wait for the police."

Mims sighed, reviewed his notes, and put the notepad into his jacket pocket.

"Is the offer of a beverage still good?" he asked.

"Certainly. What would you like?" I asked.

"What you're drinking looks mighty tasty after a long day of police work."

I poured him a Macallan, added one ice cube as recommended, and handed him the drink. He sipped it slowly, closed his eyes, and relished the rich peat flavor.

"A fellow could get used to this."

"Yes, it is quite an addictive flavor. Nothing better, unless you want to spring for the thirty-year. I have one bottle left that I have a sip or two from every month or so, but I do not want to get used to that taste. It is just too good, and the price has become ridiculous."

Mary Louise got up from her chair and went to the kitchen to check on dinner. "The food is just about ready. I prepared fried chicken with brown gravy, a wedge salad, and fresh lima beans. Lieutenant, we have more than enough food, and I would consider it an honor if you joined us for dinner. We can continue our conversation while we eat."

"Thank you, ma'am," he said. "I am starved and would enjoy the meal."

He and I walked inside, went over to the dining table, picked up a plate—the table was set for three—and served ourselves. Once seated, I poured us each some of the Newton chardonnay, and we toasted like old friends. The food was just too good for conversation, so we ate in a comfortable silence for a short while.

Mary Louise brought us back to reality with the question, "Are you from here, Lieutenant?"

"Ma'am, after this dinner, please feel free to call me Randall. I grew up in Marble Falls, played football in high school. I had scholarship offers as an offensive end to a couple of small schools and chose Sam Houston State in Huntsville. Unfortunately, I was also on the basketball team at Marble Falls, and during the state finals I injured my knee. It was surgically repaired, but I was not the same, physically. I couldn't run as fast, and I sure as hell couldn't cut like in the old days. Sam Houston rescinded my scholarship, but I decided to go on to school there. I liked the campus and the people. I had no idea what to do with my life, since my plans to play football were erased. I took a couple of sociology classes, got interested in criminology, and ended up with a major. I took the police exam in Huntsville and made it onto the police force. I worked there for a few years, but I missed this area, especially the lake, fishing, and water sports. I returned home, took the detective's exam, passed, and here I am."

"Wife? Kids?" Mary Louise asked.

"No, ma'am."

We finished our meal after Randall had second helpings. Man, could he eat! We helped Mary Louise clean up, loaded the dishwasher, took a cup of decaf coffee and our wine glasses and sat on the deck. The sun had set, but the orange glow was still present.

"I appreciate your hospitality, Doctor and Mrs. Brady." We detectives are supposed to take cases on a rotation basis, but being in charge of the detectives bureau, I can pick and choose which cases I want to personally handle. The chief of police called me into his office this morning, though, and told me I was going to handle this one. He had received a call from Dr. Buck Owens, a major supporter of the police department and a friend of you both, as I gather from the chief."

"Yes, that is true. Buck is responsible for recruiting us to Hill Country Medical Center. In the spirit of full disclosure, Randall, I must tell you that at a party at Buck's home Saturday night, he asked me to spend some time at La Cava and 'gather information' for him and his cronies who have invested a large sum of money into the project. He has offered to pay the entry fee and cover our monthly dues. We have not discussed the death of Mrs. Devlin, so I don't know if his position on the matter has changed or not. However, I wanted you to know up front that if Buck still wants me to join, I feel obligated to do so, and 'snoop around'—his words, not mine."

"Yes, sir, the chief conveyed that same information to me this afternoon. You have my full support."

"One issue that has disturbed me is—where is Mr. Devlin? Does he know his wife has been murdered?" I asked.

"He has been out of town on business but was notified by phone of the tragedy. He's on his way back as we speak."

"Would you happen to know where he's been?"

"New York, the chief said."

"Really. What's there that relates to La Cava?" Mary Louise asked.

"Hedge funds, private equity funds, real estate investment companies. In other words, money, and lots of it," I said.

CHAPTER 7

AUTOPSY

Since the morgue and the chief pathologist of the county were located at Hill Country Medical Center, I presumed my friend Dr. Jerry Reed would be responsible for Christine Devlin's autopsy. Jerry and I had worked together to solve the mysterious death of Sandy Lowell, a local oil executive and benefactor of HCMC. Jerry and I were cut from the same mold: leave no stone unturned when it comes to solving a medical mystery.

I called him at his office Tuesday morning around 7 a.m. before I began seeing clinic patients. He was an early riser, and I was not surprised that he answered the phone himself.

"Hey, friend, you must want something, to call me this early," he said.

"I sometimes call when I don't want anything from you, Jerry."

"Name one time, Jim Bob."

I hesitated for a moment, trying hard to think.

"See what I mean? You use me for what you want, then abandon me like an unwanted plaything."

"You sound like a jilted lover, Jerry."

"Pathologists have feelings, too. What do you want? I have a morgue to run down here."

"I want to see the autopsy on Christine Devlin. She was shot yesterday in her home that's under construction."

"I know about the Devlin shooting. What in the world could you possibly have to do with that?"

"I'm helping Buck out with a problem, and she might have some involvement. That's all I can say for the moment. What time is it scheduled?"

He sighed. "What time do you want it to be scheduled?"

"Now you're talking. After I finish clinic patients, say 3 p.m. Does that work?"

"Yes, oh great defender of the downtrodden and misunderstood. I'll see you then."

Belinda met me for rounds at 7:15. The post-ops from the day before were all doing well and anticipated my rule of making them get up out of bed and start moving the day following surgery. The procedure was good for preventing blood clots, and good for the mental status of the patient. Insurance companies and Medicare would no longer let a post-op patient lie around the hospital and suck up pain meds. After two or three days, they would have to go home or to a rehab unit. Fortunately, HCMC had an excellent unit for getting post-op total joint replacement patients ambulatory and self-sufficient, so most of my patients went there after hospital discharge.

That day's clinic patients were unremarkable, which was always a good thing. The post-ops were doing well, and the new patients either were signing up for a joint replacement, or asking for a refill on their anti-inflammatory meds, hoping to postpone surgery until a later date. Everyone seemed pleasant, especially since I was running on time and there was essentially no waiting. Patients hate to wait. I hate to make them wait. Not having to wait makes everyone happy.

I had Maya call down to pathology and find out if the autopsy had started at 3 p.m. as scheduled. She said that Dr. Reed was waiting patiently for my arrival—her words, not his.

The morgue was in the hospital basement, so I took the elevator down to the home of science of the dead. I donned a paper gown and booties, put a little Vicks under my nose to reduce the noxious smells in the morgue, and applied my mask.

"About time, Dr. Brady," Jerry said. "Do you know Lt. Mims?"

"Of course. We met yesterday. How are you, Lieutenant?"

"Fine, Dr. Brady. I'm surprised to see you here."

"I'm here as a favor to Dr. Buck Owens. Academic curiosity, if you will."

Jerry made the Y-incision to open the chest and abdomen. His assistant inserted a large retractor with a ratchet handle, allowing them to expose the internal organs.

Jerry dictated on a hands-free microphone for later transcription. "We have a female, fifty-one years of age, in excellent health, according to the medical records from her internist. These records were obtained via electronic transmission this morning. She has no history of diabetes or any other medical disease other than a little systolic hypertension controlled by medication. The heart and lungs appear to be clear except for the hole in her left ventricle. The bullet passed through the ventricle at close range and exited the posterior thorax and subsequently the spinal column at the T-5 level."

He lifted her over and noted the exit wound. "Was the bullet recovered, Lieutenant?"

"Yes, sir. It was embedded in the concrete beneath a recently installed hardwood floor. It is a 9 mm, very commonly used in all aspects of shooting sports, as well as in law enforcement and the military. There was nothing unusual about the shell, according to the techs."

Jerry continued with the autopsy. With a scalpel, he separated the great vessels exiting the heart, cut loose the lungs from their bindings, and separated the liver, spleen, kidneys, and intestines from their moorings. He then lifted the giant mass of internal organs out of the body cavity and set them aside on an adjacent table.

"We'll get tissue samples of all the organs, but grossly, everything looks intact except the heart."

He turned the heart over, and we saw the huge hole the shell had made in the posterior aspect of the heart muscle. The entry hole was small, about shell size, but the back side of the heart was shredded and virtually destroyed.

"At close range, this was not a survivable injury. Lieutenant, you said the shell was retrieved from the floor adjacent to where the woman was lying when discovered. She was shot on the floor, then?"

"Best we can tell, yes sir."

"That's a little unusual. Normally a person is shot while standing, and the bullet either traverses through the body or not, and the victim falls and ends up either prone or supine. Not in this case?"

"No, sir, it doesn't appear that way."

"Why would she be lying down prior to being shot, I wonder?" mused Jerry.

"Mary Louise noticed she had only one sock on. Maybe she dropped it or something and leaned down to retrieve it," I interjected.

"And the assailant shoved her over and shot her through the heart?" said Jerry. "That would be weird. This was certainly no professional hit. Pros rely on the surprise factor and take down their victims in a fashion that is most likely to kill them."

"Maybe she had encountered the shooter, and she was running and fell. He turned her over and shot her in the heart. I think that's possible," replied Lt. Mims.

"Anything is possible. Just when you think you've seen it all, you realize you have not," said Jerry. "We're pretty much done here, except to take tissue specimens. You fellows are welcome to go about your duties. If I find anything else, I'll call you. May I have a card, Lieutenant?"

Mims handed him a business card. "By the way, Doctor, you will check her for signs of sexual activity or rape, prior to signing off on your cause of death?"

"Of course, we always do. I just didn't want you both to see that part of the exam. That could ruin your evening, in case you may have intimacy plans with your wife or girlfriend."

CHAPTER 8

DEL

"Did you know her, even to just say hello?" I asked Mary Louise over dinner at Franco's, a delightful Italian bistro in Marble Falls. I ordered linguini with clams for my entrée, and Mary Louise opted for a chicken piccata. We shared an antipasto salad to start, and a bottle of pinot grigio for dinner.

"No. I had heard her name mentioned as a fundraiser, someone I might get to know if I felt the need to add on more charity work. That hasn't happened yet, because I've been so busy with the Austin charities. Driving back and forth once or twice per week is tiring enough. I just didn't think I could handle any more work, and I never made the call."

"I wonder how Mr. Devlin is handling his wife being murdered."

"I thought about that today as well. It would be devastating to me and to you, I'm sure."

"I'm just enough in the loop to know a few things, but all the details are unavailable to me because, well, I'm not in law enforcement."

"Yes, you are an orthopedic surgeon, and not a member of law enforcement, and that is where I want you to stay. How many times have you been knocked out, assaulted, or maimed while sticking your lovely nose where it does not belong? More times than I care to remember."

I laughed. I had been unlucky a few times, she was right about that. Safer to be in the hospital on the doctoring side than the patient side.

"You have a busy day tomorrow?" Mary Louise asked.

"Yes. Four total hips, two virgins and two revisions, both of which unfortunately were cemented in place. Those cases are like wrestling a bear. You may win, but you will surely be scarred in the process."

"Better get you home and in bed. You'll need your rest, sweetie."

"Sometimes when I get in bed with you at my side, I don't want to rest."

"Keep it down, big fella. There's always another time."

"You never know. I'm getting older by the day, Mary Louise."

"And so am I, dear one."

"But you look so good. You are ageless."

"When you say words like that, it makes me want to take you home and smother you with affection."

I flagged down the waiter. "Check, please."

"No dessert, sir?"

"We're having that at home, son."

I anticipated the worst with the two revision hip procedures, so I tackled them first. Bone around a loose hip prosthesis tends to erode, sometimes worse than others. The first hip I did that morning had bony erosion much farther into the pelvis than anticipated, requiring not only extra cement to hold the prosthesis in place, but bone-graft material to fill in the gaps. I was physically worn out after the first procedure, but valiantly struggled on with the help of Belinda Brooks, nurse practitioner and new best friend. We didn't put in the final stitch in the last case until almost 5 p.m.

"I couldn't have done that without you. You were a life saver, Belinda. You are some strong lady, and I mean that in all good sense of the words."

She beamed. "That was a fun day, Doc. Thanks!"

"How about a ride up to the office?"

She went out to the waiting room and brought me a wheelchair. "I was just kidding, Belinda. Although between you and me, I wouldn't mind the trip."

I visited with all the families, painting a grim picture of the case that needed cement and bone graft. I have found it, over the years, better to be pessimistic early on, then optimistic when it looked like the procedure would turn out well after all. I also thought that perhaps I should in the future refer cases like that to one of the younger fellows in the group. I had plenty of other work to do without taking on cases that were so physically demanding and that might be predicted to have a bad result.

When I finally arrived at the house, Mary Louise greeted me with an ice-cold dirty Tito's martini. I sipped, sat at the kitchen bar, and watched her prepare steak Diane.

"Want to clean up before dinner?"

"Yes, but I'm too tired to move. Has Tip been walked lately?"

He stared at me, but I didn't know if it was because he had to go out or if he was awaiting a morsel of steak Diane.

"He'll be fine until after dinner. Why don't you take a quick shower? The food will be ready in about fifteen minutes."

I did as she suggested, and the hot water did ease my sore muscles from the day's activities. We decided to eat at the kitchen bar and visit rather than eat on tray tables in the den and watch bad TV news.

"This steak Diane is wonderful. You haven't cooked this dish in a while."

"I found a new recipe. I was talking to Susan Beeson on the phone, just catching up, and she emailed me the recipe that her mother uses. I must admit, it really is tasty."

"How is Susan?"

Susan Beeson was an old friend of ours. She had been a detective in Houston and eventually became the chief of police, following in her father's footsteps. A few years back, she took a job with the Austin branch of the FBI and was now the assistant special agent in charge.

"Doing well. Gene Jr. is in his second year at Baylor, and Gene Sr. has a thriving accounting business. Susan sounded like she might be a little tired of putting so many hours in at work, but she says the FBI job is all-or-nothing work. You either give it your all, or retire. Sort of like your job."

"I know about that kind of work, that is true. But the fame and glory make it all so worthwhile," I said, jokingly. "Is she working on any interesting cases that she could talk about?"

"We didn't talk business, Jim Bob. Unlike you, I don't feel the need to stir up the pot to try and get involved in some unsolved mystery or murder. She did mention an embezzlement case, though."

"Hey, these situations just fall into my lap, Mary Louise. I do not go out looking for trouble, but trouble often finds me. Tell about the embezzlement case, if you can."

"I didn't pay attention to the details, Jim. If she needs your help, I am certain she will call you," she said, sarcastically.

Along with the steak Diane, she had prepared fresh green beans with bacon, and mashed potatoes. Although the food was great, I felt myself nodding off while sitting up at the bar. I tried to help Mary Louise clean up, but she banished me to the bedroom. The next thing I remembered was looking at the clock, seeing it register 2 a.m., and panicking about not walking Tip. I got up, looked around, found him snuggled in the bed next to his mama, and figured Mary Louise had taken care of that. I fell back into bed and went immediately into a deep slumber.

Thursday rounds went smoothly. All the patients were recovering well. Del Anderson was being transferred to the rehab unit, although she was ambulating about as well as any surgical patient I had ever seen on the third day post-op hip replacement.

"I can't tell you how good I feel, Jim. That hip pain I have suffered with for years is just gone! It's a miracle, in my opinion."

"Well, I wish all the patients could say that. Usually it takes a while for the chronic pain to subside, and a few weeks for the surgical pain to go away. I'm glad you're doing so well. Are you sure you want to go to rehab?"

"Oh yes. I'm single, you know, and live alone. I need to be as independent as possible when I leave this place."

"Okay. I'll complete the paperwork. Who's taking care of publishing the paper in your absence?"

"My chief editor, Jill Bradley. She's been with me a long time and will do fine. Say, did you hear the latest about Christine and Louis Devlin?"

"No. What?"

"My sources told me he had traveled to New York on a private jet. The Austin press people tracked him with some sort of internet tracking app on a computer and were at the Horseshoe Bay private airstrip when he landed. There's little security at the terminal, so he thought he could avoid the press by landing there instead of at Austin Bergstrom airport. The press had photographers in place, and when that Gulfstream staircase came down, guess who was first off the plane?"

"Well, it wasn't his wife, because she's dead."

"That's correct. It was the director of sales from La Cava, Patsy Simmons."

"Holy moly. He's off cavorting in New York with an employee during the time his wife has been murdered. The press will have a field day."

"Yes, Jim Bob, we will."

CHAPTER 9

DR. JERRY REED

Thursday clinic went smoothly, for which I was thankful. No emergencies had come in, so I felt safe in emailing the Friday golf-game leader that I would be available. I handled a few phone calls, dictated charts, and filled out inane paperwork that hopefully would satisfy insurance company requirements. Belinda had a few queries about some of the questions she was getting from patients. I briefed her on how to handle those issues, and I got the distinct impression she was going to be a diligent and valuable employee.

Maya buzzed me on the intercom phone and said that Dr. Jerry Reed wanted to speak with me.

"Got a minute?" he asked.

"Sure. What's cooking?"

"I've completed the autopsy on Christine Devlin. I'd like to show you something."

"Give me fifteen minutes, Jerry."

I finished cleaning off my desk and told Maya and Belinda goodbye. I told Belinda to meet me at 8 a.m. for rounds the next morning. I tried to make rounds with Belinda and the floor nurse in charge Friday mornings before the weekend. Patients got a little clingy on Friday when they realized their doctor was not on duty. It was my job to reassure them that they would be fine, but if something happened, I would be in town and only twenty minutes away.

I stopped in the clinic kitchen and made myself a fresh cup of coffee so I wouldn't have to drink the sludge they prepared in the morgue.

I located Jerry in the autopsy suite. "Want me to suit up?" I asked.

"No, I'll be out in a minute. I have slides to show you."

I found his office, sipped my coffee, and waited.

He flew in with his lab coat and mask trailing behind like he was in flight, and he started talking nonstop.

"I don't really know how to handle this, so I thought I would run it by you first."

"What are you talking about?"

"Christine Devlin was an intersex person. She had a fully formed vagina, uterus, and ovaries, but also small testicles. I did tissue studies on the ovaries and the testicles. She had functioning ova in the ovaries, and spermatozoa in the testicles. ."

"Have you seen this syndrome before, Jerry?"

"Yes; intersexuality is more common than you might think— the statistic often given is that the chances of being intersex are about the same as being a redhead—and there are more than thirty variations of the condition, each with its own medical terminology. But since I'd have to run tests at the genetic level to determine which is applicable to the victim, I'm using the general term of intersex."

"That is fascinating, truly, but what does this have to do with her murder?"

"I am required to release all relevant information about the victim to the authorities in a murder case. These findings will be reviewed by police officials and God knows who else. You know the press will get hold of this also, and then these findings will be circulated everywhere. It's an outrageous invasion of privacy, and I don't want to see that happen."

"What are you going to do?"

"I would like to release the pertinent data related to her murder as usual, but I would like to withhold the intersexuality."

"Is that allowed?"

"No. That's why I called you. What should I do?"

"I have no idea. Let me talk to Buck Owens about it."

"I have to have an answer soon."

"You will."

I called Lt. Randall Mims on Friday morning after rounds. I told him I had information for him concerning the Christine Devlin murder and volunteered to drop by his office that morning before my round of golf.

The Marble Falls Police Department sat in the middle of town close to the HEB grocery store, in a flat, nondescript building of cream-colored limestone. I went in through the civilian entry and encountered a pleasant woman with sergeant's stripes on her sleeves. She stood as I entered, not out of politeness, I suspected, but out of wariness of the presence of a stranger possibly there to do harm.

"Morning, I'm Dr. Jim Brady. I have an appointment with Lt. Mims."

Her name tag read Sarver. She was of average height and in full uniform, her brown hair pulled back into a bun. "Please have a seat," she said.

I did as she asked and when I was seated, she sat as well. She picked up the phone and made a call. "He'll see you now, Doctor. I'll buzz you through to the Lieutenant's area."

I heard a loud buzz and walked through an entry door with metal bars into a large open area with cubicles for desks. Several officers were present, some on the phone, others reviewing paperwork.

"Morning, Dr. Brady. Thanks again for dinner the other night. Your wife is one hell of a cook."

"She is that. Listen, I have a couple of items to discuss with you, in private if possible."

"Let's go to the conference room."

We walked back into the bowels of the building and entered a small conference room next to an office with an engraved Chief of Police on the door.

"Coffee?"

"No thanks, I'm fine. Two things to tell you. The first is that last Friday, I had an abbreviated tour of La Cava Golf Club, a new facility under construction. I went alone. Mary Louise was in Austin. Patsy Simmons gave me the tour, and I think you may know that name because she was seen in the company of Louis Devlin upon his return from New York. You may remember that Mary Louise and I were there on Sunday, when we witnessed the gunshot and discovered the body."

"Yes. You were there on Friday as well?"

"Yes. And the only reason I am telling you that is because after the tour, I went out to the food truck to get a bite to eat. I overheard a conversation between a man and a woman, implying the man had been in federal prison, and that he was in the process of doing something nefarious, and she was discouraging him from doing anything that might land him back in prison. He told her that this was his chance for a big score, and that they would be set for life once whatever he was doing was completed."

"Did you see them, or catch their name?"

"No. I only saw the back of their heads. They were in a dark-blue golf cart, which I assumed to be a private cart, with a vanity license plate that read HIGHROLLER. They drove off, and that was all I heard."

He made some notes. "Why do you think this is important information?"

"Well, he sounded like he was involved in a scam of some sort, and with the history of La Cava already having endured a previous developer's embezzlement, I worried that possibly the club was going to be attacked financially again. Also, I wondered if the woman could have been Christine Devlin, and the man her husband, and that perhaps their conversation had something to do with her demise."

"You mentioned Patsy Simmons, and her possible dalliance with Mr. Devlin. How did you come by that information?"

Not to be one to give up sources, I said, "A friend of mine in the newspaper business. The jet's arrival at Horseshoe Bay airport was witnessed by Austin newspaper people, so I would think it would be common knowledge by now. I did think it was odd, though, that this occurred on Monday, the day after Mrs. Devlin's murder on Sunday. I am surprised that Mr. Devlin waited until the next day to return home and tend to his wife's remains."

"He told the police officers that questioned him the weather in Teterboro, New Jersey, was bad due to thunderstorms, and his flight was postponed until Monday morning."

"Huh. I thought those expensive Gulfstream jets could fly through any sort of weather."

Mims smiled. "Thanks for the information. If there's nothing else . . ."

"There is one thing. Dr. Jerry Reed, pathologist at HCMC, performed the autopsy this week on Mrs. Devlin, as I am sure you remember, seeing as how you were there. But you may recall he completed the exam of her pelvis in private. He was looking for evidence of rape but found something else. She was an intersex person, which in her case was characterized by the presence of small testicles as well as fully developed female genitalia."

Mims was silent for a moment. "And this could impact our investigation how?"

"I was thinking that you will assume the usual, that the husband killed her, or hired someone to kill her, because Mr. Devlin wanted to run away with Patsy Simmons and live happily ever after, or until the next gold digger came along. But Dr. Reed is obligated to release such findings from the autopsy, and he felt the woman deserved privacy and hoped that you would be able to squelch that information."

He thought about it for a moment. "Yes, I can do that, unless the course of our investigation takes us down that road in finding her assailant. I seriously doubt it would, Doctor. We are focused on the husband, as you suggested.

"As far as the other information you've provided, the conversation between the man and woman in the golf cart, I can't see at this time how that has relevance in the murder of Ms. Devlin."

"You're the detective."

CHAPTER 10

FINANCIALS

The weather forecasters had erred again on the side of bad weather versus good. As I was leaving the Marble Falls Police Department, a dark cloudy mass passed over and dumped cold rain on me and the Tahoe. Playing golf began to look iffy, so I detoured through town and headed back out to the HCMC. The structures were located technically in Marble Falls but were on the west side of the county, on Highway 71. La Cava Golf Club was also in Marble Falls, but on the east side of the county, off Highway 281. That meant there were two large tax-paying structures that were located many miles apart, but in the same city. That was excellent planning and zoning by the city.

By the time I got to my office, the sky was dark and menacing. The raindrops were large and still cold. That usually meant the thunderstorm was settling in for a while. I parked under cover in the doctors' parking on level one and walked through the walkway over to administration.

"Good morning, Dr. Brady," said Lucinda Williams, Buck's admin assistant. She rose from her chair and gave me a hug. We had developed a close relationship during the trials and tribulations of her daughter, who had eventually lost her life to an abuser.

Lucinda herself had also sustained a great deal of bodily harm at the hands of the same man.

"Are you looking for Dr. Owens?"

"Yes and no. I am supposed to pick up a check. Are you included in the circle of secrets this time?"

"That I am. I have a check made out to La Cava Golf Club to the tune of $250,000. Does that sound right?"

"Wow. That's the cost of joining the club? I didn't realize it was so high."

"Dr. Buck said it was 50 percent refundable after five years, provided the club doesn't go under, in which case it will be worth nothing."

"That's a lot of expense for me to 'snoop around,' as he calls it."

"The money came from his consortium of investors. Those fellows have all sorts of oil and natural gas production, so they can afford it. Sometimes I think it's just a game they like to play, just to make sure no one else is getting the better of them investment-wise. These friends of Dr. Owens have very deep pockets, Dr. Brady, so do not worry about that."

A loud clap of thunder hit, followed by an escalation of the rain. I considered just going home. Mary Louise was in Austin on Fridays for board meetings, alternating between March of Dimes and Child Advocates. I could hang out with Tip and start the new John Sandford novel about one of my favorite characters, Virgil Flowers. However, with the bad weather, La Cava would be deserted since there was no clubhouse, and maybe I could gather some information sorely needed by my friend and mentor, Buck Owens.

I bid Lucy Williams a good day, went back to my truck, and headed to the other side of town. The rain was brutal, and the roads quickly filled with water. My sturdy Tahoe was built for the weather, and she missed not a beat on the trip to La Cava. The principals fortunately had spent the money to build concrete roads into the golf club. There was all sorts of mud and debris at the actual clubhouse construction site, but getting to the Airstream office was no problem. I had no umbrella, so I parked right by the entry door, jumped out of the truck, and entered.

I expected to find Patsy Simmons at her desk, but it was empty. I looked around surreptitiously, worried my presence would be noted by a stray employee or a hidden camera, but it seemed I was alone. First, I found an envelope in Patsy's desk, put the check into it, and placed it under a paperweight on her desk with my name on the front in large letters.

Once I had stepped over the line and opened the top drawer of her desk, the criminal side of me started looking into other desk drawers. I did not know exactly what I was searching for but thought I would know if I found it. Patsy's desk drawers had the usual administrative assistant work necessities, such as pencils, pens, paper clips, folders full of information about La Cava, a hole punch, computer printer paper, envelopes, stamps, and notepads. The bottom right drawer held her purse, or perhaps a satchel or briefcase, considering the size. I carefully peeked inside, noted keys, makeup vials, lipsticks, facial tissues, and . . . a checkbook.

Was I going to cross the line from curiosity seeker to pocketbook thief, and risk my career with a breaking-and-entering charge, compounded by theft of personal property of an employee of La Cava Golf Club? Apparently, because I snatched that checkbook out and started thumbing through the entries. The checkbook was organized with monthly deposits circled in red, and neat entries of checks written in ledger fashion. Her monthly deposit? $25,000, which seemed a lot for her job title, but she was flying around the country with her ultimate boss, Louis Devlin, so perhaps she was being reimbursed for "services rendered." That was tacky, Brady, quite tacky.

I also found a small personal calendar. I thought that was unusual, considering most of us enter that sort of data into our smart phones. I looked at entries for the past week and saw "NY!" in large red letters for last Friday afternoon. A return date of Sunday was also penned in red. Huh. Devlin had planned to return Sunday, but weather delayed that until Monday, as Lt. Mims had pointed out. I thumbed through the address book and saw a few other entries in red, indicating trips Ms. Simmons had taken; whether with Devlin or not, I did not know.

Having riffled through her purse and her desk, my courage was emboldened, and I turned around in her swivel chair and peered at the filing cabinets behind me. I opened drawers and found the first section to be full of information about the current club members. I estimated there had been over one hundred to date. At the current rate of $250,000 per member, that meant at least $25 million had been added to the coffers. I remembered from my conversation with Buck at his soiree that La Cava had only fifty or sixty members. That would produce $12–15 million. That would be a big difference in operating capital. I wondered if these numbers were correct and if Buck was misinformed.

The next section of filing cabinets was full of potential new members, with names, addresses, phone numbers, and financial information on each. It looked like the current club dues were $3,000 per month, and if a member brought in a prospective member and they joined, the referring member would get one month's dues free.

The third section was a bonanza of financial information about the establishment of La Cava, the costs of the land, construction costs, financing costs, architect fees, and golf course development costs. There were many documents showing back and forth communications between Devlin and lenders of all sorts, both local and out of state, mostly New York. I turned the chair around, looked outside for anyone in the area, then turned back to the filing cabinet and pulled out pertinent documents about the financing of La Cava. I located the copier, which fortunately was one that loaded large numbers of documents and copied them in record time. I inserted the documents I thought would be helpful, hit the Copy button, and waited what seemed like an eternity for the printing to be done. When the process was complete, I replaced the documents in what I hoped was their original position, found a large envelope for my copies, and shut the cabinet doors. Just as I stood and walked around the desk, the door slammed open and in walked Patsy Simmons. She was partially soaked, her hair askew, and her makeup streaked from the rain.

"Morning," I said cheerfully.

"Dr. Brady. What are you doing here?"

"I was just dropping off a check for membership. I assume the dues billing will start next month?"

"Uh, yes sir," she stammered. "I'm surprised. I heard that you and your wife found Mrs. Devlin's body on Sunday, and I just thought that . . . well, an experience like that could sour you on the club."

"That was a tragic event but has nothing to do with the golf course and the clubhouse. My wife and I are IN and looking forward to becoming members."

I shook her hand, tucked my stolen documents under my arm, and made a mad dash for the truck.

Tip was scared to death of thunder. When I arrived home, I found him hiding under a pair of jeans and a flannel shirt I kept in the corner of my clothes closet for such occasions. I leashed him and led him outside to the back yard at a point where the roof line extended about six feet, just enough for him to do his business without getting soaked. When he was done, he streaked back into the house, leash still attached to his collar, and ran back into the closet.

I found leftover steak Diane in the fridge and made myself a delicious steak sandwich with toasted sourdough bread. I spread the document copies from the La Cava heist and reviewed them while I ate, hoping Mary Louise would not make a surprise early return. I made a list of the pertinent facts, planning to shred the pilfered paperwork when I had the facts down. If asked, I could always respond, "What evidence"?

Land costs - $2,000,000

Soft costs - Architect costs, fees, permits, finance charges - $5,000,000

Hard costs - Clubhouse, restrooms on course, equipment and golf-cart housing - $7,500,000

Golf course construction costs - $12,500,000

Limestone formation breakdown - $5,000,000

I was not familiar with the cost of golf course development, but the total was $32,000,000. I researched average golf course construction costs online and found that the average was around $16,000,000 with land purchase. That meant La Cava was $16,000,000 over the average cost of building a golf course, outbuildings, and a clubhouse.

Maybe raising that extra money was where the Permian Basin boys and Dr. Buck Owens came in. Or maybe Devlin was trying to raise that money on Wall Street, which would explain his trip to the Big Apple. What I did not understand was where the money from membership purchases fit into the equation. One hundred memberships at $250,000 each was $25,000,000, which would go a long way to funding the construction of the golf course and the clubhouse. And there was that discrepancy in the number of memberships sold between what Buck told me and what the documents showed.

My cell phone rang, and the screen indicated Mary Louise was calling.

"Hey, are you dry?" I asked.

"No. Austin had these torrential thunderstorms go through. I wanted to get a head start, so I left early. Unfortunately, the storms are following me. I made it out of the city, and I'm headed west on Highway 71. I just passed Bee Cave Road, but I can hardly see, the rain is so intense."

"There are a few gas stations and restaurants in that area. Why don't you pull over, get under cover in case it hails, and wait it out?"

"I think I will. Mostly I was scared and wanted to hear your voice. I assume your golf game was rained out?"

"Oh yes. I made rounds, then went over to the Marble Falls Police Department and talked to Randall Mims about that conversation I overheard on Friday. He didn't think much of it. Also, there was another matter with the autopsy I wanted to discuss with him. I have yet to discuss it with you, but I will be happy to, once you're home."

"We could have ourselves a nice romantic Friday afternoon if I could just get there."

"Listen, do not hurry. Wait it out under cover for a half hour, then drive reasonably slowly and come home safely. You know me; I'll still be in a romantic mood when you get home. Deal?"

"Deal, lover. I will keep you posted."

CHAPTER 11

ROAD TRIP

Mary Louise made it home safely, although it took her close to two hours to get through the Texas thunderstorm. She was, to put it mildly, frazzled.

"Are you hungry?"

"Not really, mostly just upset with the rain and traffic."

"How about a glass of wine?"

"What time is it?"

"Time for a glass of wine," I said, and poured her a tall Rombauer chardonnay.

She sipped the wine at first, then gulped a couple of swallows.

"Better?"

"Yes. thanks. You said something on the phone about an additional finding at Christine Devlin's autopsy. Is that something you can share with me?"

"Of course," and I explained the finding that the victim was an intersex person.

"While that may have been a challenge for her to live with, I don't see how that could have been a potential cause of her death. What am I missing?"

"Maybe nothing at all. Jerry Reed called me because he was trying to protect her, even in death, and worried that the police might run roughshod over her postmortem rights to privacy. I discussed the situation with Randall Mims. He seemed to understand and said he would do his best to keep the issue out of his murder investigation, unless it turned out that her physical differences, which are hereditary, played a role in her demise."

"How could that possibly be a factor in the murder investigation?"

"You know as well as I that even though the most likely suspect is always the spouse, murder investigations can take unexpected turns," I said.

""I suppose," Mary Louise replied. "But I can't help but think her murder happened because she knew too much about her husband's doings, which takes me back to the conversation you overheard on Friday at La Cava."

"But I didn't see either the man or the woman, only the back of their heads, as I told Lieutenant Mims."

"I know that. I think someone in law enforcement should find the owner of the golf cart with the HIGHROLLER license plate, and I emphasize law enforcement, because I want you out of harm's way. If whoever killed Christine Devlin thought she was a problem, you and your amateur sleuthing might be equally offensive to them, and you might find yourself a target. It has happened before, Jim Bob Brady, and don't deny it."

"I would not deny the truth, my dear. I will steer clear."

She finished her wine and decided to take a shower and rid herself of the travel debris. I heard the shower running through the closed bathroom door, thought for a moment that I should join her, then decided she probably just wanted to get clean and take a nap. I poured myself a glass of wine and was sipping it at the kitchen bar when the bedroom door opened. "Aren't you coming?" she said.

"Yes. Yes, I am," was my response.

We drove to Dallas Saturday morning. Our son J. J., who, with his college roommate Brad Broussard, owned B&B Investigations, an upscale firm dedicated to leaving no stone unturned when it came to finding information its clients needed, specialized in background checks and uncovering financial improprieties. The firm had been hired by police departments, high-net-worth individuals, governmental agencies, even the FBI through our friend and Austin FBI ASAC, Susan Beeson. The firm had expanded over the past few years such that Brad ran the Houston office and J. J. the Dallas office, having married Kathryn Hicks, a Dallas native and SMU business-school graduate. Kathryn's father owned a chain of banks in the Dallas area, and Kathryn had gone to work for him after she completed her degree. J. J. and Kathryn's son, John James Brady Jr., was eighteen months old, and his paternal grandmother could not go longer than three or four weeks without seeing her precious grandson.

The weather had softened during the night, and Mary Louise awoke Saturday morning with a burning desire to see J. J. Jr. She called our son posthaste and said we were driving up and would spend Saturday night and return home Sunday. And that we could get a hotel room and they did not have to worry about entertaining us. I do not think she gave J. J. a chance to decline the opportunity. We were going, and that was that.

With the improved weather and driving conditions, we made the trek from Granite Falls to Dallas in three hours. J. J. and Kathryn lived in Highland Park, an upscale development north of downtown and close to SMU. J. J. and Kathryn could certainly afford to live there, based on the work they did, but I think they were mostly influenced by Kathryn's parents, who had lived in Highland Park their entire lives.

We drove up to their home a few blocks off Mockingbird Lane, and before we could get out of the car, young master J. J. was running to greet us, his dad hanging on to him to keep him from rolling down the sloped front yard and into the street. Mary Louise opened her passenger door, and J. J. Jr. jumped in and rolled about, greeting her. He played with her hair—generally a taboo—pulled on her turquoise necklace, and poked at her Oakley sunglasses. My, but was she in love with that little boy.

I hugged my grandson, but before I could say anything, he jumped back into his grandmother's lap. We finally exited the car, locked it, and strode up the incline to the front door. I was used to houses that, when entered, presented large, open living spaces with a view of something—mountains, hills, water, such as that. Their house was traditional, however, opening into a staircase leading to the second floor. As we walked down the entry corridor, there was a dining room to the left, a study with bookcases to the right, then at the end of the first level, a den with a large-screen television on the right, and a large kitchen to the left. I knew from previous visits that there were two more floors: a large bedroom suite with an office each for J. J. and Kathryn and a dual-sink bath on the second floor, and a guest bedroom and bath on the third floor for the nanny/housekeeper/cook. I felt that I was in a box in their house, something I kept to myself. They were proud of their home in Highland Park and were an integral part of a social network of friends and colleagues. Still, for my money, give me a large open great room, with sliding disappearing doors, and a view of Lake LBJ and the Texas Hill Country.

J. J. poured us a cup of coffee and we chatted while Nana—Mary Louise's appointed name, since there were two grandmothers—took off her Chanel pumps and crawled around the floor with her new best friend. What a joy it was to watch them play together.

"I hope we didn't get you out of bed too early. Your mother was up at 5 a.m. and we left the house a little before seven. Three hours to get here is making good time."

"I'm sorry Kathryn isn't here. She had a bank shareholders' meeting this morning and could not miss it. Her dad is out of town, but he's flying back this afternoon. I hope it's alright that we thought it would be fun to have a family get together tonight with Kathryn and her parents. I'm going to grill steaks and burgers, and the grown-ups can visit."

I wanted to say that he was crazy, that Nana was here for one thing and one thing only, and that was to see her grandson, and that she couldn't care less about Kathryn's parents, who always had their noses in the air because that was just the way they were. What I said was, "Sounds good, son."

Mary Louise wanted to spend as much time as possible with J. J. Jr., so we opted to make sandwiches for lunch rather than go out. He grew tired and fussy after he ate, so J. J. put him down, and we drove to the Rosewood Hotel. As we were checking in, the desk clerk mentioned that there might be a bit of secondary noise during the day while construction continued on the luxury condos going up next door, part of the Rosewood Resort, but that the evenings would remain blissfully quiet, as one would expect at the Rosewood.

I could practically feel Mary Louise's wheels spinning as we took the elevator to our room. Sure enough . . .

"So, darling husband, what about it?"

"What about what?" I said, feigning ignorance.

"You know exactly what. If we moved from the Hill Country into one of those new luxury condos—which you know we can afford—we wouldn't have to make the long drive to visit our favorite person on earth. We'd be living in the same town."

"But my job is in the Hill Country. Our new friends are in the Hill Country. Our golf club and our favorite new places are in the Hill Country. We've barely broken in the new furniture in the Hill Country."

This wasn't being received very well. So I continued, "I love our grandson just like you do. But my practice at HCMC is just how I want it. Busy, but without the pressure of big medicine. It's ideal for me, and honestly, it would break my heart a little to have found such a great position only to leave it too soon.

"Now, we'd better get a move on if we want to get freshened up and off to see that favorite person as soon as possible."

It was really the only way to get out of the conversation: dangling the idea of visiting that sweet grandson of ours. So we quickly cleaned up, changed into casual clothes for grilling, and got back to J. J.'s house a little before cocktail hour. Kathryn was home, and she was most gracious. If we were interfering with plans she had, we could not tell. She was a pretty woman, of medium height, had long blond hair she had inherited from her mother's Swiss father, and was thin with exceptionally long legs. She had been a track athlete at SMU, specializing in marathon runs, and had the physical attributes consistent with that. She had an opportunity to compete in the Olympics back in the day, but her studies were too important for her to give up the amount of time it took to train.

We had brought along a case of Rombauer chardonnay, so we opened a couple of bottles and started cocktail hour without Kathryn's parents. They showed up an hour or so late, allegedly because his flight had been delayed. Mr. Hicks, Bill to his friends, was a large man with an olive complexion and graying dark hair, whose hands nearly crushed mine when we shook. He was constantly grinning, and telling stories, and in general could be the life of the party unless he was overserved. Mrs. Hicks was more of a stern woman, tall and very thin, with black hair, very pale skin, and a perpetual scowl. When J. J. Jr. ran up to her and hugged her around the knees, she patted his head as she would a canine friend.

It was a pleasant evening weather-wise, so we gathered lawn chairs and sat outside and drank and talked for a while. Mary Louise stayed inside with J. J. Jr. and played until he got excited about his dad firing up the grill, after which they both came outside. Mrs. Hicks stayed inside with Kathryn to help with dinner preparations, maybe not knowing that her son-in-law was in fact cooking the meal. My better angels said they were probably making a salad, and my worse angels suggested she did not want to socialize with the hillbilly in-laws.

"Dad, I have to make a call. Watch the grill, please?"

I was happy to do so. I made small talk with Bill Hicks, finally asking him what sort of loans his bank dealt with.

"You need money, Brady?" he asked, and laughed.

"No, I have plenty of that. I have come across a situation I'm looking into for someone that involves lending a large amount of money."

"For what?"

"Golf course construction and probably homes down the line."

"Forget it."

"I'm sorry?"

"Forget it. Golf courses are a bad investment. You must rely on membership entry fees to get started, and the pesky members are always unhappy about something, always complaining. They get mad, quit, and go someplace else. People who join golf clubs tend to have a lot of money. They will walk away from their deposit, or whatever the golf people are calling it these days, and go somewhere else at the drop of a hat. The only thing that can sustain a golf club are dues. You must have members, and lots of them, who regularly pay dues. You must have more members than the charter allows, if you want to sustain the club."

"What about real estate? Isn't that a profit center?"

"It can be, depending on how the deal is structured. But the architect wants to make money, the builders want to make money, and the real estate agents want to make money, all of which are cutting the pie into smaller and smaller portions. The real long-term money is if you set up the principal as an agent, and they get a percentage each time a lot is sold, or a house is resold, in perpetuity. That can be worth a fortune if the club is a success. If the club is not successful, however, then who do you sell that real estate to? No one. It is a very slippery slope. I would advise against your investing in a venture like that unless someone else is footing the bill and taking all the risk. Now that's a different story."

CHAPTER 12

THE FUNERAL

We spent Sunday morning with J. J., Kathryn, and our new grandson. We went over to their house early and helped fix a huge breakfast of scrambled eggs, bacon, sausage, pancakes . . . and melon, in order to pretend we were eating healthy.

Parting was such sweet sorrow for Mary Louise. J. J. Jr. asked, in his baby way of speaking, why Nana was crying. The answer had to do with something in her eye. We hugged all around and were on the road by noon. Louis Devlin was having an impromptu memorial service for his wife, and although we did not know them, we had been invited and felt obligated to make an appearance, seeing as how our little community was tightly knit.

The service was held in the small chapel on the grounds of Hillside Cemetery, a beautiful resting place in the hills between Horseshoe Bay and Llano, off Highway 71. I was surprised to see the chapel packed. I recognized several colleagues from HCMC, including Dr. Buck Owens. I also saw Lt. Randall Mims seated in the last row and wondered if he thought he would solve Christine's murder by attending the service. Also in attendance was Patsy Simmons, which was surprising to some people, who audibly gasped at her entrance. Those in attendance who sat in the first two rows seemed to be the most disturbed by her presence.

Attendees in that section appeared to be in their thirties and forties, so I suspected they were children or other close relatives of Christine. Louis was seated in the first row as well. And then I wondered how long Louis and Christine had been married, and if they had children together, or if they had a mixed marriage of hers and his.

The minister rose, the chatter stopped, and an organist played "Amazing Grace." I heard weeping and occasional sobs during the rendition. Old sentimental soul that I am, I teared up at the music, even though I had not met Christine Devlin except in death. Mary Louise squeezed my hand, and I let the emotion fade away.

"We're here today to celebrate the life of Christine Devlin," the minister boomed, in a basso profundo voice. "I am Dr. Roger Blanchett, and I knew Christine for many years. She grew up in Carrollton, formerly a small suburb of Dallas, now a fine city of its own. We met in college at SMU. She came from a well-to-do family and was majoring in marketing, while I was a seminary student on scholarship. We struck up a friendship during our first year. We both had to take a basic chemistry course to fulfill a requirement in our respective majors. Christine was terrible with science, and just did not have the head for it. We were paired as lab partners, which was a weekly nightmare from two to five. We had to make chemical compounds using flasks and test tubes we had attempted to make with personal glass blowing. Our glassware was never level, and the chemical reactions were never consummated, as indicated by our instructor. Christine even set the lab on fire with an unexpected explosion. Fortunately, no one was injured, but the lab was never the same." The story was followed by brief respectful laughter, after which the minister continued.

"Christine and I kept our friendship until graduation, after which she returned home to work in the family retail business, and

I went on to the seminary and became a Methodist minister. Some years after, Christine looked me up in the SMU annals and asked me to perform a wedding ceremony for her. I met the young man, who was a fine sort, as was his family. That marriage produced three fine children, all of whom are here today, seated in the front row. Christine's husband died too young of colon cancer, and she remained a widow for ten or so years. Then, three years ago, she met Louis Devlin, a real estate developer in Dallas, at a builder's convention in Kansas City. Christine was then living in Dallas and had started a convention-planning business, which had become quite successful. It was love at first sight for the two of them. And once again, I got the call from Christine to perform a ceremony for her second wedding.

"I met Louis, a charming man and obviously totally smitten with Christine. He had two children from his first marriage and was also a widower, and the happy couple and their collective five children seemed a perfect match. I performed the ceremony at the Rosewood Resort, and Christine and I once again went our merry ways. When last I spoke to her, she and Louis were moving to the Marble Falls area to work on new projects.

"We continued to exchange Christmas cards, and we kept a warm place in our hearts for each other, and for our enduring friendship. And then, to get the call from Louis, that she had been murdered. What a tragedy. I must admit that I cried for two days. I finally pulled myself together for the sake of my own wife and children and prepared my words with which to address you today. Christine was a dear friend, a fine person, a successful professional, a loving mother, and a loyal wife. I have no idea why anyone would want to murder this most extraordinary woman. I hope the perpetrator is brought to justice, and swiftly."

He then continued with what I call funeral speak, a standard liturgy common to most Protestant funerals. Upon its completion, he stepped back, and the organist concluded the ceremony with a resounding rendition of "The Old Rugged Cross." When she was finished, those present politely and quietly rose from their seats and dispersed.

Mary Louise and I caught up with Lt. Mims outside.

"Looking for a murderer, Lieutenant?" Mary Louise asked.

"Well, ma'am, you never know. This would not be the first funeral I attended where the perpetrator flaunted themselves. Leave no stone unturned, I say."

"Any clues you can share with us?" I asked.

"No, not at this time, sir. I have some leads, but nothing solid."

"Let me say this, and I may be stepping on toes, but I have been involved in murder investigations in the past, and I'm good at paperwork and drudge work. If you find you need some help, feel free to—"

"Jim Bob Brady, you are OUT of the investigation business. We just had this discussion the other day. Randall, ignore my husband, please."

"With all due respect, I intend to do just that, ma'am."

We had just gotten into the car when Buck Owens tapped on the driver's windshield. "Nice service, huh?"

"Yep. Unfortunately, when you get to a certain age, they all seem the same, Buck."

"I agree, and I'm a lot older than you, so it's even more so for me. Did you take the membership fee check over to La Cava?"

"Yes. I ran into Patsy Simmons while I was dropping off the check. We had a very brief conversation, but I may have some information you might be interested in. Maybe we could meet tomorrow afternoon, after I'm done with surgery."

"Sounds good. Let Lucy know what time."

"Will do."

I started up the truck and headed to the vet's office to pick up Tip. "Want to get some lunch on the way?"

"We had a huge breakfast, but I'm hungry again. How does Bluebonnet Café sound?"

"Oh, my, a woman after my own heart."

As we drove out of the cemetery, I saw a small collection of people standing around a gravesite. I assumed those were the children, close relatives, and close friends of Christine and Louis Devlin. As I was waiting to exit, my driver window again was tapped, and there stood Patsy Simmons. I rolled the window down and greeted her.

"This is my wife, Mary Louise Brady."

"Pleased to meet you, ma'am," she said. Mary Louise just nodded, and I could feel the negative vibes from my wife fill the car. Patsy did not know how or did not care to dress appropriately for the occasion. She had on a tight, revealing black blouse, a short black skirt, black spike heels, and a black blazer.

"Dr. Brady, I would like to speak with you in the next day or two, if you have the time."

"Concerning?"

"Mrs. Devlin, me, and Mr. Devlin."

"Why me? You hardly know me."

"I know you by reputation, and you seem to be a caring and honest man. Also, I am good friends with Lucinda Williams, Dr. Owens's admin assistant, and she vouched for you."

Me, the guy who only Friday had riffled through your file cabinets and stolen and copied a myriad of documents, I wanted to say, but did not. "That's fine, but perhaps we shouldn't meet at

La Cava. How about coming to our house for a drink, and maybe a bite to eat on Tuesday? Is that a good day, Mary Louise?"

If looks could kill, I would have been a dead critter.

"Tuesday is fine, dear," Mary Louise said.

"Thank you so much, Dr. Brady. Mrs. Brady," she said, and sashayed away.

CHAPTER 13

MONDAY, MONDAY

I had five cases scheduled for Monday morning: one virgin hip replacement, three virgin knee replacements, and a hip labrum repair. Labrum repairs were relatively new. Sophisticated techniques in CT and MRI scanning allowed us to diagnose problems that were not discovered in years past. There was a time when a patient would come in to see the doc with a complaint of chronic hip pain. If a plain X-ray did not show any pathology, I would usually put the patient on anti-inflammatory medication and hope for the best. These days, with our modern scanning techniques, we were able to diagnose soft-tissue problems in the hip that would have been ignored in the past.

The labrum tear involves a tear in the ring of cartilage that follows the outside rim of the hip joint socket. It serves to cushion the joint and acts as a sealer or gasket to help firmly hold the femoral head in the hip socket. Repair was done arthroscopically with minimal incisions using miniature instruments, and consisted of excising damaged portions of the tears and repairing the remainder of viable labrum tissue. This technique was still relatively new to me, and to do the surgery under radiologic visualization without seeing exactly what I was doing under direct vision had been a challenge. I was becoming more comfortable with the procedure but did not want to have more than one of those on the surgery schedule.

Belinda met me at the hospital at 5:30 a.m. We made rounds on the inpatients, then walked over to the rehab unit and checked on our patients in phase two of their recovery. Del Anderson was the leader of the pack in the rehab process for the post-operative patients from last week. She was up on a walker when we arrived, inside the nursing station getting coffee.

"Morning, Del. I can see I don't have to ask you how you're feeling."

"Jim Bob, it's a miracle. Most all my pre-operative pain is gone. I have some soreness in the skin and tissues from the surgery, but that bone-chilling, teeth-gnashing pain I endured for years has disappeared. Thank you, Jesus! Can I get an AMEN?"

"Amen," said Belinda and I simultaneously. We were raised in church and knew what to do.

"Did you go to Christine Devlin's memorial service yesterday?"

"Yes, we did. Did you know her very well, Del?"

"I knew her, Jim Bob, but only for a short time. She and Louis had only been here for three years. They were on the social register in Dallas but hadn't been here long enough to establish those sorts of connections in our area, not that there was such a thing in our part of the world. I think they had been married for only a little over three years. I believe they moved here shortly after the nuptials because of some project Louis was working on. I think it might have been the La Cava Golf Club, but do not quote me on that. Christine and I met through a ladies' auxiliary for the SMU Touchdown Club."

"I did not know you were a Mustang. I always figured you for a Longhorn."

"Why? Because I am brilliant, charming, loquacious, and a nosy pain in the ass?"

"Something like that, Del. Listen, before we go, Patsy Simmons stopped me in the car yesterday after the funeral, said she wanted to talk to me. I could feel the ice coming from Mary Louise's side of the car. Any idea what that's about?"

"She wants to talk about Louis, and you're her choice to confide in. That would be my guess."

"She said she and Lucy Williams, Buck Owens's admin assistant, are good friends, and Lucy told her I could be trusted. Trusted with what, I wonder?"

"I don't know, but would I not like to be a fly on the wall during that conversation. Please let me know what she has to say."

"I will if I can, but can you really trust a man who is friends with a woman who owns a newspaper?"

"Now there is someone with insight. You must be a Baylor man."

"Go Bears."

We started the surgical day off with the hip replacement. When that was complete except for the closure, I went next door into my second operating room and started the first knee replacement. That routine continued until the only case left was the hip labrum repair.

Lisa Stewart was her name, and she was a mid-thirties former college athlete in basketball and volleyball. She was over six feet tall and thin, and was unable to do any sort of running due to hip pain. When I went into the identification area, Louis Devlin was standing at her bedside. He was my height, heavier, with thick silver hair slicked back with gel, wearing an expensive blue pinstriped suit with a red tie.

"Dr. Brady," he said, "we haven't had the opportunity to meet. Lisa is my daughter."

I was shocked into silence; why, I did not exactly know. "Nice to meet you, sir. Nice service yesterday, if there can be such a thing for a funeral. Lisa, any last-minute questions?"

"No, Dr. Brady, just fix me up, please. My husband had to be out of town on business, so Daddy is filling in for him here. I had scheduled this surgery before Christine's . . . well, her demise, and I offered to reschedule it, but my husband and Daddy wanted me to go ahead."

"Lisa, I will do my best to get you back in action quickly. Mr. Devlin, a pleasure sir," I said, shaking his hand.

I summarized the situation in my head, walking back to the OR. I was about to operate on the daughter of a man who was reputed to be having an affair with his secretary, who might have murdered his wife, and from whose business I had just stolen a ream of documents that could possibly convict him of fraud and embezzlement and other financial misdeeds. No pressure, Brady, I thought. Just do your job.

Lisa had a ton of scar tissue in and around the hip joint, probably from multiple micro-fractures during her athletic career. Fortunately, the manufacturer's representative was present for the case, and he brought out some new toys that allowed me to debride that unwanted tissue very quickly. I was then able to access the hip joint and visualize the damage. The labrum tear was so severe that when I rotated her hip in certain directions, the femoral ball would almost come out of the hip socket. Thus, her complaints of feeling as though her hip was intermittently coming out of joint were justified. I was able to get a nice stable repair, and I felt confident she would be able to return to athletics.

I went out to the waiting room and talked to the remaining families. Mr. Devlin was not present.

I asked the volunteer at the desk if she knew of the whereabouts of Mr. Devlin, and she handed me a business card. "He said to call him when you're done, Dr. Brady."

I called as instructed, but the call went to voice mail. I expressed positive sentiment about the surgery, and that I thought his daughter would be fine after rehab, and hung up the phone. Weird, I thought. A husband out of town, and a father out of touch during his daughter's surgery.

I went to the office, cleared off my desk, answered questions from Maya and Belinda, and headed down to Buck's office.

Lucy was about to leave her desk when I arrived. "And how are you this fine day, Dr. Brady?"

"Good, Lucy. You?"

"I'm ready for greener pastures, truth be told."

"You're not leaving us, are you?"

"Oh, no. Greener pastures like my home, my recliner, my house slippers, and a cold glass of white wine."

"Ah, that I understand. Listen, Patsy Simmons approached me at Christine Devlin's funeral yesterday, said she wanted to talk to me. Did you somehow vouch for me as someone trustworthy?"

"Yes, and I'm sorry about that. Patsy's mother was one of my dear friends, and since her passing, well, Patsy has relied on me for advice, like a surrogate mother. I hope you don't mind."

"I don't mind, but I must say Mary Louise was a little taken back when Patsy approached me while we were sitting in the car, and said she wanted to have a private conversation with me. Mary Louise reluctantly agreed to host her at our home for drinks and dinner."

"Trust me, when that exterior of bravado starts to fade, and when she doesn't try and dress like a streetwalker, she is a lovely girl and will capture Mary Louise's heart. You'll see. Now, I must run."

I knocked on Buck's door, heard the familiar ENTER, and did just that.

"How was your day, Jim? Better than mine, I hope," he said, and began a one-sided discussion of the litany of problems he had encountered that day, and how he had solved them. I did not care all that much; I just wanted to deliver my stolen paperwork and get home.

I waited for a break in his conversation with himself and interrupted with "I have some paperwork for you."

"What's this?"

"Documents from La Cava showing the financials, or at least a set of financials. I can't swear to you that they are legitimate, but I found them in a filing cabinet and copied them."

"How in the hell did you get by with that? They guard those files like a bank vault."

"Not really. I stopped by there Friday to drop off the check for the buy-in, and the trailer was empty. Usually Patsy is there, guarding the place, but she was nowhere to be seen. I snooped through her desk and did not find anything of interest except names of current members and potential members with financial statements. Then I started looking through the filing cabinets, came across these documents, took a chance, and copied them. She walked in the door just as I was stuffing the documents into an envelope."

"Well, La Cava has made a bundle from membership sales. $250,000 each with over a hundred members, that is over $25,000,000. Devlin told my people they'd only sold fifty or sixty, which would raise $12–15,000,000, and that is a big difference. If the total cost of development really is $32,000,000, then they are well on their way to covering their costs. If you have 100 members paying $3,000 per month in dues, which is what I believe they anticipated, that is an additional $3,600,000 annually, which would be, after two years, enough to cover all their costs. Only one problem, Jim."

"What's that?"

"My colleagues and I put in additional capital, and that money is not noted on these spreadsheets."

"How much did you invest?"

"Our consortium put in $25,000,000, based on the anticipated revenue shortfall. However, looking at these numbers, there will be no shortfall. I wonder where our money is allocated."

"Well, Buck, there are operating costs, which can be huge, and there will be a residential real estate development once the clubhouse is complete. Maybe that's what your group's money is destined for."

"Brady, what you have brought me is helpful, but I need more before I get hold of our lawyers and confront Devlin. Find out what you can."

CHAPTER 14

PATSY

Belinda and I made early rounds on Tuesday prior to seeing clinic patients. All the post-ops were in good stead. When I came to Lisa Stewart's room, I noted the staff, either administrative or nursing, had placed her in a private suite. There were four in the hospital, one in each corner of the floor.

"Morning, Lisa. How is the hip?"

"It feels pretty darn good, Dr. Brady. I've already started trying to move it, and I don't have that catch in it that made me feel the hip was going to come out of joint."

"You need to be a little careful. Those sutures holding the labrum together are only so strong. You're safe doing gentle, and I mean gentle, range-of-motion exercises, but you will need to be non-weight-bearing for the next two weeks. Then we'll take it slow. Deal?"

"Yes, sir. Dad came by last night and said you had called him with a post-operative report. He is grateful for the excellent care I'm receiving here. The nursing staff is superb."

"Glad to hear that. I can let you go home today if you have help. Do you have children?"

"No, sir. Just me and the husband and the dog, a frisky but lovable English bulldog. I do have a housekeeper that comes in daily, and she's arranged to stay with me for the next couple of weeks, depending on my husband's work and travel schedule."

"What does your husband do, if you don't mind me asking?"

"He works for Daddy's company. They do commercial real estate development."

"Very good. Well, I will see you in a couple of weeks."

I had felt a bit of dread after our encounter with Patsy Simmons on the way out of the funeral service Sunday afternoon. Mary Louise had bristled at her intrusion, and while my wife is an extraordinarily good person, some things set her off negatively. I hoped it would get ironed out at our evening meeting, and that would depend on why Patsy wanted to speak to me.

I walked Tip when I arrived home, showered, and was as nice and polite and helpful as I knew how to be. Mary Louise, on the other hand, was eerily quiet. It was almost a relief when the doorbell rang.

"Good evening, Dr. Brady," said Patsy, casually dressed in a bulky sweatshirt, loose-fitting jeans, and sneakers, with her hair done in a non-threatening ponytail. I could have hugged her.

"Hello, Patsy. Welcome to our home."

"What a lovely place it is. Hello, Mrs. Brady."

Mary Louise had joined us in the foyer, walking silently from the kitchen. She had a look of amusement on her face.

"Hello, Patsy. I didn't recognize you for a moment. Come in."

I poured a Newton unfiltered chardonnay for each of us, and we sat out on the deck. Mary Louise had made my favorite appetizer, clam dip with chips, so maybe I had misinterpreted her quiet the past couple of days. At least Patsy's choice of wardrobe for the evening had disarmed my protective bride, so we were off to a decent start.

"Thank you for inviting me over. I couldn't decide who to discuss this with. I don't have many friends to confide in, and I've only talked to you, Dr. Brady, a couple of times, and you, Mrs. Brady, I don't know at all. However, I did speak to Lucy Williams, who has been like a surrogate mother to me since Mom died, and she assured me I could confide in you both, and that you would keep this conversation to yourselves.

"So, let me begin by saying that Louis, Mr. Devlin, is not a nice man. I am sure you saw the daily papers after Christine's death, those pictures of me descending the steps of Louis's Gulfstream on Monday morning, the day after Christine was found dead in the new home they were building. He had insisted I accompany him on his trip to New York. We left on Friday right after I gave you the tour of La Cava, Dr. Brady. That was why I had to leave suddenly. When Louis goes on these trips to larger financial centers to attempt to raise money for his projects, he often has me go along with him. Part of the reason is that I am very well organized, and I can keep all the paperwork straight. Louis is a salesperson, but not much of an accountant. He's dyslexic, and not good with numbers and detail. So, he takes me along to make himself appear to be a sophisticated businessperson, but also to help him close a deal, to put it politely."

She hesitated, taking a sip of wine. Mary Louise and I glanced at each other and shrugged.

"To put it in perspective, take a manager from Kansas City that might be wavering on putting money from the Teamsters' pension fund into one of Louis's projects. He wines them, and dines them, and promises them extra money on the side. If that is not enough, well, I become the carrot, so to speak."

"You mean you sleep with the client?" gasped Mary Louise.

"Whatever it takes."

"But that means you are essentially functioning as a prostitute, Patsy. Why would a nice, attractive girl like you participate in something that ugly?"

"Money, Mrs. Brady, plain and simple. Louis was paying me $25,000 per month," she said, and broke down. Mary Louise and I had been sitting in chairs and Patsy in a duo recliner. Mary Louise got up, sat down beside a tearful Patsy, and held her while she sobbed.

"I promised myself I wouldn't break down, but I couldn't help it. I am so sorry."

"That is fine, we're here for you," my wife said.

I went into the bar, opened another bottle of wine, retrieved tissues from the guest bath, and went back outside. The two were talking softly and intimately, and I thanked my lucky stars that Lucy was right about Patsy. Mary Louise had taken to her, and I predicted to myself they were going to be fast friends.

I filled glasses, handed Patsy the tissues, and sat back down. Tip even got into the act by walking over to Patsy and laying his big head into her lap.

Once Patsy got herself together, she continued with her narrative.

"I have no college education. I did go to secretarial school for a while, long enough to get comfortable using a computer. I had all sorts of jobs to try and support myself: server, bartender, clerk in the post office, even a flower delivery person. You name it, I've done it. And then a few years back, I interviewed with a builder in Marble Falls by the name of Tom Foley. He was not a builder on a grand scale, but he built low- to medium-end homes, and he was good at it. He put an ad in the local paper for a Girl Friday. That term sounds so archaic to me now, but at the time, that sounded like the perfect job for me. He wanted an assistant to help with office work and other administrative tasks that needed doing that he didn't have the time to do because he was a hands-on builder.

"Tom and I hit it off right away. He gradually gave me more and more responsibility as he became more successful, and eventually I became an information and communication manager in addition to taking care of the bookkeeping and other clerical duties. We were a great team, until he got sick. He started throwing up at work, was dizzy and weak. We thought it was the flu at first, but eventually he went to the doctor and found out he had leukemia. They sent him to the oncologist in Austin, who put him on massive amounts of chemotherapy. Whatever energy he had left was gone, once he started chemo. The cancer did not respond, and he passed away quickly. He left a lovely wife and three boys."

She took the fresh glass of wine, drank half of it, and started again.

"His wife and I collaborated and tried to sell his business. We placed ads, put out computer notices, and called other builders. Tom had several good crews, and lots of jobs scheduled on the books, and she and I thought that would be worth something. It turns out that in the building business, you have your reputation and goodwill, but without construction equipment, or an office in a building you own, or some other hard asset, your business is worth nothing. Someone will come along and take over your clients and do the job you are unable to do because you are . . . well, dead.

"And then along came Louis Devlin. He was a big-time builder and developer from Dallas, mostly in commercial properties, but some residential as well. I forgot how he initially got involved in the sale. Might have been from another builder in this area. At any rate, he blows into town, talks to me and Tom's wife, looks at all our projects under construction, offers to take over all the projects and the crews and finish the houses that Tom had started. He explained he was not buying the business, but was taking it off Tom's wife's hands, and assuming her liability for all the unfinished projects. He gave her a good-faith check of $100,000 to tide her and the boys over until she had gainful employment, and he said goodbye to her. As for me, he insisted I stay on, since I probably knew, as he put it, where all the bodies were buried. I didn't really understand what he meant, since Tom was a very honest man, but I let it go.

"And that's how I came to work for Louis three years ago. He moved here with his wife Christine and took over not only Tom's building business but a couple of commercial operations, and then got the bid to build La Cava Golf Club. He has been a busy boy these past three years."

We three stood up and stretched. Mary Louise suggested we get something to eat. She had prepared chicken piccata with fettucine pasta and a Caesar salad. We sat at the kitchen bar and made small talk while we ate. I opened another bottle of wine, a pinot grigio. After a time, I asked a question.

"Patsy, has Louis been successful in building businesses?"

"Yes, very."

"And you have been paid well, as you mentioned earlier?"

"Yes, very well."

"So, I wonder why you would want to rock the boat, and risk losing all you have gained in his employ?"

"Dr. Brady, I have done a lot of things that I wish I had not done. Ugly things, all in the name of helping Louis expand his business. I think a girl like me, raised in a conservative household in a small town in Texas, can only lie and prostitute herself for so long before she breaks down. That's where I am."

"Going up against Mr. Devlin would be a difficult task," I said. "He wields a lot of power in this town, as he probably still does in Dallas."

"Don't forget about his Kansas City connections. I've been running the books for three years. I do know where all the bodies are buried, so to speak, but they are Louis's bodies, not Tom's."

"What about his Kansas City connections? You alluded earlier in the evening to those when you mentioned something about a pension fund manager."

"Dr. Brady, I'm familiar with the goings-on of Louis and his company for the past three years, but there is some connection to Kansas City that he is very private about. I try not to involve myself in those discussions, because I sense there is something evil and foreboding about his past there. Take 'the Fixer,' for example.

"His given name is Charles Fixatore, and he's the guy Louis goes to, to get things done. He calls him the Fixer. I don't know what all he does, but he is a nasty little man, and my advice would be to stay away from him."

"I am curious if any of these dealings of your boss have to do with the murder of Christine Devlin."

"Christine was a wonderful woman. I believe she was murdered for what she knew about Louis, although I do not know what that could be. If that's the case, it would be in his past, either before Dallas or between Dallas and his moving to Marble Falls. Someone with power well above my pay grade would have to look into that."

Mary Louise and I looked at each other, and said simultaneously, "Susan Beeson."

CHAPTER 15

LISA STEWART

Mary Louise and I were lying in bed, both of us sleepless and unsettled after the lengthy conversation with Patsy Simmons.

"What do you think about Louis Devlin now, after hearing all the talk of the Fixer and Kansas City and secrets?" she asked.

"Sounds like an unsavory character. I don't know anything about him since his arrival in our area, and that's been three years or so. He apparently keeps a low profile. I'd like to find out about his activities and reputation in Dallas, and about his relationship to Kansas City. With talk of Kansas City pension funds, and this guy called the Fixer, he could have underworld connections."

"I know all the signs you exhibit, Jim Bob Brady, when you are feeling like sticking your big toe in the water of an interesting investigation, but let me tell you this. You remember Dom Davis, the paralegal who was probably guilty of mugging you and giving you a concussion years ago during that malpractice case? Well, the Fixer sounds like another character of the same ilk. I want you to steer clear of anything to do with these people. Is that understood?"

"I hear you, Mary Louise. I have no plans to get involved—"

"Do you remember earlier this evening, when you went into the bar to open more wine, and you left Patsy and I alone on the terrace?"

"Yes, but what—"

"She told me that you must be an amateur snoop, because she caught you on the hidden security cameras in her office, riffling through her desk and copying documents from her file cabinet. She erased the digital memory that showed you in her office, to keep you out of harm's way. She also said those documents you copied were a smoke screen, that the real documents on the La Cava development are kept in Louis's safety deposit box at his bank. She could not imagine what you were doing, unless you were looking for items as a favor to Buck Owens, who is a worried investor and calls Louis weekly for progress reports."

I could feel my face burning with embarrassment. I did not spot the security cameras, but I guess that is why they are called hidden cameras. What an idiot. I was thankful Patsy had the wherewithal to erase evidence of my presence in her office. Now that I had heard about the Fixer, I did not want to have an adversarial relationship with him, as he would probably be called in to take care of a snoop such as myself.

"I am sorry about that. Buck has been after me to try and find out what's going on at La Cava, which is why he and his consortium funded our entry fee. I was there to drop off the papers at Patsy's office, and one thing led to another."

"You mean we are now members of La Cava?"

"Uh, yes."

"When were you going to tell me?"

"Well, when the time was right."

"How much are the dues?"

"Three thousand a month, but Buck is also paying for that."

She stared at me, turned off her bedside light, turned away from me, and nestled into the covers. I reached over and patted her on the back but got no response. I thought she would be happy we had another place to golf at no expense, but I guessed that was an error in judgment on my part. Seems that I was guilty of quite a few of those recently.

I was up and out of the house by 5:30 Wednesday morning. Neither Mary Louise nor Tip showed any emotion at my departure. I met Belinda for hospital rounds, had a bite of breakfast in the surgeon's lounge, and headed to the operating room identification area.

The Wednesday surgery schedule was light, with only three cases: two virgin knee replacements and one virgin hip replacement. Belinda and I had developed a rhythm in surgery, not unlike a band with a smooth syncopated sound. We. completed the cases a little after noon. I ordered lunch for Belinda and me and took it up to my office. I cleared my desk in order to have a place to eat and enjoyed my pastrami on rye with horseradish and mustard. It would have tasted even better with a beer, but I decided not to press my luck. Once done, I cleared off the charts, dictated notes, signed documents, returned phone calls, then propped my boots on the desk and fell fast asleep.

Maya woke me with a phone call I needed to take.

"This is Dr. Brady."

"Doctor, this is Lisa Stewart. You repaired by acetabular labrum on Monday?"

"Of course, Lisa. Is something wrong?"

"The nurses changed my bandage before I left yesterday morning, and it was clean and dry. Now there is blood leaking through, and I'm worried."

"Have you been overactive? I told you to keep the weight off and be very gentle with the movement."

"Well, my crutches caught the edge of a rug, and a felt myself falling. I tried to catch myself, but I didn't want to fall on top of my little dog, so I ended up falling on the operated hip."

Shit. "Does it hurt to move it?"

There was silence for a moment. "There is some pain, yes, but nothing terrible. Do you think it's okay? I'll be devastated if I've messed up my hip. Can you please check it for me?"

"Sure. I am out of surgery and in my office. Do you have someone to drive you here? I think you said your housekeeper was looking after you."

Another quiet moment. "Well, my husband is still out of town, and my housekeeper's little girl got sick and she had to take her to the doctor. I could try and drive myself, but now I'm afraid. Is there any chance you could make a house call?"

"I can arrange that. Give me your address and I'll stop by in an hour or so."

I had Belinda put together a care package of new bandages. She offered to go with me, but I declined. She had work to do, and I was available, so what would be the harm?

Lisa and her husband lived in the Hills of Horseshoe Bay, a beautiful area with acreage for horses and cattle. She had given me the security gate code, and I wandered through large plots of land with well-maintained pastures with three- and four-board fencing. I eyed some longhorn cattle, herds of llamas and sheep, and horses frolicking with young foals.

I found the mailbox with her address and drove up a long driveway that ended in a large overhang in front. I rang the doorbell, heard a "Come on in, it's open," and entered the house. It was a huge ranch-style house with high ceilings and exposed beams of dark wood. There was a massive grand piano in an alcove with the lid closed to accommodate many framed photographs.

Lisa greeted me on crutches and appeared a little wobbly. She had on sweats and was barefoot, and her hair looked like it hadn't been brushed in a while. The English bulldog she was so worried about crushing was hefty to the tune of about fifty pounds and looked like he could hold his own in a battle.

"That's George."

I leaned down and petted George, whose labored breathing was noticeable. "Is he okay?"

"Yes, they all breathe like that. And they snore too, so George doesn't get to sleep in the bed with me anymore."

"Let's check that hip, Lisa."

She laid down on a leather couch covered in a sheet. I put on gloves, used scissors to cut the bloody bandage, and lifted it off her hip. Fortunately, she had a towel to cover herself with, seeing as how close the hip joint is to . . . well, other vital areas I wanted no part of peering at. I palpated the hip area. There did not seem to be a hematoma. I gently moved the hip joint, and that did not produce any undue pain.

"My guess is that the surgery is intact. I would order an MRI, except right after surgery there'll be so much bleeding and scar tissue that detail would be lacking. We might think about doing that in the next few weeks if things don't go well, but for now, I'll clean it up and redress the wound."

I used hydrogen peroxide, then alcohol, to cleanse the area, and redressed the surgical area with a very thick bandage.

"You be careful, Lisa. I don't want this procedure to fail."

"I'll do my best. Thank you so much for coming over. Can I offer you a cup of coffee before you go?"

"It's hard to resist fresh coffee."

I followed her into a modern kitchen with a massive structure over the stove which held a myriad number of pots and pans. We sat at the counter and poured ourselves a thick dark brew which would be chock-full of caffeine. I gazed out the windows and appreciated the feel of the hills and the livestock.

"Beautiful place you have, Lisa. How many acres?"

"Fifty. My husband Bill does so like his privacy."

"From the looks of the folks that attended Christine's funeral, and the number of photographs you have on the piano, you have quite a blended family."

"Oh, that we do. Are you familiar with our family history?"

"Not really. I don't want to pry—"

"Oh, don't be silly. The minister at the memorial service alluded to some of it, and there are certainly no secrets. We are ordinary people, in my opinion.

"Christine Devlin was born Christine Hall to wealthy parents who lived in Carrollton, Texas, north of Dallas. She worked in the family retail business after college, but eventually got into the convention-management business and worked primarily in Dallas. She met and married Robert Johnson Sr., who owned an executive placement firm. They had three sons: Robert Jr., Alan, and Samuel. Fast forward some years later, and Robert Sr. developed colon cancer and died young. Christine raised her boys on her own and was single for ten years or so.

"Louis Devlin, my father, came from Kansas City, but eventually became successful in the building and development business and relocated to Dallas, which is where we grew up. He had married a KC girl, my mom Lynette, family name Avalon, who died young from ovarian cancer. With two daughters, Dad provided housekeepers, nannies, whatever he needed to make sure my sister Elizabeth and I were well taken care of. I married Bill Stewart, and my sister married Kirk Winters. Both Bill and Kirk eventually came to work in Daddy's business, which has many facets, but he is basically a land developer and a commercial real estate magnate. Robert Jr., Alan, and Sam also now work in Daddy's business.

"Dad was single for close to ten years, and then met Christine at a builders' convention in Kansas City. She had a company that arranged conventions, and they hit it off immediately. Theirs was a whirlwind courtship, and they married after knowing each other less than a year. Daddy and Christine were insistent that we 'children' get to know one another before the nuptials, so he arranged several weekend getaways for us. Bill and I do not have kids, but Elizabeth does and all three of Christine's sons do. Daddy insisted the kids all come along on these 'getting to know you' trips. There were three trips, I think: one to Scottsdale for a week of golf at the Princess, one to Newport Beach for a week of water fun at the Balboa Bay Club, and one to Stein Eriksen Lodge in Deer Valley for skiing. He spent a small fortune in getting the adults and the kids to know each other, and after the third trip, we all felt like family.

"Dad and Christine were so incredibly happy together. Daddy made the decision to move here about three years ago to undertake the project to build La Cava Golf Club and to create a real estate development there. Christine was able to continue managing her convention business long distance, and Daddy had Christine's three sons take over the day-to-day operations of his business interests in Dallas, and brought Elizabeth and me here, where our husbands are now working.

"And that's it, in a nutshell."

"Your dad's business sounds like a true family enterprise, with his daughters' two husbands working for him, and Christine's three sons working for him as well."

"I won't say it hasn't been an adjustment for Liz and me to move from Dallas, the shopping and entertainment capital of Texas, to the Horseshoe Bay area. But we do love it here now, and we enjoy boating on Lake LBJ, and the golf courses. The boys are working all the time and traveling quite a bit, so it's up to Liz and me to entertain ourselves."

"Why is there so much travel involved in the development business? Being a doctor, I have blinders on about a lot of occupations."

"Development involves building infrastructure, such as conduits for power, water, sewer, and drainage, commercial buildings, residential structures, all the necessities required for people to live and work in an area. One of Daddy's favorite types of development is in commercial properties. He builds a building after discovering a need for said building, and then he collects rents from tenants for a long time, unless he ends up selling the building to another developer. He always says that's the most bang for your buck, commercial tenants."

I looked at my watch. "Listen, thanks for the coffee and the Devlin history. Come in next week and let me check that wound, and try to keep it dry and free from injury until then, please."

She showed me to the door, thanked me profusely for the house call, and bid me adieu.

CHAPTER 16

THE GALA

I got home around 4 p.m. and found Tip at a back window in the great room, barking at a rabbit that had invaded his territory. The harmless bunny seemed confident and aloof with Tip indoors, but when I let Tip out to do his business, the rabbit scattered at the speed of sound. I did not know what Tip would do with a rabbit if he caught one, since he is such a gentle creature, but I really did not want to find out.

We returned inside, and I poured myself a glass of wine and waited for the arrival of my bride. She was not home by five. I checked my cell phone for messages, but nothing. Just as I was starting to worry, I heard the garage door open. I walked to the exit door from the kitchen and peered into the garage. She had her hair done up in a "do," had on paper booties with her freshly manicured toes exposed, and was wrestling with a bag in the back seat.

"Would you like some assistance, m'lady?"

"Why aren't you dressed?"

"For what?"

"Jim Bob, tonight is Sister Mads's fundraiser at Hill Country Resort. It's black tie."

I started to feel ill. "I'm sorry, I—"

"Please get your tux out of the trunk. I had it cleaned and I bought a new shirt and tie for you. You need to shower and get dressed. You know how long it takes you to tie a bow tie."

Madelyn O'Rourke, locally known as Sister Mads, was a former nun. She ran a women's shelter for the Catholic Church for many years, until ideological differences caused a rift in her relationship with the Church. Sister Mads had come across several teenagers who were pregnant from their abusers. She felt that exceptions should be made in the Catholic Church's philosophy, and she had arranged for the pregnancies to be terminated. The Church found out, and while they might have been sympathetic to the girls' situations, rules were rules. Sister Mads insisted on providing a 'full service' shelter and refused to back down. As a result, the Church threw her out for failure to uphold her vows.

Mads decided to try and raise money to build her own private women's shelter. She contacted her doctor friend, Buck Owens, whom she'd known for many years, and asked his advice. What she did not know was that Buck had been reducing his medical practice gradually over time and had been investing with his old buddies in oil and gas production. Their consortium had recently hit the big-time with a spectacular oil well, and Buck had become insanely wealthy overnight. He asked her what she needed, she told him, and he said the money is yours, whatever the cost.

And that's how Mourning Doves began, which functioned as a temporary residence for battered and abused women. It was a refuge, and it provided educational assistance, job training, and counseling in all aspects necessary for a woman to start a new life. Sister Mads held a fundraiser yearly, which was essentially a big party, where the food, alcohol, and donations ran freely. And I had forgotten and was already late. I showered and dressed, saving the tying of the bow tie until last.

I was standing in front of a full-length mirror in the hallway when Mary Louise exited her dressing room. All I could do was stare. Her hair was still up in a "do," with braids and curls interwoven with rhinestones. Her red ballgown was low cut, and she wore a beautiful diamond necklace which dipped down close to her cleavage. She wore red satin heels with an open toe, exposing toes whose polish matched her dress. What a package she was.

"Well, what do you think?"

"Does the fact that I'm speechless indicate what I'm thinking?"

"Later, buddy. You can be the one to take off the dress. Let me help you with that tie."

She stood behind me and tied the tie. All I could think about was her breasts rubbing against me, and to hell with the tie.

She had arranged for a car, not that there was a great distance to travel from our home in Granite Falls to the Hill Country Resort ballroom. Our journey would take us through Horseshoe Bay, whose police officers did not take kindly to citizens traveling their streets under the influence. Mary Louise did not want to spoil the evening by having to bail me out of jail, so we had a driver, who dropped us off at the external entry to the ballroom. He gave me a card and said to text him when we were ready to go home.

We checked in at the desk, secured our reserved table, and received a numbered paddle to be raised during live-auction bidding. Sister Mads was no fool. She waited until everyone was good and liquored up before she would start the live auction.

The ballroom had been professionally decorated, with an elevated stage for the band, streamers covering the walls, and flower arrangements on every table. Mary Louise and I made the rounds, greeting the attendees and thanking them for the money we expected them to donate. We were both on the Mourning

Doves board, and therefore had a personal interest in seeing that the event went well.

The lights dimmed slightly, and the band climbed onto the stage. They started playing a song well known to us all, "Then You Can Tell Me Goodbye," and the dance floor was immediately filled. About halfway through the song, our guest entertainer, Neal McCoy, entered the stage and began singing. He received thunderous applause from the crowd. Neal was a native son of Texas and was always ready, willing, and able to play for a charity event. I was about to take Mary Louise for a stroll on the dance floor when I felt a tap on my shoulder. I turned and, sadly, it was Louis Devlin. I introduced him to Mary Louise, then he motioned me aside for a private conversation. He had on a beautiful tuxedo, with a vest rather than a cummerbund, and a matching tie that was so perfect I could not believe he had tied it himself.

"Dr. Brady, I wanted to thank you for taking the time to check on Lisa's hip. That was above and beyond your call of duty, but it was very much appreciated. I understand everything was all right?"

"Yes, sir, best as I can tell. I will check her in the office next week, but I told her she has to be more careful these first few weeks."

"Lisa is my athlete. She does not like anything or anybody to keep her down. At any rate, I just wanted to say thank you. I heard from Patsy Simmons you and your wife joined La Cava, so if you ever need anything, let me know."

We shook hands and went our separate ways.

The crowd danced and enjoyed Neal McCoy's music for an hour or so. Then dinner was served, and when dessert came, Sister Mads entered the stage to a standing ovation. Eventually everyone sat back down.

"Thank you all for coming and spending your hard-earned dollars on seats and tables. And a special thanks to the gentleman who has underwritten the uncovered costs of this event, Louis Devlin. Louis, please stand."

He did so, to a polite round of applause. He had been in town for three years, maybe a little less, and few people seemed to know him. Maybe he was a behind-the-scenes operator and did not like public attention. Maybe he had some deep dark secret from his past and tried to keep a low profile. And maybe none of that was my business. As my dear departed dad liked to say, eyes forward—his way of saying mind your own business.

Sister Mads continued with her speech, then called up the professional auctioneer, and he started the live auction for the first of three items. It was a Mediterranean cruise on the Seaborn line. That was followed by a trip to Napa Valley, wine tours, and a stay at Meadowood with golf. Lastly was a golf trip to Sea Island, Georgia. By the time the gavel sounded for the last time, generous patrons had ponied up over $200,000.

Neal McCoy re-entered the stage, the band cranked up the volume, and once again people cleared the tables and started dancing again. Mary Louise and I participated for a while, but by 10 p.m. it was time for us to get home. I was worried about getting enough sleep to function through clinic the next day, but Mary Louise said she had called Maya and she had arranged for me to start seeing patients at 9 a.m. instead of 7 a.m. I was so thrilled with that news that I offered to go right home and help her get out of her dress.

I texted our driver to pick us up, and while we were waiting, I saw Louis Devlin exit the ballroom doors and head to a black stretch limo. The rear door was being held open by a man I'd not seen before. He was small in stature, had some sort of facial incongruity, and wore a fedora hat tilted to one side, reminiscent of Frank Sinatra. When he closed the door on his passenger, he looked straight at me, put his right hand in the position of a gun, and mimicked firing a weapon. I wondered if that was the Fixer.

Mary Louise pushed up against me with those bodacious tatas of hers, and I forgot all about the little man driving Louis Devlin.

The highlight of the evening occurred at home, where I had the privilege of dress removal. To make it more interesting, I dialed up my iPod and played an old song from the 1960s by David Rose and his orchestra: "The Stripper."

CHAPTER 17

RIP PATSY

Starting clinic patients two hours later than usual was a blessing and allowed for a great night's sleep after a great night's exercise. Once I'd arrived, I decided to forgo rounds until after I finished clinic. We saw patients through the lunch hour, and the three of us had a bite to eat as time allowed. Maya received a call from the HCMC rehab unit, asking if we would stop by and see Del Anderson at her request. We finished clinic, made rounds, and I wandered over to the rehab unit around 4 p.m. I stopped at the nurses' station and got a cup of burnt, but hot, coffee. Del was up on her walker, speeding along ahead of the physical therapist.

"I need to get out of here, Jim Bob. Today, if possible."

"What, no hello, or good afternoon? What's going on?"

"I guess you haven't heard. You were at the gala last night, and you've been seeing patients all day, so you probably haven't seen the news."

"All that is true. What happened?"

"I'm sure you don't know her. She worked as an assistant to Louis Devlin, the principal that put the La Cava Golf Club deal together. Her name was Patsy Simmons and—"

"What do you mean, was? I do know her."

"Really? I'm so sorry, but she's dead. A neighbor found her this morning when she went over to walk Patsy's dog. The neighbor called 911 and waited there for the police. One of my reporters heard the conversation on his police-band radio and arrived at the scene right after the police did. He said the officers told him the cause of death was apparent strangulation. The house was ransacked, and the victim appeared to have been tortured and possibly raped."

I had to sit down in a visitor's chair next to Del's assigned bed. I felt dizzy and nauseated.

"You don't look so good, Jim. Are you alright?"

"I'm just shocked. I knew her from La Cava. She gave me a tour there. She also happened to be a friend of Lucy Williams. In fact, she came over to our house Tuesday night for dinner to talk about some things that were . . . bothering her."

"Are you holding out on me? Is there something I should know about her other than she was on the private plane that her boss Louis Devlin took to and from New York, looking for interim financing for the golf club?"

"Del, I don't know much more than you do. She was upset about some financial irregularities in Mr. Devlin's business activities and came to Mary Louise and me for advice."

"Well, what did you tell her?"

"We suggested she contact an FBI agent who is a friend of ours, Susan Beeson. She's the ASAC of the Austin bureau. That is all we did. I can assure you I don't know anything more than that." I lied smoothly.

"Well, we have the Christine Devlin murder, now we have the Patsy Simmons murder. One a wife to Louis Devlin, the other the possible mistress of Louis Devlin. Something is going on, and I need to be back at work at the Highlander reporting the news."

"I thought you had a good staff that could handle the paper while you were gone."

"I did until we had two murders in two weeks. That is called news, friend, and I need to be back in action, leading the charge. So how about it? Home tomorrow morning?"

"I don't see a problem with it. You're walking faster than the staff."

I went directly home from my conversation with Del. Mary Louise was sitting on the sofa with the television on. She had been crying.

"I guess you heard?" she said.

"I just came from visiting Del Anderson in rehab. She told me. I cannot believe it. What in the hell is going on?"

"I don't know, Jim Bob, but with Devlin's wife and assistant murdered, I'll bet the Marble Falls Police Department will have the feds in here anyway. We should call Susan and give her a heads up, see if she can arrange to handle this herself. We just had Patsy here for dinner two nights ago. She sat right here on this couch . . ." and Mary Louise started sobbing.

"I know, I know. It is heartbreaking. I feel like somehow it's my fault, stealing and copying those documents. Thank goodness she destroyed the video clips. Otherwise . . . oh shit."

"What?"

"What if there were other hidden cameras that were focused on Patsy that she didn't know about? The installation of the first camera would give Patsy some peace of mind that her actions were not being watched. But the presence of another camera might have not only my actions on it, but her actions in erasing the video showing my activity there. I mean, if Patsy's murder was a random act of burglary and a senseless murder, then I wouldn't worry about us. But if this is somehow tied into what she called Devlin's suspicious history, then he may think we are involved somehow in his business dealings and come after us."

"Jim Bob, do not get too carried away yet. I think you need to call Det. Randall Mims and tell him what you know, admit to your breaking and entering, and see what he says. I'll get in touch with Susan tomorrow and get her up to speed on what's happening here. You're off tomorrow and can see Mims then. I do not want you to wait. Okay?"

"Yes. I'll call him first thing. He's a Marble Falls detective and would possibly draw her case, but only if she was a resident of that city. Do you know where she lived?"

"No, I don't."

"I need a drink. How about you?"

"I need more than one."

After Friday morning hospital rounds, I called Randall Mims. Fortunately, he was in his office. I told him the reason for my call.

"Ms. Simmons lived in an unincorporated section of Burnet County on an inlet to Lake LBJ, so Burnet County Sheriff's Department drew the case. Sorry, but I can't help you on that one."

"Any progress on solving the murder of Christine Devlin?"

"No, Doctor, not yet, but I'll be certain to let you know when we do."

I'd had some bad experiences with another county's sheriff's office a while back, when dealing with abused patients and Mourning Doves, so I was reluctant to call on another. The local law enforcement community seemed dialed in to each other back then, and I couldn't make headway. However, it turned out the Burnet sheriff was voted out of office and had been replaced by a woman whose attitude was completely different from that of the previous good-old-boy network in play at the time I dealt with them. I asked to meet with her that morning, and she was more than accommodating.

The Burnet County Sheriff's Department is in the city of Burnet, a few miles north of Marble Falls. The complex contained a series of one-story office buildings and the Burnet County Jail. Many of the folks I ran into Friday morning were there to visit incarcerated loved ones. It took me a while to locate the sheriff's office, but I finally located an entry that was for citizens who had business with Burnet County other than to visit alleged criminals in jail.

I found an entry desk where there sat an attractive deputy. I waited a moment until she was off the phone.

"Morning. I'm Dr. Jim Brady, and I have an appointment to see Sheriff Wilcox."

"One moment," she said, as she located the correct computer screen that apparently showed appointments. The deputy had light-brown skin, with high cheek bones and an intricate arrangement of dark braided hair. "I don't see your name, Doctor. When did you schedule the appointment?"

"Just this morning. Short notice, I know."

She picked up the phone and spoke to the sheriff directly, who authorized my visitation. The deputy escorted me through the outer office and into an inner office isolated by a cell door. She used a key to open that door, and then led me to the inner sanctum and Sheriff Joan Wilcox.

"Doctor," she said, "always nice to help out our citizenry. Please have a seat. Coffee?"

"Yes, please."

"Sharon, please get us some coffee. Black for me. Doctor?"

"Same, please."

We made small talk until the coffee arrived and discussed my history of mostly being an orthopedic surgeon, but my penchant for solving mysteries, and her past history and the circuitous route she had taken to become sheriff.

"I had some dealings a while back with Sheriff Holmes who seemed to be pals with your predecessor. I must say, this is a change for the better."

"Sheriff Holmes was in Kingsland County, and you're right, he and Sheriff Walsh, my predecessor, were two peas in a pod. They both were ousted in the last election."

"I don't remember Walsh, but I clearly remember Holmes. Essentially no one had any rights whatsoever except him. He gave me a hard time. I was trying to locate some missing women. He was an effective stumbling block for information-gathering and impeded the investigation significantly. He was a pompous ass, and a classic example of arrogance without substance."

"That he was. Well, it is a new era for this part of Texas, and about time. Tell me why you're here."

I went through the murder of Christine Devlin, and how Mary Louise and I had stumbled into that. And then I discussed our relationship with Patsy Simmons, and how devastated we were over her apparent murder. And how Patsy had discussed with us in confidence her concerns over her boss's business dealings and was found dead two days later. And that we wondered if we were in any danger.

She listened attentively to my ramblings. "I went to the Simmons crime scene myself. In all candor, it was a mess. The house was ransacked, and my crime-scene techs cannot tell me if that occurred before or after her strangulation. The victim's hands were tied behind her back. She had been brutally beaten and had facial lacerations, a fractured nose and cheekbone, and a skull injury from a blow by a weighted object of some sort. Her garments had been removed, and she had clear evidence of forcible vaginal entry with tears and lacerations that one would not get from even exuberant sexual activity.

"Without further evidence, we are calling it an attempted burglary, rape, and murder. We have no evidence that she was interrogated for information, nor do we have evidence anything was stolen. We have a woman whose house was taken apart, who was brutalized and raped, and then strangled manually. Whoever did that to her had powerful hands. There was no evidence of a cord or rope used to assist in the strangulation. The perp wore gloves, as there were no prints. And no semen, so we assume a condom was used."

"Do you think you'll call in the FBI?"

"Normally we would not, but now that you've told me this story about the victim and her role as assistant to Mr. Devlin, and that his wife was murdered a week ago, it makes me think there is more going on here than meets the eye. We don't have the resources that the FBI has, and we are short-staffed as it is. It might be nice to have the feds helping us."

"Just so you know, Susan Beeson is the ASAC for the Austin FBI, and she is a friend of ours from past days in Houston. She stepped down as the police chief in Houston to take the FBI job. I can vouch for her. She is an excellent crime solver but does not infringe on local law enforcement."

She stood. "Doctor, it has been a real pleasure. I appreciate your candor, and I will give my due consideration to calling ASAC Beeson about this case."

We shook hands, and I left the way I came. I stopped and thanked the deputy named Sharon for her assistance.

"Before I leave, I must know what it takes to make your hair do what it does. It looks amazing, but I would guess it is a time-consuming endeavor."

She leaned forward, and I leaned down. "I won't deny the braiding takes hours and hours. Fortunately, it lasts and lasts."

"Well, it is stunning. It redefines beauty."

"Thank you very much," she replied, with a smile. Then she reached into her desk, and handed me a business card. It read "Deputy Sheriff Sharon Baldwin." "Just in case you need anything in the future, Doctor."

CHAPTER 18

SEARCH ENGINE

I always looked forward to golf on Friday, but because of the stress of two murders, and the possibility that I was on Louis Devlin's radar, my heart just wasn't in it. I thought long and hard, sitting in the visitors' parking lot at the Burnet County Sheriff's Office, about what I could do to help. Unfortunately, there was little or nothing. I had no standing in the arena, no "Deputy Dawg" badge like the one Susan Beeson used to provide for me when I assisted her on cases in Houston. Lieutenant Mims and Sheriff Wilcox were polite, but there was no way I could infringe upon their investigation. Being unable to do anything constructive made me feel like a fish out of water. I exited the car and walked the lot for a few minutes. I felt a great deal of anxiety, like I was going to have a panic attack. I'd never had one, but I'd certainly seen many in my practice over the years.

I took a few deep breaths and considered my options. I could contact my son J. J. and pay for a background check on Louis Devlin and Charles Fixatore. That would give me much more information, but as close as he and Mary Louise were, he would probably let it slip, and then I would be in trouble again for veering off the path of orthopedic surgeon and into the lane of investigative work for which I was not qualified. Still, if I could convince J. J. to keep it between us, I felt I might make it work.

I also wanted to find out who the couple was that was talking about jail time after my tour at La Cava, and the owner of the golf cart with the license plate HIGHROLLER, which were probably one and the same. I was sure that Patsy knew, but it was a little late to be asking her. I wondered who might replace her at the sales office. Devlin had to keep that office open for inquiries and tours because he was still in the business of raising money for development. He would have to put someone in Patsy's place who was knowledgeable and personal, and who could be a positive influence for potential new members.

I canceled golf, got in the car, and started for La Cava. I decided to take my chances with Patsy's replacement, whoever that might be. I could be a silver-tongued devil when I tried, so that was to my advantage. If I were already in Devlin's sights, the quest would make it worse. But Buck Owens and his consortium were behind me and were heavy investors in La Cava, so that afforded me some protection. The closer I came to arriving at La Cava, the more confident I became.

There was another car parked outside the Airstream office of La Cava Golf Club when I arrived. Imagine my surprise when I opened the door and found Lisa Stewart sitting at Patsy's desk.

"Lisa?"

"Dr. Brady? What are you doing here?"

"I might ask the same, Lisa. You're supposed to be home, resting that hip."

"I know, but Daddy was desperate for help in the sales office. You heard about Patsy Simmons, didn't you? The gory details have been all over the news. What a tragedy that was. Anyway, Daddy needed someone on short notice, and I was available. What are you doing here?"

"Well, we recently joined the club, and I wanted to see if I could pick up a membership roster. I met someone here during my tour, and I wanted to get in touch with him again," I smoothly lied. "I forgot his name, but I distinctly remember he was driving a golf cart with the license plate HIGHROLLER."

"Oh, that's easy. Mr. Amato owns that cart. Johnny Amato. His wife's name is Greta. They are such lovely people. He is Daddy's business partner. They have been friends forever, before Dallas even. They go back to the old Kansas City neighborhood. As I remember, they grew up together."

"Oh, you have saved me so much time. Thanks much. Would you happen to have a membership roster anyway? I want to start playing golf here regularly, and it would be helpful to refer to the roster when I meet fellow golfers."

"Not a problem, sir." She wheeled around in her desk chair, looked through a filing cabinet and brought out a membership booklet, bound in expensive paper, and containing personal information about each member, including home address, phone number, email address, and a photo of the member and their spouse or significant other.

"Thanks, Lisa, this will be helpful. And please take care of that hip."

"Absolutely, Dr. Brady. See you next week."

The stress of lying to Lisa had stimulated my appetite. I drove over to the Hole in One diner in Horseshoe Bay and ordered a medium-rare hamburger with jalapeños, crispy fries, and an ice-cold beer on tap. The restaurant was a hangout for locals and almost always had a law enforcement clientele. That day was no exception. At one table sat a group of Llano County sheriff's deputies, and at another sat a group of Marble Falls police officers, but not Lt. Mims. It was comforting to be sitting in the presence of people sworn to serve, protect, and defend, all of whom carried weapons to make sure the peace was kept. There was no safer place in town than the Hole in One at lunch on Friday and Sunday. I filed that in my mental computer in case the Fixer was ever after me.

The carbohydrate loading at lunch and the beer made a nap a necessity. Mary Louise would be in Austin for the day doing her charity work, so Tip and I would have the house to ourselves. I headed home, fed Tip some lunch, and took him for an abbreviated walk. I literally walked back into the house, collapsed on top of the bed, and was asleep instantly.

I awoke groggy, like I had consumed many scotches. The bedside clock read 3:30 p.m. I brushed my teeth, splashed cold water on my face, and tried to gather my wits about me.

I had decided to contact J. J. only as a last resort. While I was no genius with the computer, search engines were so good that I felt I could discover pertinent information myself regarding Louis Devlin and his family and friends. I fired the computer up, put in my security code, typed LOUIS DEVLIN in the default search engine, which happened to be Google, and waited while literally hundreds of search possibilities downloaded. If I thought typing in the name LOUIS DEVLIN would direct me to the man who was building La Cava, I was sorely mistaken. There were many a man named Louis Devlin, not only in the state of Texas, but all over the United States, and abroad as well. I narrowed the search down to Horseshoe Bay and Dallas, Texas, and added Kansas City just to see what would happen. The prompt asked for any additional search features, such as age. I had no idea how old MY Louis Devlin was, but I guessed and typed in sixty years.

There was more spinning and turning on the computer, and more yawning on my part, but the search items were narrowed down considerably when the screen reactivated itself. I stared at a photograph of the Louis Devlin I was searching for, at a charity function in Dallas four years prior. He looked like he was trying to avoid the photographer, but he was with the woman who was to become his wife, Christine Johnson, and although I had only seen her twice, once in her bedroom freshly dead, and later in the morgue, the resemblance was unmistakable. I continued to click on other icons, trying to narrow my search down to get some sort of biography on Mr. Devlin. There was nothing simple about the process, no Wikipedia with a charted bio to make my life easier. I began to appreciate the work J. J. did for a living. There was no way I could sit at a computer all day and fish for information. I needed to be physically busy and preferably not having to think beyond whatever examination or procedure I was performing.

I started composing my version of a bio by using a mixture of articles from various websites. I finally was able to construct a piecemeal history of Louis Devlin. For the last three years, he had been in the Marble Falls area after obtaining the approval bid to construct La Cava Golf Club, and, it turns out, La Cava Estates, a housing development that was to begin near the end of the golf course construction. That was new information to me. There had been a previous developer involved, a firm called Hill Country Development, but that entity had gone bankrupt for lack of financing after a principal looted the escrow account and disappeared into Canada, and Louis Devlin had bid on and received approval to continue the project. There was little online about his activities the past three years other than his work on building La Cava.

Prior to his arriving in the Hill Country, he had been in Dallas. His history there went as far back as ten years. He had been a successful commercial real estate developer in Dallas, concentrating on buying land and building office buildings with the intent to collect rents from tenants. I was not familiar with the names of any of his properties, but all sounded legitimate, like North Star Properties, Dallas Midtown Office Complex, and Oak Cliff Development. There was mention of him as one of Dallas's most eligible bachelors, having escorted a bevy of wealthy society woman to various charity balls. The records I could find did not go back beyond thirteen years, which would be three in the Hill Country, and ten in Dallas. There was mention of his nuptials three years prior with Christine Johnson, formerly Christine Hall, just before moving to the Hill Country. There was documentation of Christine and Louis having a blended family, three boys on Christine's side, and two girls on Louis's side, in one of the articles I found. Most of this information I had obtained from Lisa Stewart when I made the house call.

In other words, I found a whole lot of nothing. I knew all the basics of the target of my inquiry from a combination of information from Patsy Simmons, his assistant of sorts, and Lisa Stewart, his daughter. I kept searching for any records that would indicate that Louis Devlin had background connections to Kansas City, but I could find nothing. Both Patsy and Lisa had alluded to that, but I was unable to substantiate it. My skills at computerized detecting were limited, and I felt I had wasted the time when I could have been out golfing and not thinking. I heard the garage door open, quickly exited the programs, and hopefully erased any evidence of my tracks in the search engine.

I left the study and met Mary Louise struggling with sacks from the grocery. "Hey, babe, need some help?" I asked.

"Of course. I stopped by the market to get supplies for dinner. We have a guest."

"Who?"

"Who do you think, big fella?" I heard from the garage, and I knew immediately that Susan Beeson was in town and having dinner with the Brady family. We hugged and exchanged pleasantries. Susan was the little sister I never had. I first met her in Houston years before, when she was a detective for HPD and became involved in the investigation into the homicide of our neighbor's child. That had been many years prior. Not much had changed in her wardrobe. She wore khaki slacks, a white shirt, a blue blazer, and brown orthopedic shoes.

I opened a couple of bottles of Rombauer chardonnay and poured us all a glass, and we retreated to the terrace once the groceries were in their rightful place.

"I hear you've been a busy boy again, Jim Bob. I was sitting in my office yesterday, pondering what Gene and I were going to do for the weekend, and suddenly I find myself here in Granite Falls, investigating not one but two murders you have involved yourself in. Some things just never change, do they?"

"Well, Susan, it seems on this occasion I simply have found myself in the wrong place at the wrong time through no fault of my own. I think Mary Louise would agree with that. We happened to hear a gunshot while we were playing golf at the new La Cava Golf Course and discovered Christine Devlin's body. And as far as Patsy Simmons is concerned, we simply had her for dinner two nights before she was brutalized and murdered. How did you get involved in these cases?"

"I was contacted yesterday by Lt. Randall Mims of the Marble Falls Police Department. He also came to your house for dinner, and after a discussion with you and Mary Louise, and having made no progress over the past week in solving the murder of Christine Devlin, he called me and asked the FBI for help. Coincidentally, I was also called by Burnet County Sheriff Joan Wilcox late this morning after a conversation you had with her regarding the murder of Patsy Simmons, the assistant of Louis Devlin. So, it seems that your name keeps coming up in these murder investigations."

I felt my facial skin begin to burn. Mary Louise gave me that "look" she gave me when I got caught interfering in things that were none of my business. In retrospect, instead of paying a visit to Sheriff Joan Wilcox, I should have just gone to play golf. I could not believe she had used my name and mentioned our visit when she called Susan and the FBI for help.

"I think Tip needs a walk. You two catch up, and I'll be back in time for dinner," I said, and I quickly grabbed Tip and his leash and headed out the front door with my wine roadie.

CHAPTER 19

CRIMINALS IN THE MIDST

I returned from my walk with Tip, feeling chagrined, embarrassed, and full of humility. Mary Louise recognized all the signs and symptoms of my being sorrowful, and she gave me a sincere hug. Susan, on the other hand, after my wife's kindly affection, pinched both my cheeks and said, "Stay out of my business. You have almost been killed three or four times now. Neither of us could stand to lose you. The people that are involved in this La Cava project are not nice people and hang out with even nastier people. I am just starting to get involved in my investigation, but since Lt. Mims's call yesterday, my agents have me up to speed on, shall we say, certain nefarious activities."

"Before you get too involved, let's eat," said Mary Louise.

She had prepared a beautiful stir-fry meal. She had browned sliced chicken breast filets in a pan, chopped and added broccoli, corn, snap peas, green beans, cauliflower, and shaved almonds, and tossed the mixture with wasabi paste and soy sauce. The dish had just the right amount of spice and was delicious. I had seconds, maybe thirds. We washed our food down with a cold pinot grigio. We cleaned up the kitchen, brewed a pot of decaf coffee, and went out to the terrace.

"I have printed you a dossier, Jim Bob, so you can refer to it when you have time. Louis Devlin, although that is not his real name, originated in Kansas City. He is sixty years old. His birth name was Luigi Del Tommaso, and he is obviously of Italian origin. His father was a low-level employee in a trucking company and worked for a cousin who was 'in the business,' so to speak. Luigi was a smart kid, and the parish priest tried to help him stay out of trouble. He wrangled a scholarship for Luigi to Xavier University in Cincinnati, and Luigi graduated with honors in business.

"Unfortunately, he returned to KC and went to work for Nicky Savolio, head of the KC crime syndicate, helping him launder profits from loan sharking, prostitution, and gambling through a series of fast-food joints and dry cleaners he owned. Eventually the feds caught up to Savolio and his activities and sent him to federal prison in Leavenworth on a twenty-year sentence. Luigi was found guilty of money laundering and went to Leavenworth, but only for twenty-four months.

"Luigi turned over a new leaf when got out of prison. He apparently did not want to return. He changed his name legally to Louis Devlin. He tried to legitimize himself and landed a job with a commercial real estate firm in Kansas City. He worked hard and separated himself from his former business associates, made advances in the company, and after years of hard work, rose to president and CEO of Mid-America Development Corporation.

"Our history is sketchy, but he was approached at some point in time by his boyhood chums, those who had risen in the ranks of the old Savolio organization and were not in prison. They tried to bring him back into the fold, and they felt that in his position in the development corporation, the crooks stood to make a lot of money. They controlled the electricians, plumbers, and cement workers, all the positions necessary to get buildings built. The two groups wrangled back and forth for a few years, and finally Louis just packed up, left it all behind, and moved to Dallas.

"While there were syndicates operating in Dallas, they did not control the unions and workers in the building business as they had in Kansas City, so Devlin was able to start over with a great deal of money he brought with him from the Kansas City enterprises. As they say, it takes money to make money, and Louis Devlin hit town with a bang, and started buying up, primarily, failing commercial real estate firms. Before long, he had friends with money who trusted him and helped him put together another development company called Oak Cliff, specializing in commercial buildings in the south end of Dallas.

"By the way, while living in Kansas City, he had married Lynette Avalon, whose parents seem to have been straight arrows. Louis's departure from Kansas City coincided with her early death from cancer, which could have been another reason he moved to Dallas. He brought his two daughters with him, a Lisa Stewart, and an Elizabeth Winters, both married. Their husbands are involved in Devlin's businesses, and it appears they run part of his ongoing Dallas operations. The Stewart daughter has no children, but the Winters daughter has two young girls. From what the agents doing the research determined, the two daughters' husbands are commuting to Dallas from the Hills of Horseshoe Bay, where both families live.

"We have also learned that Devlin married the former Christine Johnson, a widow he met in Dallas. She had three sons by her deceased husband, and all three are employed in Devlin's Dallas offices. Their names are Robert Jr., Alan, and Samuel Johnson."

Susan stopped for a moment, took a swallow of wine.

"This is probably a good time to interject that I operated on Lisa Stewart this past week. She is recovering well from repair of a torn hip labrum."

"I didn't know that, did I?" asked Mary Louise.

"I can't remember whether I told you or not. It was shock to my system when I went in to identify her prior to surgery, and there was Devlin, standing at her bedside. I had to make a house call on Lisa a couple of days ago. She had a fall and bled through her surgical dressing. Her caretaker had some sort of emergency and had to leave, so she called the office, told Belinda the problem, and I went over and changed her bandages. I doubt there is any damage to the repair, but I won't know for a while."

Both women stared at me like I had just committed a crime.

"You went to her house?" asked Mary Louise.

"Yes, like an old-fashioned house call. Docs used to do it all the time."

"Yes, before the age of mass communication. Did she take your picture while you changed her dressing and put it on Facebook or Twitter?" Susan asked.

"Of course not. You two are being sort of silly, aren't you?"

"I am certainly not," replied Susan. "This is the daughter of a convicted felon, a former or current member of an ancient Sicilian/Italian crime organization, which will stop at nothing to feed itself and its members from illegal activities. You might as well have gone to visit Rosalie Profaci!"

"Who's that?"

"Who's that? The wife of Salvatore Bonanno, who was the son of Joseph Bonanno, a.k.a. Joe Bananas, head of the Bonanno crime family out of New York. You simply amaze me, Jim Bob Brady."

"When I operated on her, I didn't know anything about her family. I treated her like I would any other patient."

That was met with silent stares from both women, as though I had developed a third eye in the center of my forehead.

"While I am digging myself a hole, you should also know that I went over to La Cava this morning to try and get some information on the driver of the golf cart with the license plate HIGHROLLER. I had overheard a conversation between a man and a woman the day I had the tour. He was talking about having changed his identity, and making a big score, and she was retorting that he had already been in prison and surely he didn't want to return. I was eating in front of the food truck and stepped around the other side of it to try and see their faces, but all I saw was the license plate and the back of their heads. I told Mary Louise about that the day it happened."

Susan looked at Mary Louise. "Yes, he did tell me about that. I kept it to myself because at the time I had no idea what to do with that information. But now you have it, Susan, and that's all Jim Bob and I know."

"Well, there is one more little thing. When I returned to the sales office, I figured there would be a replacement for Patsy there, and I was right. Lisa Stewart was running the desk at the request of her father. I went there to get a member roster, and she was accommodating with that. I now have a small directory with names, phone numbers, email addresses, and photographs of the members and their spouses or significant others.

"In the process of securing the roster, I mentioned to Lisa that I had played golf with a man whose name I had forgotten, but remembered he drove a custom cart with a HIGHROLLER license plate. She told me that the cart belongs to her father's business partner and his wife, name of Johnny and Greta Amato. I thanked her and left."

Mary Louise hung her head and sighed. Susan flipped through her copy of the dossier until she found the page she sought. "Johnny Amato, real name Giuseppe Fertitta, grew up in Kansas City, was a boyhood buddy of our own Louis Devlin and a known enforcer in the Savolio crime organization. He served a prison term of eight years for manslaughter and was indicted twice before for the same offense but was not convicted. He is a real piece of work, Jim Bob, and I am so glad to hear you're trying to follow him around. If you have a death wish, that sort of activity will certainly shorten your life."

I went into the house, retrieved three decorative shot glasses and an iced bottle of Tito's vodka, and took it back outside. I poured us each a tall shot and clinked glasses with Mary Louise and Susan to make sure they were still with me in spirit.

"Jim Bob," Susan said, "I hope you see the gravity of the situation. Devlin's wife was murdered, and now his assistant has met the same fate, with little or no clues regarding either, but surrounded by these shady characters you read about in books and see in movies. But this is no game, friend. These people are not cartoon caricatures. Some are probably stone-cold killers and would not hesitate for a New York minute to do you in, if you interfere with whatever business they have going here."

"While we're confessing our sins, I might as well throw out another name that Patsy mentioned to Mary Louise and me when she was here for dinner. She called him the Fixer. She said his name was Charles Fixatore, I think. She said he was a longtime friend of Devlin, and that he was living in the area."

With the mention of that name, Susan stood up, shook her head and walked away. Mary Louise and I looked at each other. Not knowing what to do, we refilled our shot glasses and downed them quickly, as though we were bad children awaiting our punishment.

CHAPTER 20

THE FALL

I was up early Saturday morning and opted to avoid getting in the line of fire of my two housemates. I was certain that Susan stayed over, since she was probably in no shape to drive home. I had gone to bed when I finished the final shot of vodka after mentioning the presence of the Fixer in our normally safe and secure community. Usually, after a cleansing session where I tell all, I would have waited for Susan's return to her outdoor chair for further discussion, but I had been castigated enough for one evening. Susan and Mary Louise were both right. I had no business meddling in the affairs of Louis Devlin, especially with the unsolved murders of two of his intimate partners. There were so many questions I would have liked to ask, but the message I had received was "leave it alone."

I brewed a pot of coffee, put it in a Thermos, and headed for the golf course. Horseshoe Bay Golf Club did not open until 7 a.m., so I enjoyed the solace in my Tahoe and sipped a brew named Mediterranean Sunrise. I parked in a remote sector of the massive parking lot, near a grouping of oak trees and a small spring aptly named Slick Rock Creek. The caffeine level in the coffee was quite strong, and in short order my heart was racing. Then nature called, so I exited the truck and found a nearby tree and relieved myself. The foliage and grass were wet, which meant rain had fallen during the night. I tried to balance myself as best I could, taking care of my business and trying to hold my coffee at the same time. But between the thick dew, and the slope of the hill, and the slick rocks in and around the creek, I felt gravity begin to take over just after zipping up. I let go of the coffee cup, grabbed onto a small branch of one of the oak trees I was next to, and tried to pull myself back to level ground. Unfortunately, Sir Isaac Newton's theorems about gravity proved true as I fell onto my bottom and started sliding down the hill.

I thought my golf shoes might hold me back, but those plastic soft spikes were worthless on a wet and muddy descent. Low-hanging oak tree limbs slapped at my face and body, but again gravity was the victor as I slid toward what looked like a pond. The driving range was off to my right, and I chastised myself for never having noticed the steepness of the decline. I extended my legs in front and tried to get purchase with the golf spikes again, but to no avail. I was reminded of the slide I once made down Ajax, the final ski run at Aspen Mountain, before I crashed into a concrete berm that supported the large outdoor bar. I got a standing ovation. But there was no berm to stop me this time.

I hit the water hard. I felt rocks scrape my buttocks and the back side of my legs. The pond was small and fortunately level, so my slide was stopped by the opposite side of the accumulated water. I stood carefully and felt for injuries to my legs. All seemed to be well. I got down on all fours and climbed out of the pond, walked to a flat space, and sat on a clump of oak leaves. My clothes were soaked and muddy, my shoes as well. I looked around for a flat place where I could start my ascent, but there was nothing. I sat back down to restore my bearings when I noticed a shiny metal object near the surface of the pond, glimmering in the early morning sun. I crawled to the edge and tugged on what appeared to be a locket. It was attached to something, so I reached my other hand into the water to try and release the object, and up floated the head of a woman.

My cell phone was wet, but functional. I dialed 911 and related my findings to the dispatcher who answered, who happened to be from the Marble Falls Police Department. I described my location and recommended the first responders take care in reaching my location, given the treacherous topography.

I heard the sirens before I saw the vehicles arrive. By then, the golf shop had opened and the parking lot was starting to fill up. There were looky-loos that I could see above me, but I was still hidden by oak trees and I hoped it would stay that way before my cronies discovered me.

Ropes were tied to trees, winches on rescue vehicles activated, and workers shimmied down their lines quickly and without sliding. "You alright?" asked a young firefighter, first to arrive at my location.

"Yes, I think so."

"What happened? How did you end up down here?"

I related my saga. I think he might have chuckled but tried to keep a straight face. He tied a rope around my waist, and I felt the winch slowly turn, which allowed me to walk back up the hill. Once I was back on level ground, I noticed yellow crime-scene tape around the area, and golfers craning their necks to see what was happening.

I heard someone yell "Brady!" but I ignored it and set about trying to figure out how to get some clean clothes.

"Dr. Brady," said a tall man who had just stepped out of a police vehicle.

"Lt. Mims. I wondered if you might get the call."

"Yes, sir. Seems like you and I keep running into each other. Want to tell me what you were doing at the bottom of the hill, and what you found?"

I related my story, including the discovery of the dead woman in the pond. "She has a locket, probably around her neck, but I could not get it loose. It might have some clue as to her identity."

"Thank you, sir. We will take it from here. Anyone I can call for you?"

"No, but thanks. I need to get home and get out of these clothes. Thanks for the quick response."

"You are quite welcome, and thanks for not messing up my crime scene."

I called Mary Louise from the truck, told her the situation, and asked her to meet me in the garage with a large bath towel. I gave her a synopsis of the morning's events. I could tell she didn't know whether to laugh or cry. When I arrived home, I stripped down to my skivvies in the garage, wrapped the towel around me, and carefully exited to the shower for a cleanup.

Once I was free of debris, I put on fresh jeans and a T-shirt and Docksiders and went to the kitchen for fresh coffee.

"Your clothes are ruined. Sorry."

"Too bad for even Goodwill?"

"I do not think any self-respecting homeless person would wear them. The stench from the pond is awful. Think that's the dead body or the muck in the pond or some combination of the two?"

"Probably. Mims shooed me out of there quickly, so I have no idea who the dead woman is, or how she died, or anything."

"And is that your job?"

I hung my head. "No, simply curious. Is Susan still here?"

She nodded. "In the shower. I bet she can't wait to hear your news."

About that time Susan exited the guest room, came into the kitchen, gave me a hug, and said "Sorry about last night. You know I love you, right?"

"Yes. Always."

"Good."

"He has news," said Mary Louise.

I explained my morning adventure to Susan. She used her cell phone to call Lt. Mims, they connected, and she said she would meet him at the morgue once the crime-scene team had done their business.

"Did you see her face, or what was on the locket?"

"No. The water was muddy. All I could see was the glint of the locket reflecting against the sun. I tried to lift the locket, but it was stuck. I tried to free it up with my other hand, but that maneuver caused the head to surface. I decided to call 911 at that point."

"Oh, my. You're leaving the detecting to the detectives. Can this be happening?"

"Hopefully, Susan."

"The saints be praised. It's a miracle!"

"Don't be too happy. I called 911 because I knew there was no way I could climb back up that hill. If the ground had not been so slick and wet, I might have tried to haul the dead woman up myself. I have a great intellectual curiosity, Susan, and despite whatever measures you use to quash that, it will not go away. Which, by the way, brings me to another topic. I want to attend the autopsy. I want to know who the woman is. I want to know if her being in that pond has anything to do with the deaths of Christine Devlin and Patsy Simmons."

"Now why would you think that? You have no idea how long that woman has been there, you have no idea of her relation to—"

"It's the trifecta, Susan. At least three women know, or knew, something about the plans of Louis Devlin. Christine his wife, Patsy his administrator, and, possibly through Johnny her husband, Greta Amato. Three women are dead, all tied to Louis Devlin. Whatever he's up to must be worth a lot of money to risk losing it all by killing three women."

"You don't know that, Jim Bob. And you surely don't know the identity of the woman found in the pond."

"I have a suspicion, Susan, that's all I am saying. It would be easy to call up Johnny Amato and ask him if his wife is missing."

"We'll find out the identity of the most recently deceased tomorrow, hopefully. And I will take responsibility for calling Mr. Amato. It was nice of Dr. Reed to agree to do the autopsy on a Sunday."

"It was, although he might have been influenced by the barrage of phone calls from you and Lt. Mims."

"Mims and I called, but two calls does not a barrage make," she said.

Surprisingly, Susan allowed me to tag along for the autopsy at HCMC on the unknown victim. Once the body was extracted from the pond, the first responders discovered the woman was nude. They confirmed she was dead and transported her to the morgue. They searched the small pond for any form of identification—a wallet, or a cell phone—but nothing was found.

The only jewelry on her person was the locket. Dr. Jerry Reed removed it from the deceased's neck and opened it. Inside was a photograph of a young child. There was nothing on the back of the photo to indicate the identity. Lt. Mims was in attendance, as he had been on Christine Devlin. It was Sunday morning, and rather than enjoy the smells of Mary Louise cooking breakfast, we breathed in fumes of formaldehyde and dead-body smells.

Dr. Reed made the Y-incision and inserted retractors to hold the split rib cage out of the way. He perused the great vessels and the heart, lungs, and abdominal organs from the throat down to the rectum. As usual, he detached the great mass of the human interior in the chest and abdominal cavities and set it aside on another table. The technician went about sectioning and separating the organs.

"Doctor Reed," said his assistant, "the lungs are full of water. She drowned. Or at least that was probably the cause of death. She had to be held underwater until she died, otherwise I don't know how she could have drowned in a pond that was, what, a foot deep?"

Jerry sectioned the lungs and agreed with his assistant. "The microscopic sections will tell the tale for sure, but the lungs point to drowning."

"No other signs of foul play?" asked Lt. Mims.

"Not that I can say at this time. Once I have the micro specimens, I can tell you for sure. I'll perform a dissection of the perineum but plan to reserve that for when the tech and I are alone, as you know."

"Yes, I remember, and thanks for doing that portion of the autopsy without us."

"Also, I'll run a tox screen for completeness and will have that report in a few days. There is a chance she had drugs in her system and was out for a walk, and she could have stumbled and fallen and hit her head, not unlike your fall, Jim. If there is nothing else . . ."

"Can you tell how long she had been in the water?" Susan asked.

"Not for sure until the slides are back, but no more than twenty-four hours would be my guess."

CHAPTER 21

ASAC BEESON

After the autopsy, I returned home, picked up Mary Louise, and took her and Susan to lunch at the fabulous food truck at the new La Cava Golf Club. Why I chose that dining venue, I did not really know.

I was curious about the identity of the dead woman. There had been no reports on the news, or from Susan, about calls regarding a missing female. I thought that strange as well. Everything about the deaths of the three women was strange. The Marble Falls-Horseshoe Bay-Kingsland area was no metropolis, and as a result, a killer could not go around offing people without that being noticed. Maybe in New York or Chicago, where murders were commonplace, could a killing spree occur without anyone paying much attention. But in our small area, that just did not happen.

Del Anderson had written a column in her paper the Highlander about the deaths of Christine Devlin and Patsy Simmons, with perhaps some link to the development of La Cava. However, she was careful not to step on anyone's toes until there was evidence of some conspiracy. I could hardly wait to read what she would publish Monday after a third woman had been found dead. I had not spoken to her since her discharge from the HCMC rehab unit, but I suspected she had some information about the parties involved. And I also suspected she might have a touch of fear, thinking about the possibility of a killer on the loose in our little piece of Hill Country heaven.

We each ordered a Mexican breakfast of scrambled eggs, onions, peppers, and chorizo, with flour tortillas. Thirst was upon us, so we each had a spicy Blood Mary. While we were enjoying the scenery and stuffing ourselves, I saw a man drive up in a custom golf cart. He got out of the cart, strode to the food-truck window, and placed an order. He had a dark complexion, Mediterranean I guessed, with silver hair, wearing black shorts and a turquoise golf shirt. He went back to his cart and waited for his food.

Curiosity overcame me, and I got up from my sumptuous breakfast and walked over and checked out his license plate . . . HIGHROLLER. He noticed me looking at his cart, since I was only three or four feet away from his fender on the driver's side.

"May I help you?" he asked.

"Just admiring the cart. I have seen it a few times before. What's the color called?"

"Midnight blue."

"It's a beauty. My wife and I just joined the club. Jim Bob Brady," I said, and extended my hand.

He responded to the handshake and said "Johnny Amato."

"I know that name. I went to the sales office and spoke to Lisa Stewart about your cart, and she knew exactly who you were. She was filling in for Patsy Simmons. Terrible story. Anyway, she mentioned you were friends with her father, Louis Devlin. I thought I might get in touch with you and ask about the cart customization. And here you are. Small world."

The vendor brought his food, and Mr. Amato looked ready to leave. "I don't want to miss my tee time. I'll get you that information on the cart upgrade. I can leave it with the locker room people if you like, or with Lisa in the sales office. I'm not sure the locker room is fully functional, so why don't I just leave it with Lisa."

"Sounds great. Pleasure to meet you. Playing alone? I see only one golf bag on the cart."

"No, with a friend. Usually, my wife and I play together on Sunday, but she's out of town visiting a grandson. See you another time," he said, and drove away toward the first tee.

I did not know if the woman from the autopsy that morning was Greta Amato, but if it was her, Mr. Amato was an awfully cool cucumber if he knew she was no longer with us. I walked over to our table and sat down.

"Friend of yours?" asked Susan.

"Hardly. That is Johnny Amato, husband of Greta Amato, who I thought could be the unidentified dead woman from the autopsy this morning. He told me she was out of town visiting her grandson, so I guess you don't have to make that call now."

"And you involved yourself with Mr. Amato under what pretense?"

"I simply asked him about his custom golf cart. I may want to get one."

Mary Louise and I had brought our clubs and intended to play at least nine holes of golf. Susan had followed in her vehicle and intended to personally view the three crime scenes. Christine Devlin had been murdered in her new house under construction, Patsy Simmons in her home on a lake inlet, and the unknown female in or near the pond at Horseshoe Bay Golf Club driving range. Truth be known, I would have rather gone with Susan on her investigative jaunt. But it was Sunday afternoon, traditionally a time for Jim Bob and Mary Louise bonding, whether on the golf course or elsewhere.

I had yet to play the back nine holes, and since the time was after 3 p.m., the kindly starter allowed us to begin on the tenth hole, which was normally forbidden, due to the risk of golf traffic piling up with folks who had teed off on the first hole. But there was a high chance of precipitation, so the course was relatively empty, and the starter didn't think there would be a problem with us starting on the tenth hole. He said there were only two players on the course, each with their own golf cart, and who had already played the front nine and were probably on the green of the tenth hole.

The tenth hole was a par five, as was the first hole. I could see the pesky creek on the south side of the first hole and guessed that it would interfere with the tenth hole as well, but on the north side of the fairway. I aimed left and duck-hooked the ball into oblivion, precipitating my first mulligan. Mary Louise of course hit an easy driver about 150 yards right down the middle, then another shot toward the green, a third shot onto the green, and had an easy two-putt for a par. I lost two balls and ended up with a swell double bogey. I once again wondered why I played the game at all.

The back nine of La Cava was beautiful. There was a gentle slope downward for the first six holes, then the inevitable climb back up the hills to the eighteenth hole and the unfinished clubhouse. We noted that an effort had been made to make the tee boxes as beautiful as possible. Each hole had five tee boxes depending on the skill of the golfer, but each had colorful blooming flowers, including geraniums, irises, poppies, and petunias.

The clouds started to roll in on the seventeenth hole, and by the time we were approaching the green on the eighteenth hole, the wind had picked up and the sky was spitting a cold rain. We veered off the fairway and onto the cart path and were heading toward the green when we spotted two men in separate golf carts off to the left of the green. Their gestures did not indicate a pleasant conversation. I stopped the cart, pulled out my range-finder binoculars, and gazed at Johnny Amato and Louis Devlin in a heated argument. Amato shoved Devlin, and Devlin hit the ground. As he was getting up, he swung his putter at Amato's leg, and Amato went down. I then watched the two grown men roll around off to the side of the green, connecting blows when possible.

It started to rain harder, so we sped along, passing the two men who, by then, were staring at us.

"You fellas all right?" I yelled as we passed by the brawl.

"Yes," yelled Devlin, as he rose, walked to his cart, slammed the putter into his bag, and drove off.

We did not hang around to see what Amato did, because the clap of thunder indicated the lightning was close by, and a person with any sense does NOT want to be outside on a golf course in Texas with lightning in the area. Like the Charles Bronson series, it would be called Death Wish.

We sped to the portico at the front entry to get out of the rain. I had parked nearby, so I risked life and limb to retrieve the truck, left the cart in the adjacent parking space, and swung back around and picked up Mary Louise.

"Ooh, a rainy day. You know how I love rainy days," cooed Mary Louise. "You might want to get me home, Jim Bob, so I can get out of these wet clothes and into a hot shower."

The roads were slick, so I tried to avoid speeding. But I drove as fast as I could.

By the time we woke up, it was after 7 p.m. and we were starving. The rain was still in force, but the wind had died down.

I let Tip out, but he hated the noise of a storm and was back in a flash. I poured his kibble into a bowl and cut up some leftover chicken for increased flavor and bulk. He was grateful for the thirty seconds it took him to eat it, after which he sped back into my closet to hide under the pile of clothes destined for the dry cleaners.

Mary Louise ambled into the kitchen in a thick bathrobe, with sleepy eyes. She nestled up against me and said, "What's for dinner?"

"We have some leftover chicken. We could make sandwiches. It's Tip's food, but I doubt he would care."

"I bought a couple of large cans of gourmet pozole with chicken, which is Mexican hominy soup. I can add cabbage, radishes, avocado, cilantro, and lime."

"Say no more, my dear. That sounds great."

We had just sat down to eat when Mary Louise's phone rang. She said a few okays and fines, then disconnected. "Susan's coming back over to spend the night."

"I don't blame her. Not a great night to drive back to Austin."

Susan Beeson arrived quickly after the phone call. Fortunately for her, it was in time to have pozole before I had devoured the remainder. She was disheveled from the weather, with damp clothes. "Thanks for putting up with me another night," she said.

"Happy to have you," I said. "Want to clean up first?"

"No, I'm starving."

"Did you make any great discoveries today?" I asked.

"This soup is to die for, Mary Louise."

"Glad you like it. Part can, part homemade."

We sat at the kitchen bar and watched Susan slurp her soup. I was dying of curiosity and could hardly wait for her to finish eating.

"So, first I met up with Lt. Mims at the new-home site of Christine and Louis Devlin. The crime-scene tape was obviously gone, and there were footprints about, so either there were trespassers looking at the murder scene, or workers have resumed the construction. I went over Mims's report and noted that she was shot nearly point-blank in the chest and was missing a sock, perhaps from running away from her attacker while she was putting on her shoes. Mims could not say. He has no suspects. You two are the only witnesses to a gunshot, but you neither saw nor heard anyone when you entered the house, not even the sound of footsteps running from the crime scene. The murder was so clean, I would vote for a professional hit. Mims agrees. His investigation is at a dead end.

"He then accompanied me to Patsy Simmons's house on the lake. Such an idyllic spot on the water for such a tragic end. Sheriff Joan Wilcox from Burnet County met us there. Again, the crime-scene tape was gone, and there were tracks in the house. I do not know if that came from neighbors, or the crime-scene people, or looky-loos. Wilcox has found no next-of-kin to question. The sheriff told me about the murder in vivid detail. The house was ransacked. The victim had her hands tied behind her back. She had been severely beaten and had a fractured nose and cheekbone. Her skull was fractured, probably from a heavy object swung with a great deal of force. She had severe vaginal tears, indicative of a violent rape. There was no semen, so the sheriff assumed a condom was worn, or there was no climax on the part of the attacker. The victim appeared to have been strangled, and without prints on the body, the sheriff assumed the perp wore gloves. Again, no one saw anything, or heard anything. The neighbors are not close together, which is ideal unless a resident is in trouble. This looks clean, much like the Devlin woman's crime scene, and makes one again think of a professional job. The attacker was definitely looking for something, since the house was torn apart.

"Lastly, our mystery woman from the pond. The locket with a photo of a small boy was all she had on or near her person. She was nude, and from the autopsy findings, Dr. Reed thinks she drowned. There were no signs of bruising or other trauma, so if she in fact drowned, then someone held her head under water, which means she might have had drugs in her system. He will not have those results for another day or two. What is interesting is that she had the same congenital anomaly he found in Christine Devlin, just not as developed."

"You mean intersexuality?"

"Yes. I had never heard of it. He told me that Christine had three sons, so not knowing the family history, I can't say if they were biologically hers or were adopted."

"Could this mean the two women are related?"

"He didn't know, but it is somewhat unusual, and to find it in two unrelated deceased women in the same general geographic location, that would be . . . rare. He said he was going to check the DNA and see if by any chance the two women have a match of some sort. I cannot see how this has anything to do with the murders, though we're hoping it may help lead to the identification of the third victim. It did get me to thinking, though, that my friend Jim Bob here is a doctor, and he is constantly interfering in investigations, and maybe if I gave him a project, he would stay out of the professionals' hair but at the same time occupy his time and perhaps get some needed information for law enforcement."

"And what would that be, Susan?"

"I am putting you in charge of research of the genetic variance."

"Intersexuality."

"Yes, I am putting you in charge of finding out about how common it is, and what might possibly help us find the identity of the unknown victim. And if that somehow leads us to the reason for her murder, or Christine's murder, or Patsy Simmons's murder for that matter, then it is a win-win for all concerned."

My first thought? Be still my excited beating heart.

CHAPTER 22

SURGERY

The alarm's irritating buzz woke me from a dead REM sleep at 5 a.m. I sleepily performed my ablutions, got dressed in clean scrubs, made a pot of strong coffee, and was out the door by 5:30 a.m. There was no traffic on the route to Hill Country Medical Center. I had beaten the paper carrier, the milk delivery drivers, and the truckers to work, although I was not sure there still were paper carriers and milk delivery drivers. Nonetheless, if there were, I was for sure ahead of them.

Belinda had neatly stacked the patients' charts for Monday surgery on my desk. We had a virgin hip replacement, a redo hip replacement, and three knee replacements on the schedule. I had been on call over the weekend, and she had added two more fracture cases, one a femoral-neck fracture in the hip, the other a femoral-shaft fracture. Huh. Seven cases. A busy day. I cleaned up my desk, then went over to the hospital to make rounds. When I looked at my patient list, I realized that I had no patients left in the hospital. The last four had been transferred over to the rehab wing over the weekend.

Unlike the regular hospital, where the nurses and patients were up most of the night, giving and receiving medications, making IV fluid changes, performing blood pressure checks, and a myriad of other required patient care items, the rehab unit was quiet. These patients were past the acute-care phase of their treatment and were on banker's hours. I tiptoed through the tile floors, checked on all four of my patients, and saw all were sound asleep. I stopped by the nursing station to refill my coffee and found the head nurse dozing at her desk, with last night's stale coffee still gurgling in the pot. Just the smell of slowly burning coffee would have kept me awake.

I went to the surgeon's lounge, found that coffee only partially burned, and refilled. It was already 6:30 a.m. and we started surgery promptly at 7 a.m. I walked into the pre-op identification area and found Belinda standing at the first patient's bedside. The area was full of patients being prepped for surgery, so it was loud and full of activity.

"Morning, Dr. Brady. I hope you had a good weekend," said Belinda.

"I did, although it was a little busier than I like. How about you?"

"I had the call beeper, so you know how that goes."

"I didn't hear from you, but I see you added a couple of cases onto the schedule."

"Yes, sir. Both had medical issues that had to be cleared prior to surgery. Neither patient was ready yesterday, so I didn't see any reason to bother you."

"I think you did a great job. Did you have a lot of other admissions that didn't belong to us?"

"Yes, sir. Twelve."

"Twelve? What the hell was going on over the weekend?"

"Motocross event, which is essentially off-road motorcycle racing, a dangerous sport. We were lucky to get only a hip and a femur fracture. The hand service was swamped. We saw ten hand, wrist, forearm, or shoulder fractures that had to be admitted for surgery over the weekend. That doesn't count the ten other fractures I saw that I was able to treat and release."

"Whoa! Are you kidding me? You were here by yourself taking care of all those patients? You should have called staff for help."

"Staff came in for all the operative procedures. And thank goodness I had Josh Barnett helping. He's a third-year ortho resident from Dell Medical School in Austin on a three-month rotation here. He's knowledgeable, and I could not have taken care of the outpatient fractures without him. He is looking for a job, and I think he likes our facility. He's a golfer and a fisherman, so he would fit right in. I can introduce you."

"Okay, sounds good. You must be asleep on your feet. Can you make it through all these cases?"

"You bet, Doc. Bring it on!"

Whoever said it was a shame to waste the beauty of youth on the young knew what they were talking about. While the cases went well, there was a lot of strength and stamina required to do hip and knee surgery. Patients weighed different amounts, obviously, so leg weight was an issue. And it seemed in the business of hip and knee surgery, the leg was always being lifted, rotated, or moved side to side, all to ensure proper alignment once the procedure was complete. After the five joint replacements, I was ready to be put out to pasture.

We saved the two add-on cases—two teenaged boys from the motocross competition—for last. The femoral-neck fracture we fixed with multiple pins, and the femur fracture was stabilized with a rod. I basically exposed the fractures in both cases and let Belinda put in the hardware. That girl was great with power tools and a hammer, essential equipment in my business. She sewed the wounds up and applied the dressings, while I mostly sat in the corner being amazed at her stamina. She was the best nurse practitioner I had ever seen. She should have gone to medical school but told me finances were an issue when it came time for that decision to be made.

It was after 7 p.m. when we left the operating room. I sent Belinda home and I did post-op rounds duty. There were a couple of patients still in the recovery room. The remainder were back on the floor. I dutifully saw everyone and spoke to families again if they were at the bedside. By the time I completed patient rounds and checked my desk for urgent messages, it was 8 p.m. I limped to my truck and started home. I was just about to exit the parking facility when a car came out of nowhere and blocked my exit. I had been accosted before, both in person and by automobile, so I sat still and waited. I made sure the doors were locked, opened the glove box, and pulled out the Smith & Wesson .357 Magnum revolver I kept there for safety reasons—my safety, not the safety of others. I had a concealed-weapon permit, and I knew how to shoot. Back in the wild days of Houston, when I thought it was cool to be a part-time investigator, I had been knocked out, shot at, and run off a freeway overpass. I had learned the error of my ways. Always carry a bigger gun than your assailant.

A man stepped out of the car, leaving the engine running with his bright lights shining in my face. He strolled over to my driver's side door and knocked on the window. He kept his hands in his pockets. He motioned for me to roll down my window. I did not, choosing instead to speak through the closed window.

"What do you want?"

"I need to speak with you."

"I have an office and an assistant that schedules appointments. Look me up."

"I just want to talk, Doctor. Please?"

I cracked the window with my left hand, quietly cocking my weapon with my lowered right hand.

"Pretty suspicious fellow for a medico."

"You are not my first rodeo, sir. Again, what do you want?"

"You've been asking around about my employer, Louis Devlin. Mr. Devlin is a fine man who has recently experienced a great deal of sadness in his life. His wife was murdered, then his assistant was murdered. He has endured a great deal of emotional trauma, and he continues to be painfully sad. We understand you have been asking questions about his business, the real estate business, and we wonder what concern it is of yours. He is an honest businessman, working hard to complete the La Cava project. For this project to be completed, and be successful, he needs the confidence of the city officials, his investors, and the residents of the community. He does not need any bad publicity."

"The public relations people say there is no bad publicity."

"We would disagree, as would our investors. I come to you in peace, asking for a favor, and that is to let Mr. Devlin get about his business without interference or interruption. You are a doctor, a fine surgeon and talented, from what I hear. Stick to your job. Take care of your patients. Do not interfere in other people's business, lest you become a patient yourself."

"Is that a threat, sir?"

"Of course not. Just advice from one friend to another."

"I do not believe we are friends. I do not even know your name."

"You are Dr. James Robert Brady. I am Charles, and my last name is irrelevant. Have a pleasant evening, sir. And I hope you know how to use that pistol you are holding in your right hand. It would be a shame to shoot your foot off, or worse, a vital organ."

"How do you know I'm carrying a pistol?"

He laughed. "This is Texas. Everybody is carrying a pistol."

He casually walked back to his vehicle, which was a black nondescript Lincoln Town Car. He backed up, made a turn, and left the parking lot.

I was certain I had met the Fixer.

CHAPTER 23

LOVELY CLINIC DAY

By the time I had showered and eaten dinner, I was ready for bed. Mary Louise knew I would be whipped, so she had turned down the covers in advance, placed a bottle of water and some Advil on my bedside table, and turned on a couple of night lights. I think I was asleep before my head hit the pillow. I had neither the time nor the inclination to discuss my brief encounter with the man called Charles, last name irrelevant. Some things are better left unsaid, especially when there is little or no time for discussion or explanation.

I was back up at 5 a.m. and at the hospital by 5:45, where I met Belinda for rounds. The post-ops had all survived the evening, and although everyone was in pain, there were no complications thus far. I picked up a breakfast sandwich in the surgeon's lounge after rounds and headed over to the office-building side of the campus to see patients.

My first patient was Del Anderson, owner and publisher of the Highlander newspaper. Her X-rays looked good, and her wound was healed, so Belinda took out her sutures while I gave Del instructions for the next month. I could tell she wanted to talk, but I had no time. She mimed the words "call me," gave me a big Texas hug, and walked out of the exam room carrying her walker over her shoulder. Oh, to have all the patients be like Del, I thought to myself.

Next was Lisa Stewart, daughter of Louis Devlin. She was emotionally up, and friendly, so I doubted her father or one of his minions had poisoned our relationship. She had an excellent hip range of motion, and her wound was healing nicely. I told her to keep the weight off the hip until the following week, and after her sutures were removed, she could start partial weight bearing. She also gave me a hug.

Unfortunately, after those first two patients, the rest of the day went gradually downhill. Everyone seemed to be in a bad mood, either from post-op recovery pain, or from pre-op pain, or from waiting for their doctor to see them, who was behind by then and in a bad mood himself. Maya, Belinda, and I took a short break for lunch, thinking that having some calories on board would make the whole world seem rosier. We were wrong. Our patients were still an unhappy lot. I hoped there was a full moon, often the cause of masses of people becoming unpleasant at the same time, and not the general dissatisfaction of planet earth's inhabitants with Dr. Jim Bob Brady.

But like all good things and bad things, there is an end, and we did manage to finish seeing clinic patients around 4 p.m. It was close enough to cocktail hour for me, and I slouched into my office and poured a couple of fingers of a single-malt Macallan scotch into a Waterford crystal glass. Years prior, a grateful patient gave me a set of those beautiful glasses, and it was too bad she was not in the clinic today. She was always up, and friendly, and kind, and constantly bringing gifts to me and the staff. Camille was her name, and what a lovely human being she was. She had passed away from issues unrelated to her orthopedic problems. As usual, before I sipped the scotch, I raised the fine glass she had given me and gave her a toast. After the day we had, I would like to think Camille returned the gesture.

There were several messages on my desk, two of primary interest. One was from Dr. Jerry Reed, the other from Del Anderson.

I called the pathology department and asked for Dr. Reed.

"Long day?" he asked.

"The longest. Is it a full moon?"

"Funny you should ask. I have had some strange cases come in today, and yes, I looked it up. Full-moon time, Brady."

"Glad to know it's not just me. I feel better knowing that, at times, even the dead get strange."

He laughed. "More often than you think. Listen, about the autopsy on the unidentified woman victim from the pond. I spoke to Susan Beeson, since she is top of the chain of command, but I wanted to let you know the new victim was an intersex person as well, though her external variances were less developed than Christine Devlin's."

"Susan told me. Her intersex traits were vestigial testicles and an enlarged clitoris. Is that it in a nutshell?"

"Very well put, Jim. That of course made me wonder if by chance the two women were related, because, quite frankly, intersexuality in two local murder victims killed within a week of each other is rare. As a result, I took the liberty of ordering a DNA screen on both. That will take a few days."

"What about the tox screen?"

"Nothing yet. Unlike you and me, many of these technicians do not work on the weekend."

"Imagine that."

"That's all for now. I will keep you posted."

"Okay and thanks."

Next, I called Del. "Is it true?" she asked.

"Is what true?"

"That the unidentified female discovered in the golf club pond is related to Christine Devlin?"

"Del, I have no idea. Honestly. Dr. Jerry Reed called me, said there were similarities in a . . . genetic expression, if you will, and that warranted further testing. He took DNA samples from each of the women, but the results aren't back yet. That's all I know. How did you hear of the similarity?

"I have my sources, that's all I can say."

"Del, Dr. Reed, the detective in charge of the case, and I have been careful not to allow spread of this information to the general public for many reasons, the main one being personal privacy for the deceased. You are speaking of Louis Devlin's wife, a man with resources you can only imagine. I would hesitate to spread rumor and innuendo in your newspaper, for fear of retaliation of some sort."

"Jim Bob, remember freedom of the press?"

"Yes, I do. And do you remember The Godfather and Goodfellas?"

"Of course. Are you saying . . .?"

"I do not know what we are dealing with, but until Susan Beeson, ASAC of the FBI in Austin, sheds more light on the subject, I would tread lightly."

"Well, I don't intend to have the voice of the Fourth Estate thwarted."

"Del, from one friend to another, I am asking you to give it a few days until more information can be obtained. You are the only newspaper person I converse with, and you will have an exclusive, regardless of whatever this situation turns out to be. I just want to make sure you are healthy enough to write the story, if you get my drift."

"This newspaper owner and editor is not afraid of—"

"Del?"

"Fine. I will keep my silence until next week. I will write around the edges of the story, print nothing that has not been proven, and keep supposition to a minimum. As a favor to you, by the way. Personally, I am afraid of no one, and would not hesitate to print what I think I know about these deaths, were it not for our friendship. But if anyone scoops me, there will be hell to pay, Jim Brady."

"Thanks Del. I'll be in touch."

I looked at the schedule for Wednesday, saw we had a reasonable schedule of four operations, and my mood immediately lightened. I would have some time in the afternoon to research intersexuality, and maybe make a positive input into the now-complicated cases of three murders.

While HCMC had a medical library, it was primarily composed of current journals in all the fields of medical and surgical specialties represented at the hospital. I walked over to the library, located on the first level back by the administrative offices, and admitted myself. As I suspected, there were only a few weighty tomes from which to glean information. I also found a few cursory articles and treatises about intersexuality, but not to the extent that I needed.

I placed a call to the Houston Academy of Medicine and was directed to the Jesse Jones Library, one of the finest medical libraries anywhere. I had used them before in a murder case involving the death of my neighbor's child. I spoke to the medical librarian, telling her what I needed. She said to give her half an hour, then she would call me back.

I wandered over to the coffee shop and had a double shot of espresso mixed into a regular coffee. It was called a "hammerhead" at some coffee places, but at times that order was met with a blank expression, so I usually just went with the less exciting but more descriptive "double shot of espresso in regular coffee." Within ten minutes, I was finally actually awake.

I went outside to get some fresh air and walk off the caffeine high. I saw a black Lincoln Town Car turn into the drive off Highway 71 and slowly approach the portico to the hospital. Out of the rear seat stepped Dr. Buck Owens, chair of the board of HCMC. I turned back from my walk and met him at the car.

"Hello, Buck. Out for a drive?"

"Louis Devlin scheduled a walk-through on the property south of La Cava Golf Club. He's nearing completion of the clubhouse, and once that's complete, he'll bring in crews to excavate and start building the infrastructure necessary to develop homes. He bought 300 acres and has plans for 200 high-end custom homes with minimum one-acre lots. His plan is to bring in workers from the outside and house them in trailers while the work is being done."

"What sort of work would they be doing?"

"Building infrastructure, as I said. Roads, power lines, water lines, sewer lines, phone lines, and fiberoptic cable lines, all of which will be buried so the development is free of those pesky electrical lines and towers. In the grand scheme of things, the cost of burying all those lines is minimal compared to the cost of trying to install them later, once the home-building has begun. Plus, the property will be so much more appealing without the above-ground eyesore.

"By the way, have you found out any information from being a member at La Cava? Anything to help our financial guys understand what's going on with our $25 million investment?"

"Let me think. In a word, no. Devlin's wife was murdered. His assistant was murdered. Now an unknown woman was murdered, relation to Devlin undetermined. Three murders over the course of two weeks takes precedent over your investors' money problems. How in the world did you get involved with Devlin in the first place?"

"Friends from Dallas who had done business with him in the past. He made them a lot of money, and the deal sounded good to my consortium."

My phone rang, and I saw it was the Houston library. "I need to take this, Buck. Talk later."

"Hello. Dr. Brady here."

"Yes, sir, this is Yvette in the Jones Library. I have gathered quite a bit of data on intersexuality for you. I could email it to you and you could print it, or I could overnight the information to you. Which do you prefer?"

"It sounds like printing it would be a one-cartridge process. Correct?"

"Maybe two, the way those cartridges run out of ink so quickly. How about I overnight it to you?"

"Sounds good, Yvette. Thanks much." I gave her the office address, since there was always someone to sign for it if need be.

I went back upstairs to my office, checked in with Maya and Belinda to make sure all was well, then headed home.

Tip greeted me with enthusiasm, since I had been home such a short time the day before. I took him for a long walk down to the dog park, where I let him run rampant without his leash. He stopped over what he considered was a delicious smell and perked his ears up at me like he was about to roll in whatever animal poop had his interest. I yelled "NO!" sternly, and he backed away, then ran toward me to receive a "Good boy!" and a vigorous head pat.

Mary Louise had opened a Far Niente chardonnay. I gave Tip some kibble laced with fresh chicken, then I sat at the counter and sipped my wine. "Smells good. What's for dinner?"

"Chicken piccata with fresh broccoli and carrots. A wedge salad to start."

"Yum. At least I feel more alive than I did yesterday. I could not have made it without Belinda."

"You may be getting a little old to try and do seven cases in one day. That is a lot of work for a man your age."

"A man my age. I love it. I am not old, at least in spirit."

"You're right, there," she said, as she walked around the counter. She had on tight blue-jean shorts and a white long-sleeved blouse with the sleeves rolled up. Her hair was in a long ponytail. She had scant makeup on, just a little lipstick to accent her full lips. She nestled up against me between my legs, put her arms around my neck and gave me an open-mouth kiss.

"We have about fifteen minutes before dinner is ready. How do you want to spend that time?" she asked.

"I can shower and be ready—"

"No. Sometimes I just like it dirty," she said, and waltzed me into the bedroom for dessert before the main course.

I showered after, and put on shorts and a tee shirt. We ate on the patio and observed the full moon rising.

"Clinic was wild today. Jerry Reed said the full moon affects his patients as well."

"Jim Bob, his patients are dead."

"Just goes to show you how far that full moon will go to affect earth's people."

"I had a similar experience today at the grocery. This little man came up to me and started talking about different forms of sausages, like bratwurst, chorizo, Andouille, and Kielbasa, but then said the best kind is Italian sausage and winked at me. I think he was coming on to me, but not in a nice way. I left him standing at the meat counter and checked out quickly. He was scary."

I had stopped eating by then. "What did he look like?"

"He was dark, in a Mediterranean sort of way, about five foot eight inches or so, and wore a fedora. Anyway, he gave me the creeps."

I shared my experience from the previous night when I was leaving the hospital. "He sounds like the same fellow. He told me his name was Charles. He works for Devlin; supposed to be his right-hand man, at least according to Devlin's daughter, Lisa Stewart."

"I cannot imagine what he would want with us, but I would prefer not to see him again."

"I will try and grant your wish."

CHAPTER 24

DNA

I did not sleep well and tossed and turned due to Mary Louise's encounter with the man I assumed was the Fixer. I got up early and was at the hospital by five thirty. Rounds were time-consuming, considering all the cases we did Monday. I intended to call Louis Devlin and give me a piece of my mind when surgery was done.

Belinda and I went through the four cases with ease, considering there were two virgin hip replacements and two virgin knee replacements. We were done by 1 p.m. I stopped in the surgeon's lounge to get lunch and ended up sitting next to Jerry Reed.

"This is the surgeon's lounge, Jerry. I didn't know you were a surgeon."

"You've seen me operate. I am a surgeon for the dead. Besides, I have news for you. The tox screen on the unidentified woman was positive for Rohypnol, the so-called date-rape drug, and fentanyl, a general anesthetic. Both were in high-enough concentration to put her out. I don't know if the police checked for drag marks or lines. It's probable that her assailant dragged her down the hill, although she could have been pushed. They more than likely held the victim's head underwater until she quit breathing. As a result, I am calling it a murder.

"Also, the DNA testing came back. The two women, Mrs. Devlin and our unknown victim, shared 25 percent of their DNA. First cousins generally share about 12.5 percent of their DNA, and full siblings share around 50 percent. In my opinion they were half-siblings, sharing DNA either from the same mother or father but not from both. They were related, however. I don't know what that means for the investigation, but I'll send the information to Lt. Mims today and let him worry about it. My job is done."

Once I was back in my office, I called Louis Devlin. I didn't know his personal number, so I called the sales office. Lisa Stewart was still filling in and answered the phone.

"Dr. Brady, how nice to hear from you!"

"Hey, Lisa. Are you taking care of that hip?"

"Yes, sir. What can I do for you?"

"I would like to speak to your dad. Do you happen to have his number?"

"Is there something I can help you with?"

"No, thank you. I need to ask him a question about a potential investor."

"Of course," she said, and recited his number.

"Thanks much. See you next week," I said, and disconnected.

I called Louis Devlin. He answered on the third ring.

"Devlin."

"Mr. Devlin, this is Dr. Jim Brady. I got your number from Lisa, your daughter. I wanted to tell you that I do not appreciate being accosted by your factotum by the name of Charles. And I really do not appreciate his innuendos toward my wife at the grocery store. You have been in Texas long enough to know how people here like to be treated, and being threatened by a cartoon-like character is not one of those ways."

"Brady, I have no idea what you are talking about. I do have an employee named Charles, and he does all sorts of odd jobs for me. As to him possibly threatening you or your wife, I know nothing of that. You are my daughter's doctor, and I have no reason to harass you in any way. As far as your wife is concerned, I cannot imagine Charles approaching a lady he does not know in the manner which you just described. I believe you are mistaken, and while I will discuss the matter with Charles, I should think I am owed an apology. I am a busy man, so I will bid you a good day."

And he hung up.

I arrived home in a bit of a tiff. I did not appreciate the way Devlin had spoken to me, as if I were an underling of some sort, working in one of his businesses. I shared my feeling with Mary Louise, and she of course agreed with my take on the subject.

"Also, the tox screen came back on the unidentified female and it was positive for Rohypnol and fentanyl. She was therefore drugged and drowned, according to Jerry Reed. And one more thing: the DNA showed a familial match between her and Christine Devlin, likely a half sister."

"Do you think their intersexuality has anything to do with the murder of either woman?"

"I can't imagine, at this point. The librarian at the Jones Medical Library in Houston is sending me a packet overnight with all I ever wanted to know about intersexuality. It should have arrived today."

"The package is on your desk, husband. Why don't we eat something before you tackle that project?"

"Sounds good to me. What are we having?"

"French dip sandwiches."

She served the thinly sliced roast beef on a baguette topped with swiss cheese and onions, as well as a dipping container of beef broth made from the cooking process. It was a culinary delight.

I was embarrassed that I ate two of those sandwiches, but I enjoyed every morsel of each.

The research regarding intersex patients was not anything I'd seen in med school, let alone as an orthopedic surgeon, but it was enlightening. Intersexuality is an inherited condition, an autosomal dominant mutation. The outdated term "hermaphrodite" is pejorative, though some intersex people still find the word employed in their medical records.

I read for a while, and the more I read, the less it seemed to me that this congenital anomaly had anything to do with the deaths of the two women beyond the fact that it indicated they might have been related to each other, and whatever that may have implied. It seemed more important to find that their DNA matched at a 25 percent level. As Jerry told me, that implied sisters from a different mother or father, with only one parent the same. I was unable to research the unidentified woman, but having Christine Devlin's name would allow me to research her online. However, after my last attempt at researching a subject fell woefully short, I thought that perhaps sharing the information in hand with Susan Beeson might aid her in the investigation and produce some familial history that might help solve Christine's murder and identify the other woman.

I returned to the bar, poured myself a short Macallan scotch, and called Susan on her cell phone. I heard Mary Louise laughing in the primary bedroom and wondered which inane television sitcom with a laugh track she was watching. She was a sucker for that kind of show.

"Are you behaving yourself?" Susan asked.

"Absolutely. I just wanted to share something with you that Dr. Jerry Reed told me. The presence of intersexuality in both Christine Devlin and the unknown drowned woman caused him to test their DNA, in hopes of helping to identify the second woman. The two victims had a 25 percent match, indicative of a common mother or father, but a different second parent. They were half-siblings. I don't know if that will help you with the murder investigation, but your people could do a background check on Christine and see if something like a half sister turns up. Where that would lead, I have not a clue, not being a detective and all."

"Sounds like you are not behaving yourself."

"I had this conversation with Jerry at lunch. He was just sharing with me. He said he would call you with what he had discovered. Did he?"

"Yes."

"Why didn't you say something before I rambled on with my paltry information?"

"I wanted to try and decipher how involved you still are with this investigation."

"Let me tell you this: I do not know nearly enough to satisfy my curiosity!"

"Down, boy. I will share with you what my people find out. How's that?"

"That would make me feel . . . included, Susan."

"Oh, good, Jim Bob. It is my goal in life is to make you feel included."

CHAPTER 25

REAL ESTATE

Thursday-morning rounds were a breeze compared to the previous couple of days. The patients had less pain, therefore there were fewer complaints. The five joint replacements would be moved to the rehab unit, and the two fractures would be discharged. Both boys who had fractures in the MX event were racing the hallways on their crutches. They were supposed to be non-weight-bearing, but from the looks on their faces when I saw them up on crutches, it was apparent they were not following the instructions. I sat them both down and had a heart-to-heart talk about the complications of their respective fractures not healing properly. The boy with the femoral-neck fracture had the highest complication risk, with the development of necrosis of the femoral head a real possibility. A total hip was in his future if the break didn't heal properly. The other boy with the femoral-shaft fracture and the rod would be fine unless he really went off the beaten path.

The boys seemed to listen to what I had to say, but then they were teenagers, so how could one know the degree of absorption of my impromptu lecture? I discharged them both back into the care of their parents. It was out of my hands at that point.

Belinda and I returned to the office and began the clinic day. We had a full schedule, so we didn't see the last patient until almost 5 p.m. I leafed through the mail, answered correspondence, and signed a few checks. Belinda and I agreed to meet for "late" Friday morning rounds—at 8 a.m.

On the drive home, I thought about Louis Devlin and the financing of his grand development project at La Cava Golf Club. The clubhouse was near completion, and from what I could tell, the golf course was completed. There were outbuildings needed for cart and equipment storage. I had not seen those structures, but I assumed they were nearing completion or complete as well. From the numbers I had seen in the pilfered documents, there was enough money to complete the building of the course, the clubhouse, and the required outbuildings. And the dues from the existing 100 members would produce enough revenue to make the initial investment whole, if those numbers were correct.

The next step was to begin the residential real estate project. From talking to Lisa Stewart, it sounded like building the infrastructure was either underway or about to begin. I was no civil engineer, but it made sense that water, sewage, electrical, and cable conduits had to be in place prior to building homes. I questioned whether Devlin would function as the developer and would partner with a builder to market the houses or whether he would handle the building himself. And then I wondered how much land one needed to build houses and how much the building process would cost. And then I wondered what the overhead costs of running an upscale golf club would be, and how much of the initial investment would that eat away until the club was up and running and the requisite number of members were paying their dues and using the club for food and beverage. Too many questions without answers made me thirsty, so I was happy that I had driven on autopilot and was near my driveway.

"How's my boy?" I said to Tip, once I entered the house, although when I reached down to pat his head, I smelled an awful aroma. "What in the world . . .?"

"He's been bad, Jim Bob, very bad," said Mary Louise. "He found a squirrel carcass in the yard today. It looked like it had been mauled by a bobcat or a coyote, and then chewed on by birds. Anyway, before I could stop him, he had run away with the dead squirrel and was gnawing on it, and throwing it up and down, and rolling on top of it. I finally got it away from him, but he growled at me! Can you imagine our sweet dog growling?"

"No, I cannot. It must have been a real prize for him."

"I guess. I am on the way to the groomer at the vet's office. She said she was willing to stay for Tip's cleanup, which of course means more money. There is roast in the oven with carrots and red potatoes, or you can make yourself one of your famous roast beef sandwiches on white bread slathered with mayo, covered with lettuce, tomato, and pickles. Your choice. I cut up the condiments you might need and covered them in plastic wrap."

"And how could any man not love you?"

"And don't you forget that. See you in a while," she said, and bussed my cheek and dragged a pitiful Tip to the car by his leash.

I made the "Dagwood" of all roast beef sandwiches, took it to my home office, and cranked up the internet search app. I read several articles about maintenance of several levels of golf courses, from daily-fee courses to top-of-the-line courses. Considering La Cava was intended to be a high-end club, my research suggested yearly maintenance without major complications like droughts, fires, and insect damage ran at least $1.5 million, sometimes more. This would explain my son's father-in-law Bill Hicks's comments on why golf courses are difficult to make money from. The current membership of 100 at La Cava paying $3,000 monthly would generate $3.6 million per year in dues; more than adequate to pay for the upkeep, but dependent on the membership remaining stable.

The sandwich was divine, and I had to interrupt my research in order to sample more of Mary Louise's roast beef. How could a woman who looked that good also be such an amazing cook? I was a lucky man and reminded myself to tell her that when she returned home from having MY dog groomed, at night, no less.

After fortifying myself with more roast beef, I read a little about the residential real estate business. Someone had told me, whether it was Buck Owens or Lisa Stewart I could not remember, that the Devlin group had purchased 300 acres just south of La Cava Golf Club and planned to build 200 homes, each on a one-acre parcel. The homes were intended to be upscale, which according to my readings would cost anywhere from $300 to $1,000 per square foot to build. If there was a minimum house size, like 3000 square feet, or 5000 square feet or more, that would bump the cost up even further. If one figured the max cost at the highest end, 200 homes sized each at 5000 square feet at a cost of $500 per square foot to build was a staggering $500 million. Of course, not every home would be at the max size or the max cost to build per square foot, but at even half the max, the cost would be $250 million.

And that was when I saw the light. The big money was in real estate. You can sell memberships to the golf club, and folks can go to dinner and have a martini and a nice bottle of wine, but the revenue from food and beverage pales when compared to potential real estate sales revenue. I believe that is what Bill Hicks was trying to explain to me. In our conversation he hinted there was also a bit of skulduggery or hanky-panky at play in creating upscale housing subdivisions. With the right construction crew, costs could be shaved. With the right builder, square footage costs could be reduced. With the right man in charge, permits could be granted even if the specs were not up to code. In other words, cutting costs was critical to maximize profit. And what better group of people to be involved in such a process than Louis Devlin and his cronies, with their history of having served jail terms followed by name changes. And they would protect their investment at all costs.

I was about to pick up the phone and call Susan Beeson with my newly found insight into the real estate development business when the door opened and a dog smelling of hyacinth bounded into my office. I rubbed his big fat head and scratched his sides, and he stood there paralyzed with the joy of attention.

"He certainly smells good now," I said.

"He should. How was the roast beef?"

"Incredible. How a woman can look as good as you and cook like that, I will never know."

"I look a mess. I'm going to go and shower. Did you save me any food?"

"Of course. A couple of bites," I said, and smiled. "Need any help in there?"

She gave me the look, the one that implied I should not ask about taking a shower together after she had been to the vet getting YOUR dog cleaned up from wallowing in dead squirrel remains.

I poured her a glass of chardonnay and watched her depart to the showers . . . alone.

After Friday morning rounds, the day was mine. I stopped by Lucy Williams's desk and asked to be let in to see the grand potentate of HCMC, Dr. Buck Owens.

"He's on the phone. How about a cup of coffee, and you can sit and chat with me?"

Lucy looked good, outwardly seemingly recovered from the brutal murder of her daughter a few years ago. She was wearing makeup and lipstick again, and getting her hair styled, and she looked younger and healthier.

"I would like nothing better, Lucy."

She brought us each a steaming mug of hot java, thick and full-bodied with a hint of spice. "Wow. This is good. What is it?"

"Cajun Delight. What do you think?"

"Great. This will keep me going for a while."

"I have a cup of this in the morning, and one after lunch, and I can get all my work done and tolerate His Highness in there. What are you seeing him about?"

"My surreptitious investigation of La Cava Golf Club and the future La Cava Golf Estates, I think the project is called."

"Why wouldn't he get his CPA and his attorney to look at the books? I mean really, Jim, what can you realistically do?"

"I've told him the same thing, but he will not listen. I was able to get a few documents to review, but I am not big on breaking and entering."

"I don't blame you. How is Mary Louise?"

"She's good. Friday is her day to make the trek to Austin for a charity board. She usually gets home right at cocktail time, frazzled from the drive. I usually play golf around noon and meet her at the house, wine in hand."

"You are such a good man. I wish there were more like you."

"You might be in the minority there, Lucy."

"His private phone light just went off. Want me to let him know you're here?"

"I guess, although you are much more fun to talk to. Thanks for the coffee."

"Most welcome. Go on in."

Buck's office was a home for western art. He had two original oils by Remington which he had purchased forty years prior. He also displayed works by Malcolm Furlow, Donna Howell-Sickles, Louisa McElwain, and Oleg Stavrowsky. It was a wonderful display, and I could not help viewing each painting when I entered.

"You have news for me?"

"I don't know. I am no expert in the golf course business, and neither am I an expert in how to screw your partners in the real estate development business. I do have some ideas, though, as to which giant hole your investment money might have disappeared into."

I quoted him the figures I had gone through the night before, and emphasized they were estimates of highs and lows.

"I can't believe those numbers. From $250 million to $500 million to build a subdivision with 200 custom homes. That would be an accounting and logistical nightmare. That would require borrowing a lot of money, Jim. Of course, some of that cost would be defrayed by the future homeowner putting up money at certain agreed-upon stages during the construction."

"What I can't believe is that smart men like you and your buddies got into the deal without knowing all the ins and outs. Maybe you should stick with drilling oil and gas wells. You seem to be good at that. How did you get involved with Devlin in the first place?"

"One of my associates is from Dallas and made a killing on the sale of a shopping center deal that Devlin put together. My friend invested at the front end, collected his portion of the rents for three or four years, then sold at a large multiple of rent revenue. He thinks Devlin walks on water."

"Well, Buck, he might, because this deal is just getting started. A little patience on your part could solve all your problems."

"I just don't want to lose my share, which was $5 million. We each put in that same amount."

"Wow. That would be a big loss. But I guess you can afford it, otherwise you would not have invested."

"True, Brady, but still. That's a lot of money down the drain."

"Didn't you have enough to begin with? I mean, what's the point?"

"The thrill of the chase, buddy. For an old man like me, there are not many thrills left to enjoy. Hitting a big-time investment is one. It is one of those things you just do not forget."

"Neither is losing $5 million, Buck. I would be the type that remembers the losing venture much longer than the winning venture. Especially if the men I was in business with were crooks."

"Why would you say crooks? There's no evidence of that."

"What would you say if I told you that Louis Devlin served time in Leavenworth for money laundering in his twenties? And that his real name before he changed it was Luigi Del Tommaso?"

"Where did you get that information?" he asked, as he slowly began to pale.

"From our friend Susan Beeson, ASAC of the Austin FBI. I've been waiting to tell you for a few days, knowing it would make you apoplectic. And that's not all. His business partner is a childhood chum of Devlin's from Kansas City. He has also been to prison and changed his name from Giuseppe Fertitta to Johnny Amato."

Poor Buck had lost most of the color in his face by then. "I met that Amato guy at one of the investor meetings. He is allegedly in charge of the real estate construction portion of the project. So, what do we do?"

"There is no 'we,' if you are referring to me. You and your cronies will have to wait and see what happens. He had a good reputation in Dallas, so maybe his past is truly behind him. Trust me, Susan is on it. She is an expert in financial crimes and has had her eye on the Savolio family for a while."

"Savolio? Who is that and where does it fit in?"

"That would be Nicky Savolio, head of the Savolio crime family out of Kansas City, and another one of Devlin's childhood friends. From what Susan told me, Devlin and Savolio were partners in the building and development business back in the day. Apparently, one of the main reasons Devlin left Kansas City and moved to Dallas was to get away from the hooks of the criminal syndicate and try to run a clean commercial real estate business. Whether he has been successful at that or not, Susan does not know. But trust me, she is an expert in this field and will get to the bottom of the matter. Whether she'll be able to preserve investor money or not, I do not know. My advice is to sit tight and see what comes about."

CHAPTER 26

FRIDAY GOLF

had invited my golf group of sixteen to play at La Cava that day. We had tee times starting at eleven thirty. I was not surprised when Louis Devlin showed up at the practice range while we were warming up. He greeted each guest, shaking their hands as though they were best friends. He saved my greeting for last.

"Dr. Brady, thank you so much for bringing your guests to La Cava. You're a new member, and if all new members supported the club in such a manner, we would be assured of success. I apologize for my behavior on the phone the other day. It was uncalled for. I took out my aggression over another problem on you, and I regret that. Perhaps we could schedule a dinner soon, with you and your wife as my guest?"

"Well, Mr. Devlin, I—"

"It's Louis, please. Next week, on Friday, we'll have dinner at my penthouse. Christine and I were going to sell it in anticipation of moving into our new home on La Cava number one, but now I'm not sure if that's in my best interest. There'll be too many memories. At any rate, you and your wife will be my guests. Plan on 7 p.m.," he said, and handed me a business card with the address.

"Thank you very much. We'll be delighted."

As he walked away, I wondered if I was very smart or very dumb. Getting close to an alleged criminal could not be a good thing. My curiosity was always just beneath the surface, and in time it would probably kill the cat.

My golf group had a spectacular time at La Cava. The course was pristine. The rain stayed away, and at the turn, prior to teeing off on the tenth hole, the staff provided sandwiches, chips, and beer, compliments of Mr. Devlin, the valet told us. We finished the last hole unscathed and met in the men's locker room once all four groups had completed their rounds.

While I reviewed the score cards to calculate the winners, the staff brought in plates of mini hot dogs, pizza slices, egg rolls, and fried dumplings, again compliments of Mr. Devlin. The open bar was compliments of yours truly, so for one day, I was everyone's best friend. We had each put $50 into the pot, which totaled $900. There were multiple games going on at the same time: best two-ball score, best four-ball score, closet to the pin on all pars 3s, and skins on every hole. By the time I completed the scoring and the money was divided amongst the winners, we were all feeling no pain. I distributed the cash winnings and bid everyone adieu a tad before 6 p.m.

I decided to roam through the almost-completed parking lot but did not find an exit that led directly to the future housing development. I finally exited the property, drove south on a freshly asphalted road, and after a mile or so, found a sign for La Cava Golf Estates. At the entrance, the road turned to dirt, and I could see construction vehicles scattered about, with earth movers in the distance still working, despite the hour.

I saw a cluster of vehicles a couple of hundred yards away and drove toward them. There were several workers gathered, smiling and laughing as only one could at the end of a workday, especially on a Friday. The conversation stopped when I walked toward the group, as did the laughing.

"Afternoon, all. You're working late," I said. They looked at each other as though no one had understood my comment. They spoke to each other in a language I did not recognize. I had lived in Texas my entire life, and I knew enough Spanish to get by, but this language, I did not understand.

"Boss man?" I asked

"Si, si," said one of the men with a radio. He spoke to someone on the other end, then said to me, "Soon."

I walked back to my truck, their conversation resumed, and I waited for the supervisor. Before too long, a man drove up in a dusty pickup. He pulled up beside me but stayed in his seat. His skin was olive, and he wore a wide-brimmed hat and sunglasses, but he looked familiar.

"Help you?"

"Afternoon. My name is Jim Brady, and I'm a new member of the club. I'm interested in the homes in this subdivision. How would I get information?"

"Sales office. Closed now. Try tomorrow."

"You look familiar. Have we met?"

He paused. "At the club. You asked about my golf cart. Johnny Amato."

"That's right. I didn't recognize you with the hat and sunglasses. Are your guys putting in the infrastructure?"

"Yes, but we're about a month from completion."

"Wow, that was quick work. I would have thought it would have taken longer."

"Depends on the crew. I brought all the crew in from out of town and housed them in those trailers you see down by that copse of trees. They're all Italian, the best workers in the world.

Besides, we've been working on the infrastructure for a while. There was all that limestone . . ."

"I heard about that. Caverns and large deposits, as I understand."

"Yes, it was a bitch to dig up all that rock, although we have plenty now for building houses. The real problem is the granite."

"The granite?"

"Nothing, just talking about bedrock. Not a big deal, with our equipment."

"Do you use your imported workers for building houses as well?"

"Yes, but we'll bring some new ones in for that, specialists in the building processes. Once the infrastructure is done, the roads will get paved and be made smooth so the buyers in their fancy cars won't get too dusty," he said, with some degree of sarcasm.

"I don't get how it works. Do builders come in and build custom homes, or do you build spec homes to attract customers?"

"The plan is for 200 homes to be built. There'll be ten styles of houses. We have our own builders, and our own labor. We'll begin construction on one each of the styles available. If a buyer wants to make some changes and purchases a house in the early building phase, we can accommodate adjustments in the architectural plan. However, in my experience, with ten options available, you can make most people happy without too much variance."

"I guess the sales office will have the information about the styles and prices?"

"Yes. Lisa Stewart runs the office. She comes in at nine in the morning."

"Okay, Johnny. Thanks much for the info." I reached up to his window, shook his hand, and headed home.

Mary Louise was barely able to greet me before Tip just about knocked me down. He demanded attention and got his way.

"How was your day?" I asked. "The weather was good here, so I hope you had no issues getting home."

"Yes, it was a beautiful day compared to last Friday." She put her arms around my neck and kissed me. "You smell like alcohol."

"I took the guys to La Cava today. We had beer at the turn and drinks after the round. Louis Devlin showed up and greeted each player and provided us with food both at the turn and after the round. He also insisted we come to dinner next Friday night in his penthouse."

"What did you say?"

"I was cornered. He does not take no for an answer. I think we're stuck."

"I am leery of him. I don't know that I can trust a man like that."

"You are not alone," I said, and related my conversation with Buck that morning.

"I went down to the building site for La Cava Estates and met the building foreperson. It's the guy with the HIGHROLLER plate on his golf cart, Johnny Amato."

"Wasn't that the guy that was fighting Devlin on the eighteenth hole when we played over there?"

"Yep."

"Strange people. One minute he and Devlin are fighting, the next minute Amato is the construction foreperson."

"He said he had brought the entire crew in from Italy for the Estates construction and was housing them in trailers on the property."

"Hmm. He's leaving out the local workforce, it sounds like to me. I wouldn't think that would sit well with the city and county government people."

"Probably not. There might have to have been an exchange of funds for those building permits to get approved, unless they didn't know about the imported workers. But I don't believe that. Seems to me that cities and counties approve new building projects with the employability of its citizens in mind."

"Maybe you can ask Devlin those sorts of questions at dinner on Wednesday. You can ask him about his superintendent Amato, and maybe ask about them fighting. You can also ask why Mrs. Devlin was murdered, and while you're at it, you can ask the same about Patsy Simmons."

"Mary Louise, I do not think those questions would be appropriate for dinner conversation. As I remember, Amato has a wife named Greta, according to Lisa Stewart."

"See, there is another question you can ask, if Amato is at the dinner. Where is your wife, sir? You can glean all sorts of information from these people. I can just sit back and watch the master interrogator at work."

"I detect some smart-ass to your tone, Mary Louise Brady."

"Who, me? Never! I am your biggest fan."

"We will see, young lady. Are you hungry?"

"Starving. I stopped at the Bluebonnet Café on the way home. How does fried chicken with cream gravy and fried okra sound to you?"

"Like I died and went to heaven. Did the food come with a coupon for a discount on a cardiac catheterization?"

CHAPTER 27

GRETA

Saturday was another glorious day in the Hill Country, and golf with my Horseshoe Bay Golf Club group carried on without weather interference. Casting aside my worries about possible criminals in the midst, I was in a good mood. I played well and won a few bets. My colleagues again thanked me for hosting them at La Cava. I would be in good favor for a while . . . until I was not. Life was like that. What have you done for me lately?

I arrived at home to find Susan Beeson's car parked in the middle of the driveway, blocking my entrance into the garage. I could never understand why a guest blocks the host's driveway. Another one of life's little mysteries.

"Hello, all," I said, as I entered through the front door.

"Hey, babe. Why are you coming in the front door?"

"Because someone is blocking the driveway and I was unable to get into my spot in the garage."

"Oh, sorry, that would be Susan. She never thinks of things like that. I'll have her move the car once she's off the phone. She's on the terrace."

"Good thing that wasn't a test question on the exam for special agent in the FBI. Do you or do you not block the driveway of a home where there is NO crime scene?"

"Jim Bob? You aren't in one of your weird moods, are you?"

"I was perfectly happy until I could not park in my own garage. I was having a great day until then."

"You are acting like a baby, sweetie. How about a beer, or a glass of wine?"

"It is a Macallan kind of moment, Mary Louise," I replied, and stepped into the bar and constructed myself an eighteen-year mood elevator.

"Well, I think I have it figured out," said Susan, as she entered the house and slammed the door. "Jim Bob! How is my favorite non-detective?"

"Fine. Having a drink while waiting to get my car in the garage."

"What!? Oh, I am such a dunce. I was so excited about some new information that I couldn't wait to tell you. Let me move it and then you can fix me what you're drinking."

I fixed Susan what I was drinking, only I gave her the Macallan twelve-year with two ice cubes. She would not know the difference.

She re-entered, and we three moved to the terrace to drink and talk.

"Thanks for the drink," she said as she sipped, "but it just doesn't have that marvelous peat taste the eighteen-year has."

I hoped she didn't notice the reddening of my face.

"Christine Devlin, family name of Hall, grew up in Carrollton, north of Dallas. She went to SMU where she met Robert Johnson Sr., who became her first husband. She worked in the family business, which was retail, but eventually branched out into the convention business. She had three sons, Robert Jr., Alan, and Samuel. According to her medical records, which we were able to access using her social security number plus some other identifiers I cannot discuss with non-agency personnel, all three of her children were delivered via C-section. She had a significant anomaly in her pelvis that prevented natural delivery. I assume that is associated with her intra . . ."

"Intersexuality," I said.

"Yes. It is interesting to me she was able to conceive but could not deliver a child."

"That's not unusual, Susan, according to what I've read. But the decision to perform a C-section usually has more to do with a narrowing of the pelvic entry/exit in comparison to the width of the baby's head than intersexuality specifically."

Susan looked at me curiously. "How do you know about obstetrics?"

"I went to medical school, and during the clinical years every student is required to rotate through eight weeks of OB-GYN. Some things you just do not forget."

"Fine. At any rate, after her children were grown, she apparently found a website devoted to intersexuality which provided a private forum for intersex people. Christine communicated with a lot of people on the website but was drawn to one woman with whom she just seemed to click, like they'd known each other for years. That woman happened to be looking for her biological family, as was Christine, each having been adopted as infants. The woman had moved to Dallas a few years ago. She and Christine eventually met in person, and low and behold, it was someone Christine already knew. What neither of them had known, though, was that the other was an intersex person. But having exchanged that more-detailed information, they realized they also had a physical resemblance to each other, and each decided to get DNA tests. And sure enough, they had a 25 percent match, suggesting they were half sisters with one common parent.

"They undertook a project together to try and find the source of the common DNA, but it proved to be fruitless. Christine's parents were deceased, and she had no known siblings. Her newly discovered half sister's parents were also deceased, and she had no known siblings either. She had known she was adopted but had never searched for her birth parents until she met Christine. The DNA search company did what they could to help the two women, but all roads led to the fact that some things are just not meant to be discovered."

"I assume you know who the half sister is. Is there some reason you can't tell us?" I asked.

"At this point, I do know who she is. I do not see any reason why you and Mary Louise shouldn't be told her name, seeing as how you both have been involved in these matters from the outset. Her given name was Margaretta Sinclair. But after she married, she went by . . . Greta Amato."

"What?! She's the wife of Devlin's friend and partner, Johnny Amato!"

"That is correct. We have been trying to contact her. Her husband told my agents she was out of town visiting a grandson, but we were unable to substantiate that with their son and his wife. We interviewed the husband twice, and he seemed terribly broken up by what would be his wife's disappearance.

"Meanwhile, your pathologist Dr. Jerry Reed had been working to find the identity of the woman in the pond using dental records and comparing the dead woman's DNA to DNA the crime-scene techs recovered at the Amato house, specifically in her bathroom. Jerry called me today. The woman in the pond is in fact Greta Amato, Christine's half sister."

We three stared at each other for a silent moment or two.

"Let me get this straight," I said. "Christine Devlin, wife of Louis Devlin, was murdered in the primary bathroom of her new home, still under construction, by an unknown assailant. Patsy Simmons, assistant to Louis Devlin, was raped and murdered in her home shortly thereafter. And now, Greta Amato, wife of Devlin's business partner and long-lost half sister of Devlin's wife Christine, was drugged and drowned in a pond adjacent to the driving range at Horseshoe Bay Golf Club."

"An excellent summary, Jim Bob. Three women, all close to Devlin, have been murdered in the past two weeks, with nary a clue as to why or by whom. If these were 'hits,' they were all handled by a professional, in my opinion. If we knew the why, we might be able to find out who. As it is, our investigation is stymied."

"You're telling us there is nothing left for the FBI to investigate? You people are supposed to be the experts in solving crimes," said Mary Louise, almost tearing up as she spoke.

"That is where we stand right now. We have served a subpoena to Mr. Devlin for all his business records since he arrived in this area. There may be a clue in there somewhere as to what these three women knew that would result in their demise. Otherwise, this case will be called the work of a random serial killer."

"How could the murders possibly be called 'random' when the victims knew one another and had connections to the same men, Devlin and Amato? That would be ridiculous."

"Jim, I deal in realities, not suppositions. 'Facts not in evidence' is a legal term used for good reason and applies to these cases."

I went to the bar, poured Mary Louise a glass of Rombauer chardonnay, and refreshed the Macallan for myself and Susan. I used eighteen-year-old for both of us.

"Is Devlin responsible for killing everyone necessary to accomplish his goal of . . . what? One must assume he is responsible for all three murders, but what is the end game, Susan? Any ideas? Any guesses?" I asked.

"My agents think it must have something to do with the building project at La Cava. Devlin has been operating a commercial real estate business for years, three here in the Marble Falls area, and before that, ten years in Dallas. He has a murky past in Kansas City, but as far as we can tell, he's been running an honest business for the past thirteen years. He had excellent credentials and a stellar reputation in Dallas, which prompted his being welcomed into this area by the city hierarchy and private investors. As far as we know, he did not find it necessary in the past to kill off anyone here or in Dallas in order to operate his businesses. The question I need to answer is, what's different now?"

"Mary Louise, remember last Sunday when we played the back nine at La Cava, and we came in early because of the weather? And we saw two men fighting adjacent to the eighteenth green? And when we got close, we saw it was Devlin and Amato going at it?"

"Absolutely."

"You see, Susan, that's evidence of something!"

"Two men fighting does not a murderer make, Jim. Do you know what they were fighting about?"

"Of course not. It had just started to rain, so we were in a hurry to get in. I didn't stop and try to break up the fight, if that's what you're asking."

"Was the fight you saw about their respective wives being murdered?"

"Susan, I have no idea."

"So, you have no evidence?"

"No, but . . ."

"Jim, these are the kinds of questions I ask my agents every day. We need evidence, we need proof, we need facts. Without that, we have only supposition and innuendo, which is what defense lawyers feed on for their clients. I would suggest you concentrate on your work and on your golf, and leave the FBI to do its job, unless you think you can do better that the federal government in solving this case."

"If I had reliable resources, this situation would be different, but I have none."

"If you come up with some sort of evidence, you let me know and I will run with it. Otherwise, you are sticking your nose in some unsavory business with alleged underworld figures possibly involved. A smart man would steer clear."

"Amen to that," chimed Mary Louise.

CHAPTER 28

ROBERT JOHNSON

We slept in Sunday morning, seeing as how we were up late talking and tossing ideas about as to the reasons why three women close to Louis Devlin would be murdered. Mary Louise prepared a late breakfast of scrambled eggs with ham and Havarti cheese, hash browns, bacon, sausage, and sourdough toast. We ate so much, we thought about going back to bed. However, adult reasoning prevailed, and Susan showered and got herself together and headed back to Austin to her family.

Mary Louise and I cleaned up and dressed for our traditional nine holes of golf on Sunday. We had decided to play at Horseshoe Bay rather than La Cava. There were just too many negative vibes at the new course, plus I did not want to take a chance and run into Devlin or Amato there.

We had just teed off on Apple Rock when my phone chimed. The screen read Robert Holmes. The name did not ring a bell, so I let it go to voice mail. We played at a good pace until the seventh hole, when we encountered a foursome of slow players, looking without success for balls in the woods. I dialed voicemail on my phone and waited to hear the only message.

"Dr. Brady, my name is Robert Johnson Jr. My mother was the former Christine Johnson, and at the time of her death, Christine

Devlin. I live in Dallas and am a part of the management of Oak Cliff Development and Commercial Realty, owned by my stepfather Louis Devlin. I have two brothers, Allen and Sam, who also work in the family business. We were obviously very disturbed over the murder of our mother, but we have grown even more concerned over the newspaper and television stories about the deaths of two more people close to Louis, Patsy Simmons his assistant and Greta Amato, wife of Louis's business partner Johnny Amato. We knew Patsy and Greta very well. They were both like family to us. Johnny Amato has been Louis's business partner for longer than I have been alive, and Patsy was like a sister to us. We spoke almost every day via telephone or text about some business issue in the corporation. The reason I am calling is that I understand you and your wife found our mother just after she was shot, and we wondered if we might get together for a conversation, maybe on Zoom or Skype. I called the Marble Falls Police Department and spoke to Det. Mims, but he said he couldn't discuss the case because it was an open investigation. Since we're often there, we subscribe to the Highlander online, and the editor, Del Anderson, recently wrote an article about the case and included your names as the discoverers of Mom's body."

He left me his number and instructions of how to get together via video call. The wanderers in front of us finally quit looking for balls, dropped new ones in the fairway, and managed to complete the hole before I was an old man. We finished the hole and drove around to the eighth tee, and there they were, hacking away. They looked behind at us and motioned us through, so we took advantage of their largesse and teed off. Fortunately, we both hit spectacular shots down the middle. I saluted the gents as we passed them and they tipped their hats toward us, then happily returned to looking for balls. We finished the hole before they ever hit their second shots, so we were done with eight and nine in fifteen minutes. We decided to take a break from golf and have lunch.

We found an outdoor table in the shade and each ordered a Bloody Mary and fish tacos for lunch. A new clubhouse had been built at what is called Cap Rock, a confluence of two golf courses, Apple Rock and Ram Rock. The patio was beautifully constructed and had vistas that extended for many miles into the Hill Country.

I gave Mary Louise the details of the message from Robert Johnson Jr. "What do you think?"

"I don't see any harm in talking to him, do you? The police are stymied, the FBI is at a standstill, and maybe he has some information that could break the case open. And it's not like you're confronting a mass murderer. You're just having a conversation with a deceased woman's son. He's not a suspect, is he?"

"If he were, I would think that Susan would have said something to us about that."

"Then I say make the call."

I left a message on his cell and suggested 7 p.m. for our video conference. He texted me back shortly thereafter and agreed to the time. He said his two brothers would be present as well and asked me to please keep the conversation to ourselves.

We finished our tacos, decided that nine holes was enough for the day, and went home. After a shower, we were tired again and decided a nap was in order. Mary Louise came to bed with nothing on but a transparent camisole, so being an ardent member of the male species, I took full advantage of the situation. We fell asleep afterward but were awakened by a shrill beeping of my computer. We took just a minute to arrange ourselves for conversation mode.

"Hello," I said. "Jim Bob Brady here. This is my wife, Mary Louise." She put her face into the camera and said hello.

"I'm Robert Johnson. This is Alan, and Sam," he said, and both men took turns appearing on the screen. The three of them looked alike, all with dark hair and tanned skin and good facial features.

"Thanks for agreeing to speak with us. We just needed to talk to someone, and figured you, being a doctor and all, would at least be a reliable person to communicate with."

"Well, I didn't know your mother. The day we found her was our first encounter. I have since had a few conversations with Louis Devlin."

"Mom was a great lady. She raised us as a single mother after my dad died of cancer. We were on our own for ten years. She got us through high school and college unscathed, and rarely even went on a date until we were out of the house and working. Then she met Louis about three years ago, and suddenly our lives were disrupted. We three boys were business majors at SMU, and all had good jobs in Dallas working in commercial real estate. Then she meets Louis, and he decides he wants us to go to work for his company. He had two daughters, Lisa Stewart and Elizabeth Winters, and both their husbands, Bill and Kirk, were working for Louis, and he decided he wanted to make his business a family affair.

"He had heard of La Cava, which had a previous name that I now forget, and their bankruptcy problems, and put us all to work in raising money to take over the project. Lisa and Bill and Elizabeth and Kirk had to move to the Hill Country and help Louis with the project. Alan, Sam, and I were selected to stay in Dallas with our families and manage our commercial properties here. Next thing I know, Louis and Mom also moved to the Hill Country. Bill and Kirk then had to travel between Dallas and Marble Falls on a weekly basis, depending on what was needed at the time, so it's been much more disruptive for them.

"In spite of the changes in our lives, the company was doing well. Louis got the contract to build, or rather complete, La Cava. He got the permits needed to finish the project, then went through the process to get approval to create the subdivision of La Cava Estates, and while that took a couple of years, we finally had the project and all its facets underway as planned.

"And then something changed. Louis, who was normally a cool, calm, collected, and happy guy, became sour, moody, and difficult to get along with. He became obsessed with raising money for the project, even though our projections showed that with his investors' contributions, and with an even mediocre number of memberships sold and dues paid, we would be fine. Louis got a line of credit from a New York bank, to be used only if necessary. That is where he was the weekend Mom was murdered, giving those investment bankers a financial update on the project. Patsy had traveled with him. She knew the finances backwards and forwards, so he never went to a financial meeting without her.

"And then, Mom was murdered in their dream house they were building. Patsy was murdered as well, and then Greta Amato was found drowned in a shallow pond. We are all freaking out."

"Can you tell me what the relationship is between Louis and Johnny Amato?"

"Old friends from the Kansas City neighborhood, was what they always told us. Louis made Johnny the building superintendent of the La Cava project. He knows all these Italians from working in the building business his whole life, so he gets good deals on employee compensation. He has a bunch of those guys working at La Cava now, living in Airstreams on the property."

"What do you think was the source of Louis's personality change?"

He looked away from the camera, and I heard he and his two brothers having a heated discussion.

"We have differing opinions about that. Louis, and Johnny for that matter, have a past. They were both in prison in their younger days. Louis turned over a new leaf and changed his name. Johnny Amato did the same. They became honest businesspeople, developers of commercial properties primarily. Johnny always worked for Louis. They were friends back in the 'Kansas City days,' as they would say, and would be friends forever. They had some trouble with a criminal element in Kansas City, but I thought that was all behind them when they moved to Dallas. My brothers think differently. They think that this so-called criminal element has raised its ugly head and has been trying to extort money from Louis and Johnny. That would explain Louis's need for additional money in excess of what is required by the project. I do not totally agree with Allen and Sam, but I can see their point."

"Have you or your accountants and lawyers been through the books? I mean, you are principals in Louis's development business and certainly have a right, if not an obligation, to have your financial people go through them."

"That's the thing. The La Cava records are in an entirely different system. Patsy had control of that aspect. I don't think that either Bill Stewart or Kirk Winters have access to all the financials. I had a conversation with them yesterday, and they admitted they've been kept in the dark about a lot of transactions that they normally would be involved in."

"Wow. It does sound suspicious, even to me, a doctor. What can I do to help?"

"Ideally, get ahold of the financials on the La Cava project. If any of the three of us or Bill or Kirk start asking questions, Louis will get suspicious. And with the mood he's in, no one wants to aggravate him further. But he is very partial to Lisa, and I think she's taken over Patsy's job. She might be the key."

"You know I just operated on her hip?"

"We did. That's one of the reasons we called you."

"I have no relationship with Lisa other than as her doctor. I don't see what I could do."

"She knows where the paperwork has been hidden, we feel sure. She may not know what she has, but she probably knows something. We cannot call the cops and we cannot call the accountants. You might not be our only hope, but our options are few. We're hoping you can help us out."

"I'm just a doctor with limited resources."

"We know your reputation and have heard otherwise. Our family is counting on you."

CHAPTER 29

GUNSHOT

When the call ended, I looked at Mary Louise. "You didn't reject their request as I thought you might. You tend to take a negative view of my so-called investigations."

"They sounded desperate. I felt sorry for the family. You have Susan on your side, and she can be very accommodating when she wants to."

I sighed. "Both of you tell me all the time I should emphasize my work and my golf and stay out of involving myself in other people's troubles. I think that is especially good advice considering there are three murdered women involved with a possible criminal syndicate connection."

"You seem to get along with Lisa Stewart. She's running the sales office at La Cava, and she is your patient. You can be a silver-tongued devil when you want to be. I think you could ask her some questions in an innocent sort of way that hopefully would keep you off the Devlin radar. The young man you were speaking to seemed to think that his mother's murder is at the root of the issue. I won't tell you how to approach Lisa, because you are the expert at that sort of thing, but it would be nice if you could get some information without exposing yourself too much."

"Let me think about it. I'm beat and feel like lying in the bed and watching something mindless while I doze off."

"What a great idea. I'll make popcorn," she said.

I grabbed a bottle of water from the fridge, made myself comfortable amongst the pillows, and settled in. Mary Louise brought freshly popped corn, and we laid together and munched and laughed at a show celebrating the Best of Carol Burnett. I found myself getting somewhat hysterical over a skit with her, Tim Conway, and Harvey Korman involving a parody of Gone with the Wind. I tried to wipe my eyes, but the salt on my fingers overcame that plan and I half-blindly stumbled into the bathroom to wash my face.

As I was drying my eyes, the leaded glass window over Mary Louise's bathtub shattered. I crawled into the bedroom and pulled her down onto the floor and out of the bedroom. Tip went crazy and tore out for his hiding place in my closet.

"What was that noise?"

"Sounded like a gunshot to me. Didn't you hear it?"

"I heard what sounded like glass breaking, that's all. Are you OK?"

"Yes. I think someone shot out the window over the tub. Where's your phone?"

"In the charger by the bed."

I crawled back into the bedroom, took the phone into the bathroom, and dialed 911. We then crawled into the nearest closet and waited. When we heard the sirens in the front yard, we crawled out and saw the red, white, and blue reflections emanating from the front drive and assumed it was safe to exit the closet.

"Still want me to talk to Lisa Stewart about Devlin's business?" I asked Mary Louise.

The Granite Falls police cruiser had arrived in less than ten minutes. The two young officers surveyed the property and saw nothing out of the ordinary. I explained about what we thought was a gunshot. They entered the house and saw the broken window over the tub.

"The bullet was probably a small caliber, since we see a hole there, with broken glass around the entry point. A larger caliber weapon would discharge a round that would probably have taken the whole piece of glass out. I would guess a .22 or even a .25 caliber pistol. Did you look for the slug, sir?"

"We did not. With someone firing at us, that seemed a little risky. Did you happen to see a vehicle speeding away from our house when you were at the gate?"

"No, sir. There was no traffic at the gate, or past the gate, or in the driveway on the way up to your house," said the man in charge by the name of R. Jones, according to his nameplate. "I figure the perpetrator might have parked down the road by the dog park, walked up your driveway, shot out the window, and ran back down the hill. Sunday nights are usually quiet around here. We rarely get calls in this neighborhood. Did your dog give you any warning prior to the shooting? Like a bark or something?"

"No. Tip is no guard dog. He is friendly to everyone, especially if you have food. What's next, officers?"

"Let us look for the slug, sir. We'll take some glass samples as well. I have no idea if they'd be useful, but better safe than sorry."

The two men scoured the bathroom, found the distorted piece of metal, and put it in a plastic bag along with glass fragments.

"Sorry, sir," said the other man, with J. Peters on his nameplate. "I can call in a detective if you like, but as far as I can tell, there's not much to find here at the scene. I would suggest you have someone put plywood over the window until you can get it repaired."

"All right, gents. Thanks much for your promptness."

They left, and we poured ourselves large glasses of wine.

"Are you okay to sleep here?" I asked Mary Louise.

"Of course, this is our home. Do we keep any weapons in the house?

"Yes. I have two Krieghoff K-80 shotgun sets, with interchangeable barrels of .410, .28, .22, and .12 gauge. I used to shoot skeet with those guns. I have ammo as well. In addition, we have several handguns. I have a short-barreled .38, which is light and has little kick, ideal for you. You just point and shoot if you're close enough, and it'll get the job done. I have a .357 Magnum revolver that my dad left me, as well as a 9mm Glock with an eighteen-shot magazine."

Mary Louise looked at me in absolute shock.

"How can you have these weapons and I don't know about them?"

"You never have been a gun aficionado. I keep them in the back of my closet. I go out and shoot occasionally, usually after a short surgery day."

"I want to learn to shoot. I feel vulnerable right now. Can you take me to the shooting school and get me certified?"

"Of course. I've had a concealed/carry permit for years. I can take you to the classes, practice with you, and get you certified. I just never thought you had any interest in the shooting thing."

"That was before some asshole shot at me. And he shot the window over my bathtub, of all things. Whoever it was, tried to kill me."

"I'm not sure he or she was trying to kill you, but certainly that might be a warning."

"You mean a warning for you to stay out of Devlin's business?"

"What else could it be? I've had some unhappy patients over my many years in practice, but no one has ever tried to shoot me over a bad result."

Mary Louise and I tried to get to sleep, but the trauma of the evening kept the sandman away for most of the night. I finally drifted off around 2 a.m., but the obnoxious shrill of the alarm woke me at 5 a.m. I showered and dressed and left my bride in repose with our poor excuse for a guard dog lying next to her.

I was at the office by 5:30 a.m. We had five operations to do that day: two virgin hips, two virgin knees, and an ankle replacement. No one else in the area would tackle an ankle replacement, and I was tired of sending them to Austin or San Antonio, especially if the patient lived in our area. I had gone to a couple of continuing education schools and had done a few cadaver ankle replacements. The case was to be my first live patient ankle replacement.

Belinda and I started with a total hip replacement, then another, then a knee replacement, then another, moving back and forth between two operating rooms. Last came the ankle replacement. The biomechanics of an ankle replacement are different from a hip or knee replacement. The ankle has two bones, the tibia and fibula, to account for on the top of the joint, and one below called the talus. The manufacturer's representative was present at the case, and as it turned out, the technology and the templates were of superior quality, and the replacement went smooth as glass. I enjoyed the new procedure and felt comfortable performing the surgery at HCMC. Who said you can't teach an old dog new tricks?

We went to the office after seeing the post-op patients and their families. Belinda answered messages, and I cleaned off my desk. As I was reminiscing about how smooth the day went, Maya entered my inner sanctum and gave me a note.

"What's this?"

"Dr. Owens wants you to call him."

"Did he say what it was about?"

"No, sir."

"Okay, would you get him on the phone, please, Maya? Thanks."

She did, and Buck greeted me with, "I heard you were shot at last night."

"Now how in the world would you know that? We didn't tell a soul."

"The police captain at Granite Falls is a friend of mine. He called me and thought maybe I would like to know one of my docs was the target of a discharged firearm. He said the shooter aimed at the primary bathtub and partially blew out the window above. The slug was a .22 caliber, valuable, and dangerous only at close range. My guess is it was a warning, unless they were trying to shoot Mary Louise. I assume you're not much of a tub guy?"

"I'm a shower man, thank you."

"Well, I think it was a purposeful miss, just to get your attention. It no longer seems safe for you to prowl around La Cava. I'm sorry I got you involved."

"I appreciate that. You should know that Christine Devlin's oldest son Robert Jr. called me yesterday and asked me to snoop around for him and his two brothers. They think the La Cava deal is what got their mother killed, and probably the other two women as well. They would like to get a look at the financials for the golf club and La Cava Estates."

"I think many people would like to see those books, but I suspect Devlin keeps them tucked away in a safe."

"You know that Lisa Stewart took over Patsy Simmons's job. Robert suggested I try and sweet-talk her into letting me look at those books, but I think that's risky, considering that someone shot our window out last night. The only strategy that might work would be to tell Lisa that Mary Louise and I are considering becoming investors in the project. Devlin might have to show me what's happening financially."

"Brady, I think that's very risky. That first copy of La Cava's financials may have been fictitious, at least according to Patsy, remember?"

"Yes, I do. I could approach Lisa, give her the spiel, and see what happens. Even Mary Louise suggested that I could approach her. She felt sorry for Christine's sons after our phone conversation."

"I can't believe your wife would encourage you to do that. She's always steering you away from your involvement in mystery and intrigue."

"I'm just as surprised as you. Tell you what; let me mull it over for a day or two. I'll let you know something Thursday."

"Meanwhile, Brady, you might want to invest in a bulletproof vest and a hardhat."

CHAPTER 30

WORK

We were lost in a morass of patient issues on Tuesday. Belinda, Maya, and I worked through the lunch hour to get people seen and taken care of. There was so much business, and so many people who needed operations, that a suggestion was made by my staff that I should consider working on Fridays again, at least for a while, until my backlog of patients needing joint replacements was diminished.

"How far backed up are we, Maya?"

"At your current pace of six to eight cases on Monday and Wednesday, if a patient came in today and met all the criteria and wanted surgery, twelve weeks to get on the schedule."

"What? Three months to wait?"

"Hey, in Canada, it's a year or more."

"Well, that's socialized medicine. We don't have that here."

"Yet," Maya said.

"What are my other partners doing? We had two other hip and knee replacement surgeons, and last year we added two more."

Belinda and Maya looked at each other. "Your associates are not as . . . productive as you. None of them will do more than three cases per operating day."

"What? Why?"

"That is their routine. I've spoken to the booking secretaries of each doctor about the pace they work at, and each is comfortable with nine to twelve cases per week, and about twenty or thirty patients per clinic."

"Then we need more docs, don't we?"

"It's not easy to find qualified docs who want to live in this area. Wives and children want the big city when they're young, then plan to retire somewhere like Horseshoe Bay when they get older."

"So why am I working so hard? Aren't we all on salary?"

"Yes. There is a bonus system for doing more work than the other docs, but basically, at the pace you work, you are paying their salaries."

"Then I'm not being very smart."

"Doctor Brady, for the three of us, it's all about the patients. Belinda and I do not mind working harder to see that the patients are taken care of. You are paying me an extremely generous salary, and you have Belinda on salary, and that plus the money she makes on assistant fees in surgery puts her in a six-figure bracket. We are taken care of. And we thank you."

"I don't think I knew Belinda could get assistant's fees. That is great for her."

"Because of her degrees and her nurse practitioner status, she's treated just like a physician when it comes to billing as an assistant."

"Amazing. Well, let me think about the Friday surgery thing."

"You wouldn't have to pack them in like you do on Monday and Wednesday. You could do four cases between two rooms, and be done by 1 p.m. If you did that for two months, you would catch up to your backlog."

"And then I would get behind again, right?"

"We could start next week, see how you feel after a month, and go from there. You might also have a discussion with Dr. Owens and the other four physicians in your section, see if you might get a little more work out of them."

I could not believe I was speaking with my admin assistant about getting doctors to work harder. "Okay, Maya, set up a meeting. And thanks for caring. You're the best."

I spoke to Mary Louise that evening about Maya's idea of temporarily giving up my day off every other Friday and operating on the backlog of patients to catch up. Her thought was that since I was using at least part of Friday to stick my nose where it did not belong, maybe plying my real trade of a bone doctor was a better use of my time. I could still play golf in the afternoon if I chose, or I could meet her for lunch and take in a movie, or if it happened to be a rainy day . . .

Wednesday was another seven-case grinder, and Thursday another large clinic day. I saw Lisa Stewart late in the day. She was doing well.

"You may begin putting weight on the operated leg, Lisa, but start with just touch-down weight first, and progress VERY slowly. It's not too late to tear out those labrum stitches. I want you to stay on crutches for the next two weeks, regardless of how much weight you put on the leg."

"So even if I'm not having pain, use the crutches?"

"Yes. You have a high pain threshold and quite frankly, I do not trust your pain levels to tell you when to back off the weight. That was to your credit prior to surgery, but now . . . I just don't want to risk any damage. Okay?"

"Yes, sir. I will be a good girl, even though it pains me to do so. Sorry, no pun intended."

"By the way, Mary Louise and I may want to become investors in La Cava. Do you think that's possible?"

"Do I think it's possible that my father would accept money from an outside source for his project? I think I have answered your question."

"Maybe I can stop by in the morning at your on-site office, look at the financials, and come to a decision. Would that work?"

"Yes, sir, absolutely."

"I have to make rounds, so why don't we say between nine and ten?"

"I will be there. And thanks again—my hip feels great."

I was too tired after Thursday clinic to go home and dress, so I changed into fresh scrubs and met Mary Louise at the Yacht Club for an early dinner. We selected an outdoor table since my scrubs blended in well with the shorts and Tommy Bahama shirts of other patrons. We ordered Tito's dirty martinis and a boiled shrimp platter to start. Once the alcohol started to ease the pain in my aging body and head, I perked up a bit.

"You really look beat, Jim Bob. I'm not so sure adding another day to your work week is the right decision."

"It sounds good in theory, but the kind of work I do is very physical and takes a lot out of me. If I just sat around all day in the operating room and performed hand or foot surgery, it would be different. The surgeries require me to manipulate heavy legs to get those hips and knees replaced. I did an ankle replacement on Monday, and talk about a difference in the physical requirements to complete the surgery. I sat for a good part of the case, and there was nothing to lift until the implants were seated, and then I just had to put the ankle through a range of motion. What a difference!"

We peeled and ate shrimp and caught up with each other. The server asked if we wanted another drink, so we ordered a bottle of pinot grigio to go along with a dinner of crab cakes, soft shell crab, and fresh mussels. I had missed lunch, so I ate my share and half of Mary Louise's. By the time we were done, I knew I had a window of only an hour or so before I crashed and burned. I followed her home, which was only fifteen minutes or so down the main drag of Horseshoe Bay and into the hills of Granite Falls.

She volunteered to walk Tip while I showered and readied myself for bed. The next thing I remembered was having a full bladder that needed emptying. The bathroom clock read 4 a.m. I got back into bed after making sure Mary Louise and Tip were present, and conked out again. The smell of bacon frying woke me up at 7 a.m. I jumped out of bed, showered and put on clean scrubs, and made an appearance in the kitchen.

"Rounds at 8 a.m., right?" she said.

"Yes. I have just enough time for a quick bite. Thanks for fixing breakfast."

"What's on for you today?"

"Rounds and golf, but in between, a meeting with Lisa Stewart about us becoming investors in La Cava. Yesterday, or the day before, you thought it would be a good idea to help Christine's sons by trying to get more financial information."

"After having been shot at, I'm not sure."

"Technically you were not shot at, Mary Louise. A small .22 caliber gun was discharged through our bathroom window and was unlikely to be intended to injure."

"Still, part of me wants to run off to another part of the country where it's safe."

"I think it's safe here; I just have to watch what I say and do. Are you going to Austin for your charity meetings?"

"Yes, and I don't even want to do that. I just want us to be safe."

"You should go ahead and honor your obligations in Austin, and I'll go see Lisa and try and extract information in a pleasant, fatherly sort of way. I'll play with the boys this afternoon, provided we don't get rained out, and we'll meet back here for cocktails around 5 p.m. And don't forget we have the dinner at Louis Devlin's penthouse at seven tonight."

"Yes," she said, as she stood behind me and hugged my neck tightly. "Yes, I remember. Please be safe."

"I will. Be careful driving. See you this afternoon."

CHAPTER 31

THE DEVELOPMENT

Rounds went well despite the census of twelve, which represented the surgeries from Monday and Wednesday. As usual, some would go to the rehab unit until they were ambulatory, and some would go home if they had adequate family support. As always, my biggest worry after lower-extremity surgery was blood clots in the legs that ended up traveling into the lungs, causing a pulmonary embolus. They were not always fatal but often enough they were, so all patients received anticoagulants. And on rounds I was always diligent to squeeze every patient's calf muscle on both extremities. A swollen calf was the harbinger of disaster.

I made it to Lisa Stewart's office by 10 a.m.. She was still housed in an Airstream trailer. She wore jeans and a black turtleneck and had her crutches leaning against her desk.

"Morning, Dr. Brady," she said, as she greeted me. "I have coffee."

"Excellent. Sorry I'm late. Rounds took a while."

"I don't know how you do it, taking care of the volume of patients that you have. I would not be able to keep everyone straight."

"That's why I have Belinda and Maya. They are my collective memory box."

"I pulled out our latest financial report for you. It covers the costs of buying the land, building the golf course, building the clubhouse and outbuildings, limestone removal and abatement, and all the other extraneous fees that went along with the purchase. I also have the summaries of land costs for La Cava Estates, building costs, and extraneous fees, as well as granite abatement and other costs. You might want to take some time to review the reports. You are more than welcome to use my desk, and I'll leave you to your privacy while I take care of business in the main clubhouse."

"Very kind of you, Lisa. That'll be fine. I do have a question. I know about the limestone caves and limestone deposits that were essentially littered through the land where the golf course and clubhouse were to be built. What's this about granite abatement?"

"Well, granite is bedrock, and when Daddy decided to buy the property, he knew that a certain percentage of the land mass would have to be built on granite. As you probably know, building on granite or other bedrock is very stable, but also . . ."

"Very expensive, right?"

"Yes, sir. We were able to carve 100 acres of land out of the 300 acres purchased that would not require building on the granite outcroppings, but no matter how we platted the land, there would still be 200 acres remaining where the homes would have to be constructed at least partially on granite. That would increase the building costs considerably, as well as the time required for construction."

"You know, Lisa, that reminds me that I spoke to Johnny Amato the other day. I brought a crew of golfers over from Horseshoe Bay to play golf here at La Cava, and after the round I drove down to the construction area. I asked some questions of Johnny, but his simple response was that you were going to build ten spec homes, each with a different floor plan from which buyers could choose.

How would you position those ten homes if you had 200 acres to work with, and each home had to have one acre of land?"

She leaned toward me as would a co-conspirator, and said, "Carefully. We chose the ten spec-home building sites on the first 100 acres of land that did not have a granite bedrock to build upon."

"Just to be clear, you'll build ten spec homes on the terrain that's normal for this area, then convince future buyers that building on granite is a good thing, even though it costs much more?"

"Well, we won't advertise the granite base. There are few outcroppings, which make the presence of granite obvious, but those are relegated to the second 100 acres that we won't be building spec houses on, only custom residences. The third 100-acre parcel is for common grounds, a park, an Olympic pool, tennis and pickleball courts for residents, and a spa that rivals anything in Beverly Hills. And while the underlying granite will increase the cost of building, it's not significant, since there aren't any homes to be built in the common ground area."

"That means, Lisa, that you'll hopefully end up with 100 homes on a granite base, and 100 on normal Hill Country soil and rock."

"Yes, sir, that is correct."

"I guess I don't see the problem, so long as potential buyers know their respective homes will cost more to build upon due to the subsurface granite."

Lisa sighed. "The crux of the problem, Dr. Brady, is that when Daddy borrowed all this money to fund the purchase of the club and to develop the land south of the club, he didn't include the additional interest costs to the lenders and various investor groups because he thought that might scare everyone off. So now he's short on funds. I'm worried he's looking at some unsavory investors to complete his project. I have seen some characters come into this office, describing themselves as investors. I just hope he hasn't gotten himself into trouble. I worry about him all the time."

"Where did the extra interest costs come from, Lisa?"

"Partly from rising interest rates. Daddy has been working on this project for almost three years, and rates have risen during that period. Also, estimated building costs have skyrocketed due to considerations of granite mitigation. And to compound the situation, we realize now that we only have an 'easy' 100 acres to build houses on, not 300 like we originally thought."

With that, she hobbled out on her crutches, and left me to my reading. I kept an eye on the trailer door, hoping not to see Devlin, Amato, or the dreaded Fixer. I wondered why Lisa was so cooperative. Was she that open a person? Or naive? Or was she reeling me in like a catfish?

I reviewed the current financials of La Cava Golf Club. Devlin had spent $32 million on golf course construction. He had 100 members signed up, each of whom paid $250,000 to join the club. That was a total of $25 million. Plus, those same 100 members were paying $3,000 monthly for dues, a yearly total of $3.6 million. Those numbers would surely rise over time, but if they did not, with the entry fee and the monthly dues, he would have had his investment to build the golf course and clubhouse returned in two years. There was the maintenance of the course to contend with, and other expenses, which would run about $1.5 million per year, but still, a tidy profit yearly, based on the current number of members and not including member growth.

But the land for building houses, that was another story. According to Lisa and the documents I reviewed, Devlin had purchased 300 acres for building the houses. 100 acres was dedicated to common areas, 100 acres of homes was for building on "normal" soil content, and 100 acres was going to have to be built at least partially upon granite bedrock. According to the specifics, 100 houses on one acre each, with a required minimum size of 5,000 square feet, at a building cost of $250 per square foot, would be $125,000,000 total building cost. If the builders, which was Devlin's company, charged $500 per square foot to the potential owners, that would roughly be $250 million, which would be $125 million in profit.

The houses on the granite foundation, however, were going to cost $500 per square foot to build, which totaled $250 million. I did not know how much folks were willing to pay per square foot to live in the community, but I thought that $500 a foot was steep. If that was correct, then Devlin would be in a break-even mode on the 100 homes to be built on granite in the best of circumstances.

The way I saw it was that Devlin, and his partners, originally stood to make $250,000,000 on the home-building project until it became known that there was a granite problem on over half the buildable acres. And then, he was down to a paltry $125 million profit, which sounded like a lot of money to me. That did not include revenue from the golf club dues, and new member joining fees. The project still looked to be viable, unless there were issues that were not obvious. If the death of Devlin's wife, and Amato's wife, and Patsy Simmons were somehow related to the La Cava project, I did not see how or why. There would be interest to be paid on the borrowed monies, at what rate would only be a guess, and payback to investors such as Buck Owens's group and whomever Devlin had borrowed money from. Still, there had to be in excess of $100 million profit in the deal.

I committed the facts as best I could to memory rather than risk copying the documents that I had reviewed. I would be able to report to Buck that it looked to me like his investment was safe, not so much from the golf course revenue, but more than likely from the home-building revenue over the next few years.

I wasn't sure what Lisa meant when she said she was worried about her dad. That he was short of funds, and that he might possibly be borrowing from unsavory types, which I assumed meant investors from what might be called organized crime. It looked to me like there was plenty of money to be made as future golf members and other customers bought the lots and built the houses. Devlin should make about $125 million on 100 acres, break even on the granite 100 acres, and use the outcropping 100 acres for common areas, parks, pools, and the like to sell the cosmetics of the property.

All would be well if residents bought the houses, and why wouldn't they? The setting was beautiful, in the heart of the Hill Country. There was a beautiful golf course, and an almost-completed modern clubhouse. But then I wondered over what period of time the houses would be built. One year? Five years? Ten years? If the home-building process was slow, interest on borrowed or investor money could be a deal breaker. And what if, as Lisa suggested, Devlin had involved himself with "unsavory" types? What if there was "Kansas City money" involved from Devlin's old days? I was no financier, nor an expert on underworld types, but I had read enough books and seen enough movies to know about vigorish, or "the vig," another word for exorbitant interest. What if he had involved himself in that sort of scheme? Devlin could be hemorrhaging cash from interest payments, which would make the numbers I had seen meaningless. I scanned through the documents that Lisa had left me and there was nothing grossly indicative of anything out of order. But Louis Devlin and his business partner and old friend Johnny Amato spent time in prison for money laundering, so . . .

Christine's son, Robert, suggested some type of malfeasance, but he couldn't pinpoint it, and he worked for the company. I got the impression from our phone conversation that he was thwarted in what he could say. I assumed his two brothers who also worked for Devlin in the Dallas operations were in the same position. Which then made me wonder about Louis's two daughters' husbands, Bill Stewart, Lisa's husband, and Kirk Winters, Elizabeth's husband. They were involved in the La Cava business full-time, according to Robert Johnson.

My review of the prospectus had taken longer than anticipated and I was getting nervous. I left the documents on the desk and headed to my truck. I did not see Lisa on the way out. Once safely in the truck, I considered the possible locations of other documents pertinent to the La Cava development. If Devlin had a safe deposit box at a local bank, they would be untouchable. Who else might have a copy? The most logical choice was Patsy. Maybe she had a safe at home. I wondered if Lt. Mims had checked, and if he had, what did he find? Did Patsy have relatives in the area? Had someone claimed money, like insurance proceeds, or safe deposit contents? Did she even have a will?

I called the Marble Falls Police Department and asked for Det. Randall Mims. The dispatcher told me he was out on a call and would return my message as soon as possible. All that reading and thinking had given me a headache, so I headed over to the Horseshoe Bay Golf Club for the best burger in town. Several of my golf group were eating as well, bulking up for our golf outing. I joined them on the patio, above the driving range. I was tired of thinking about La Cava and the murders, so I had a beer to wash down my burger.

We teed off in groups of four, sixteen players total. I checked my phone at the turn and saw a message from R. Mims. I was having too much golf fun to ruin the day by talking to the police, so I switched the phone to silent and labored on. I was paired with a retired preacher from Houston, name of Riley Eubanks. He had a terrible limp, and limps were my specialty, so I asked him what had happened to create the problem.

"Oh, Doc, I had a bad fall getting out of my fishing boat. I live right on the water in a little cove off Lake LBJ. I caught my deck shoe on the edge of my dock, tried to twist it free, but that torqued my hip, and when I fell backward into the boat, my hip broke. Fortunately, my wife was at home, heard me screaming, and called 911. Otherwise, I don't know how long I would have laid in that boat. This was when HCMC was just starting out, so the fire department took me all the way to Austin to get the hip fixed. The doc over there said I had a bad break in the hip joint and told me the bone in the ball might die and I would need a replacement. Well, I can tell you, that is what happened. It hurts me all day every day."

"Why don't you get it replaced? We're good at that procedure these days."

"Well, I keep asking the Lord to heal me, and I keep waiting patiently."

"Maybe the Lord answered your prayers and paired you with me so we would get to know one another, and I could fix that hip for you. Ever think about that, Rev?"

"I've been to several docs, and they said that the ball is so degenerated that a replacement might not work. That dead bone has caused a problem on the socket side of the joint as well. I've heard words like 'bone graft' and 'surgical allograft,' which scares me to death."

"I see. You should come in and see me, let me take some X-rays, see what's what in that hip joint. It can't hurt to look."

"Well, I just figured the Lord gave me this pain as a trial, like the prophet Job and his trials and tribulations and torments."

"Maybe I can fix that hip and the Lord can find you a new trial to deal with. How does that sound?"

He laughed. "I will think about it. Thanks for the advice."

I fished around in my golf shorts for a card, found a dilapidated one, and handed it to him.

"Dr. James Douglas Brady. You are named after Jesus's brother, Saint James."

"But I am no saint, Reverend, just a bone doctor put here on earth to help God's children out."

"Man, if you can fix this hip, that would be like walking on water, as far as I'm concerned."

"That is too high of an expectation, sir. I'll just stick with the hip repair, if you don't mind. I know I can do that."

CHAPTER 32

DINNER

Mary Louise and I arrived home at about the same time. She looked haggard from the drive to and from Austin. I immediately went to the bar and constructed us iced dirty Tito's martinis, which cures what ails one, at least for a while.

"A-h-h-h. The pause that refreshes," she said, as we clinked glasses carefully. Tip was jumping so much that we had to take extra sips to avoid spilling. We walked out to the terrace and let him run without the leash. If Tip was younger, he might be able to jump the wall, but at his age, three feet might as well be a mile. It was a beautiful afternoon, temperature in the low 80s with low humidity. The skies were mostly clear with scattered clouds, and the Twin Sister Peaks were visible in the distance.

"I was afraid to ask what you did this morning after rounds, but since you're alive and well, I would assume you did nothing to get yourself in trouble."

"Alive and well, madame," I said, and gave her a synopsis of my time at Lisa Stewart's desk.

"In essence there is a problem with Devlin's home-building plan due to this granite formation at half the building sites, which has caused prospective cost overruns, which may have led him to seek financing from organized crime sources he has known since childhood. Is that it in a nutshell?"

"Yes, as far as I can tell. I have no experience with this sort of business, being a humble orthopedic surgeon . . ."

"Orthopedic surgeon, yes; humble, I'm not so sure about," she replied, with a smile.

"I put in a call to Randall Simms, which reminds me, he called me back. Let me check my messages."

He had indeed left a message telling me to return the call and giving me his cell phone number. I dialed the number, and he picked up on the first ring. I put the call on speaker.

"Doctor Brady, how can I help you?"

"Randall, sorry to bother you, but Mary Louise and I were wondering if Patsy Simmons had left a will distributing her assets, or perhaps had a safe deposit box with valuables assigned. This is none of my business, I admit, but I have been doing some independent research and have wondered if there might be another set of books for the La Cava development that she was in possession of."

"Well, that's interesting, Doctor, because I have run into a rather odd situation with regards to Ms. Simmons's worldly possessions. She did have a will, filed with her attorney, which was in order. She has, or rather had, a grown niece. She left her house, a couple of bank accounts, a savings account, and an insurance policy to her, which total about $1.5 million. But oddly, her attorney told me that a couple of weeks ago, and I think it was the morning after she had dinner with you and your wife, Ms. Simmons added a handwritten codicil to her will. In it, she named you and Mrs. Brady as beneficiaries of the contents of a safe deposit box she kept over in Johnson City. According to the attorney, the codicil has been notarized and is entirely legal."

"Really? Did you just now find this out?"

"Yesterday. What a coincidence that you would be calling me about a safe deposit box the day after I found out about it. Your timing in uncanny, Doctor."

"Well, it's just that I spoke to Lisa Stewart, Louis Devlin's daughter, who has taken over Patsy Simmons's job, and got the impression that there might be trouble in paradise with regards to the development of La Cava Estates. I was able to look through the books—"

"Now how did that come about, Doctor?"

"I might have mentioned to Lisa that Mary Louise and I would be interested in becoming investors, but we needed to understand the finances better."

"So, she just opened up the books and let you have a look?"

"Lisa trusts me. I recently operated on her hip, so we have a doctor-patient relationship."

"Doctor, I might need to confirm this with Mrs. Brady."

"I'm here," she said. "Jim Bob has us on speaker."

"And you can confirm what your husband is telling me?"

"Yes, sir, I can."

"Very well. When would you like your key to the box?"

"You mean we can get into the box? At this point in time? What about probating the will?"

"By law, it's your box now. The assets were held in trust, and therefore the probate process was not required, or so the deceased's attorney told me."

"How about tomorrow? We can stop by the station and pick up the key, and maybe we'll take a drive down to Johnson City and see what's in there."

"You of course will apprise me of the contents, especially if there is any information in the box that I can use to find Ms. Simmons's killer?"

"Of course, Lieutenant."

"Doctor Brady, I again caution you, and Mrs. Brady as well, that there may be forces here that we do not yet understand, and I am concerned for the personal safety of both of you. Tomorrow is my day off, and if you would like, I would be most happy to accompany you. I owe you for that fine meal you prepared, so I could buy you both lunch at Ronnie's BBQ. I can pick you up at, say, 9 a.m., and save you a trip. And I'll bring the safe deposit key."

We chose to sign off without mentioning our evening plans.

Devlin lived on the top floor of a six-story building off Island Drive, which sat directly over a large boat dock on Lake LBJ. A valet was stationed at the elevator entry and asked to see our invitation. We had been emailed invitations earlier that day— we were relieved to see the dinner party for the three of us had turned into a much larger party—and I presented mine to the elevator operator. All must have been in order, as he opened the door, stepped into the car with us, used a key which allowed us to rocket to the top floor, and deposited us outside Apartment 601. There were two entrances, and we chose the one with a female server holding a tray of glasses filled with what we assumed was white wine. We each took one and stepped inside.

A normal apartment on the top floor had around 2,000 square feet of space. Devlin had removed most of the wall between 601 and 602, had opened the stucco walls separating the two balconies, and had created a magnificent space over at least 4,000 square feet, with 270 degrees of water views. When Mary Louise and I stepped out onto the balcony, we could not believe the vistas.

We wandered back inside, as we were the first to arrive, and found a marvelous walk-in kitchen with all varieties of canapés covered in plastic wrap on the granite countertops. Just prior to my tearing off the plastic and diving in, a voice behind us said, "Welcome."

"Good evening, Mr. Devlin," Mary Louise said, and demurely shook his hand.

"You are looking lovely, Mrs. Brady. I am Louis Devlin, and I do not think I have had the pleasure."

Mary Louise did not look lovely; she looked, well, hot. She wore her hair down that night, and having naturally springy hair, it was a mass of curls. She had chosen a black knit sweater with a low neckline, a black leather skirt, and black pumps. She wore diamond studs in her ears, and wore a tasteful diamond bracelet on her left wrist. I immediately was jealous of Devlin's Italian charm, his black silk suit, and his thick silver hair brushed back and ending in a small ponytail.

"You've done wonders with this place," said Mary Louise.

"Christine was responsible for the work. She had an eye for beauty. I don't know what I'll do with the place under construction at La Cava. I'm not sure I can live there, after what happened. At any rate, thank you for coming, and have a pleasant evening."

"Charming," she said to me.

"Yes, right after he pulls the knife out of your heart."

"Jim Bob, be nice. We are guests here, and I do not want to ruffle any feathers . . . or get another bullet through my bathroom window. I would like to think the best of our host until proven otherwise."

Several other arrivals wandered in, most agape at the view from the living room and balcony. Some we knew, some we did not. My mentor Dr. Buck Owens arrived, with Lucy Williams, his admin assistant. That was a shock. Lisa Stewart was also in attendance and was using her crutches, to my surprise.

"Dr. Brady," she said, and gave me a chaste hug. "You must be Mary Louise. So nice to meet you."

"You too, Lisa. I've heard good things about you."

"I'm just thankful I brought these silly crutches so I could stay in Doc's good graces. I really don't need them, you know, Doc. I want you both to meet my husband Bill. Let me find him."

As she walked away, Mary Louise commented, "Talk about a looker. Wow. She is gorgeous. Now I'm jealous about that house call you made. Jim Bob Brady, alone with a young woman that looks like a youthful Sophia Loren."

"I am her doctor, Mary Louise. Besides, I am alone with a beautiful woman every night."

"Good comeback, husband," she said, as she smiled and bussed me on the cheek.

We snacked on boiled shrimp wrapped in bacon, California rolls, and fried asparagus spears, drank more wine, introduced ourselves to all those present, and finally sat down to dinner. Seating had been arranged. Devlin was at the head of the table, and seated Mary Louise next to him. I was on her other side, seated next to Lisa. Next to her was her husband Bill, and next to him was Lisa's sister Elizabeth. Then came Kirk Winters, Elizabeth's husband, Lucy Williams, Buck Owens, and lastly, on the other side of Devlin, Bishop Jeffrey Walker of the Austin diocese of the Roman Catholic Church. He was pinned between Devlin and Buck Owens, an unenviable position for a man of the cloth.

The meal was begun by a short prayer and blessing by Bishop Walker.

It was one of those dinners that had more plates, silverware, and glasses than I knew what to do with. Over the years, Mary Louise had developed hand signals so that I would know which utensil to use for which course. Luckily, we were seated next to each other. I dreaded those dinners when spouses were separated and I had to use obvious gestures across or down the table to Mary Louise so I would not make a mistake.

Devlin must have been an entertaining dinner partner, as I saw and heard Mary Louise laughing quite a bit during the evening. I wanted to lean over and whisper, this guy is probably a murderer, but took the high road and refrained. Instead, I made nice with Lisa and made idle conversation with her husband Bill, who was a nice guy but boring as watching paint dry. I somehow thought that commercial real estate development would be exciting, but only in the sense that you could make large sums of money after a project was completed without doing much work. Bill termed it "clipping coupons," referring to checks received from tenants every month, not unlike collecting money from bonds every month, the original source of the term clipping coupons. Some of my friends called it "mailbox money," implying royalties from an oil or gas well.

Before dinner, Lisa had introduced me to Bill as well as her sister Elizabeth and her husband Kirk Winters. Elizabeth was a couple of years older than Lisa and had two children and was married to a man who was equally as boring as Lisa's husband. He and Bill both worked for Devlin in Horseshoe Bay, now primarily on the La Cava project. I asked both husbands numerous questions about the project, and how it was going, and neither had much to say. I knew that looks were deceiving, but I did not feel I was in the presence of financial felons. My "smart antenna" registered low on the scale for both sons-in-law.

I mouthed "how are you doing?" to Lucy, stuck between Kirk Winters, who had not said a word to her, and Buck, who was in rapt conversation with Bishop Walker. Maybe he was using the opportunity to have an informal and free confession session. Lucy smiled back, sipped her wine, and rolled her eyes.

After the first course, a cold vichyssoise, and the second course, a delicious seafood salad, both served with a delightful Tesoro pinot grigio, Devlin stood up with his wine glass and tapped it with a spoon.

"Welcome to my guests this evening. It is a pleasure to have you all here. I think you have had adequate time to meet and greet each other. If not, these are my two daughters, Lisa and Elizabeth, with their respective husbands, Bill and Kirk, both of whom work in my company. We have Dr. and Mrs. Jim Brady with us tonight, as well as Dr. Buck Owens and his companion, Lucy Williams. And last is Bishop Jeffrey Walker from Austin, an old friend. The next course is a traditional family recipe, veal with linguini and pomodoro. I hope you enjoy. Thank you again for coming."

He sat, and I proceeded to eat the most incredible veal I had ever tasted. It was done to perfection, as was the pasta. I was used to eating linguini with a clam or cream sauce, so the tomato-based sauce was unusual, but incredibly good. I am not an expert on Italian wine, but the brunello that was served with the entrée was beautiful.

I was stuffed to the gills but managed to scarf down a dessert of cannoli, along with a glass of port wine, after which I started to fade. I gave Mary Louise all the usual signs that I needed to go—yawning, stretching, standing up and leaving the table, looking around for a bathroom. In the old days, I would activate my beeper, a sure technique for leaving a dinner party. I no longer carried one, but rather had my calls delivered via my smart phone, which was smarter than me because I could never figure out how to call myself and get out of a situation I no longer wanted to be in.

I did find a bathroom, which was occupied. I waited for a moment, then Lucy Williams exited.

"How did you end up here, Lucy?" I asked.

"Paying for past sins, I guess, Dr. Brady."

"Are you and Buck dating?"

"Oh heavens, no. His date canceled on him at the last minute, and he asked me to go. I had nothing to do, rarely ever do, so I agreed."

"Well, you look great." She had her hair up in a bun and had on a nice red dress with low heels. She never dressed like that at the office. I wondered about her social life, then decided I had enough on my plate to deal with.

"Thank you, Dr. Brady. You are too kind. I hope this shindig is over soon. I am not used to late nights and all this alcohol. My goodness, I do not see how people drink that much. I can barely stand."

"Practice makes perfect, Lucy. It takes time to build up those alcohol-dissolving enzymes. I have had years of practice. Smoking encourages those little boogers to dissolve the alcohol molecules quicker, as I learned in my old smoking days, but alack and alas, those days are gone."

"You are too funny. Oh, look, here comes Dr. Owens. Maybe we can escape."

"What are you two doing?"

"Figuring out ways to leave. Are you about ready to go?" asked Lucy.

"I think so. I'm not a Catholic, so the bishop was not interested in hearing about all my past sins. He wasn't a bad sort, though. He's going to play golf with us tomorrow, Brady. He has a six handicap, so he must play often. I'll put you in the foursome with us."

"Sorry, but I have to make a trip out of town tomorrow. A rain check with the reverend for golf, if you please."

The table had gradually emptied, and while folks lingered about to be polite, the evening was essentially over. I tried to lead Mary Louise out first, but other members of the dinner party were quicker than we were. As we were saying goodbye to our host, he pulled me aside, leaving Lisa, his daughter, to speak to Mary Louise.

"I know what you're up to, Brady; it's the why that I don't know. You have no stake in La Cava other than a membership, and that bullshit story you gave my daughter about wanting to become an investor in La Cava, is just that: bullshit. I hear tell you like to stick your nose into things that are of no concern to you. I would repeat the advice I am sure you have heard many times in the past: You leave me alone and stay out of my business, and I will grant you the same favor. Do we understand each other?"

I separated his hand from my elbow and stood as tall as I could. "Would that mean no more conversations with your factotum Charles? And no more gunshots through our bathroom window?"

If looks could kill, I would have been a dead man, but Devlin said nothing. He shook my hand, as well as Mary Louise's, and we made a quick exit.

CHAPTER 33

SAFETY DEPOSIT BOX

The next morning, Randall Mims pulled up to our front door in a giant pickup truck, a Dodge Ram 1500. I sat in the front while Mary Louise lounged in the back seat, which had enough room for a recliner.

"You could have a party back here, Randall. This back seat is enormous."

"Yes, ma'am. The biggest rear compartment that truck manufacturers make."

"Why do you need all this room? As I remember, you don't have kids."

"No, I don't, but you never know when you're going to need to haul stuff for friends and family. Besides, this is Texas, where Bigger is Better."

The truck had a decent ride for a vehicle its size. We were so high up in the air, I was almost eye level with the drivers of the semis that passed us driving south down Highway 281 toward Johnson City, Texas, birthplace of Lyndon Baines Johnson, our thirty-sixth president.

Johnson City Bank was a squat one-story building close to the Main Street Grill. There were shiny marble floors marred by plastic sheeting covering desks, evidence of a remodeling process going on. We were greeted by a senior bank officer and taken to the safe deposit box area. Our driver had called the bank and forewarned them of our arrival. The safe deposit room was a windowless enclosed space, so quiet it could have been a funeral parlor. I inserted the key Lt. Mims had given me into the lock of the appropriate box, as did the bank officer with her companion key. The lock turned, and the box was removed and placed on a central table. The bank officer departed and left us to the contents.

In the box was a letter addressed to Mary Louise and me, along with a file folder and a small cassette recorder with a tape inside. No valuables were present.

"Is that a cassette tape?" asked Lt. Mims. "I've heard about those."

I rolled my eyes. "I haven't seen one in a long time. The cassette tape replaced the 8-track tape for your listening enjoyment," I answered.

"Eight-track?" Mims said.

I looked at him like the child he was but said nothing. I wanted to stay on the good side of law enforcement.

I hit the Play button and waited a moment for the tape to spin.

"Dr. and Mrs. Brady, I'm sorry to tell you that if you're listening to this audio tape, I am most probably dead. I documented in writing the abnormalities in the books at the La Cava Club. While I have been Louis's confidant and sales officer for the project, there are forces at play now that preclude me from being involved in certain aspects of the finances. He has been forced to shut me out, under threats toward not only me, but himself. Now that you have this information, be careful. You can trust no one, in my opinion. I am sorry to burden you both with all this, but I could not let the honest investors down. They have a right to know what's going on. Good luck."

I put the cassette back in the plastic container, took it and the envelope, and gave them to Mary Louise.

"You're not going to read the letter?" asked Lt. Mims.

"Not here. Maybe after lunch on the way back home, in the safety of your truck."

We had an early lunch, although my normally voracious appetite was dulled somewhat by the letter left to me by the deceased Patsy Simmons. The pork ribs and brisket were exceptional, however, and we took home two pounds of each for later consumption.

I opened the letter in Lt. Mims's truck. It was three typed pages. It read:

Dr. and Mrs. Brady, I am sorry you are reading this. It probably means I am dead. I dropped the codicil to my will off at my lawyer's office the morning after our dinner together. If I've been careful, you should be the only two people who know of the existence of this letter and the cassette tape.

Louis Devlin and I were lovers. I am not proud of that, considering my upbringing, but nevertheless, it is true. I tried to present myself as his business associate to the general public, but truth of the matter is that I was madly in love with him. As I told you at dinner, Louis did use me to "close" deals if the situation arose, and it was a conflict for me to sleep with his investors when he asked me to, but I still loved the man dearly, despite that. We had our relationship for about three years, which began shortly after he arrived in Horseshoe Bay and continued until the present time. We tried hard to keep it from Christine and the girls, but whether we were successful or not, I cannot say. They were suspicious, of course, especially because of all the traveling we did together. Nonetheless, we carried on together sexually and worked on the La Cava project together. And then along came an old friend of Louis's, Nicky Savolio, and everything changed.

Louis would not tell me the whole story of his activities back in the Kansas City days, before he moved to Dallas and became totally legit. He had served time in prison for money laundering for the Savolio crime family. Nicky was his best friend from childhood on, and they have been close most of their lives. Nicky was very unhappy when Louis got "out of the life" and made his start as an honest businessperson, first in Kansas City, then in Dallas. Again, Louis would not share all the details with me, but the commercial real estate business he ran in KC had ties to the underworld, even though he had made every attempt to keep his old friends at arm's length. He had to leave town and leave his friends behind to ultimately make a clean break.

Louis was successful in Dallas and ran a legitimate operation, such that by the time he moved to Horseshoe Bay, he was clean as a whistle, or so he thought. When he put the deal together to develop La Cava, he was excited. That project was going to be his swan song. He planned to make enough money to get out of the business completely and retire. What he did not know was the true story behind the collapse of the first version of La Cava. He knew the initial investors had gone bankrupt, and that the general manager, or accountant, or a principal had absconded out of the country with funds from an escrow account. What he didn't know was that the Savolio organization was behind the whole scam, that his old friend Nicky was the principal investor through a shell company, and that one of Nicky's men stole the money and left the country but was able to funnel it back to Savolio through a dummy corporation. And that the money people in Dallas who brought Louis the deal were Savolio's factotums, and that the project was doomed from the start, due to, at first, the limestone issues, then secondly the granite issues. Louis knew about limestone caverns and large deposits, but not being from Texas, he had no clue about how the granite deposits would affect home building.

Also, his main investor came from New York, but as it turns out, he was a front for Nicky Savolio's organization. Once Louis started drawing down on the line of credit allotted for the project, these exorbitant interest charges arose, to the extent he was having to pay ten percent per MONTH on the unpaid balance of the line of credit. He had borrowed $100 million from Savolio's shell company, which made his interest costs $10 million per month. He was then drowning in debt that was unsustainable, considering the cost overruns on the project from the limestone problem, then the granite problem, then the exorbitant interest charges.

Savolio's intention was to break Louis to make him pay for turning his back on his old friends, and he had positioned himself to do just that.

I don't know all the details about the threats that Savolio made, but Louis's wife Christine was killed. It was a message from Savolio to Louis: Anyone you may have possibly told about our arrangement dies. If you do not cooperate with me and send me what is my due, someone close to you dies. Next will be your children, and then their children.

I copied some of the most damaging financial data for Louis's La Cava project, and those are enclosed. I am sure his "partners" would hate to see the figures publicized, which would put them all in serious jeopardy. Do what you will with the paperwork, but I am certain the FBI would be able to bring charges against the Savolio crime family after a review of this data.

Mrs. Brady, thank you so much for your hospitality. You opened my eyes to the fact that there are good and kind people in the world. I have not been associated with very many of those in this line of work, but I hope this letter does some good in the long run.

Yours truly,

Patsy Simmons

P.S. I have a niece that is near and dear to my heart. She is my deceased sister's child. I have looked after her the best I could. I have kept her identity secret except with my attorney, who drafted this document. My passing should put her in good stead, as I have left her my home, the funds from two checking accounts and a savings account, and a life insurance policy. I would appreciate it greatly, Mrs. Brady, if you would visit her on occasion and look after her when you are able. That will not be difficult for you, Dr. Brady, as you see her almost every day. My niece is Maya Stern, your administrative assistant. She thinks you hung the moon, and I am in your debt for your kindness to her.

"I do not believe it. Maya is Patsy's niece. Neither one of them ever said a word to me."

"I think I know why, Jim. Once Patsy became involved in Louis's dealings, and became known to the Savolio crime family, she probably felt Maya's life could be in danger. That was a smart move on her part. We should, at least for the time being, keep that information to ourselves. That would include you as well, Randall Mims," said Mary Louise.

"You'll get no argument from me on that issue, Mrs. Brady. There have been enough murders in this town to last me a lifetime."

CHAPTER 34

OAK CLIFF DEVELOPERS

We three were quiet on the ride home. There was too much information to handle, at least for me. My first thought, and Mary Louise agreed, was to call Susan Beeson and get her involved. As the FBI ASAC in Austin, she was in the best position to decipher the puzzle of the Savolio family's involvement in Louis Devlin's development of La Cava. I was no expert in financial crimes, or the loan sharking business, but Susan was. I figured that with the new information from Patsy's will codicil, Susan would be able to move forward with some type of case against the Savolio family— perhaps not murder, but at least financial malfeasance.

We said goodbye to Det. Randall Mims and called Susan Beeson at home on that Saturday afternoon. We put the cell phone on speaker, and Mary Louise and I took turns telling her about the will and the La Cava financial arrangement between Devlin and Savolio, as well as their past business dealings. Susan listened without asking any questions and was silent for a time after we quit talking.

Then, "Oh boy! The feds have been trying to nail the Savolios for a long time. We may have them this time, thanks to you and Patsy Simmons. I need to make some calls. I might have to make a trip over there today or tomorrow. Might I have a place to stay?"

"Of course," said Mary Louise. "We'll look forward to seeing you."

"Listen to me, you two. The Savolios are a nasty bunch. They will do anything, and I mean ANYTHING, to get what they want. Keep a low profile until you see me. I intend to bring a couple of extra agents to look after you both. If you have an extra bedroom they could share, that would be excellent. I really do not want to let you two out of my sight."

"We have a third bedroom with twin beds that has its own bath."

"That will be perfect, Mary Louise," Susan said. "Anything else I need to deal with?"

"I need to make a trip to Dallas," I said. "I want to talk to the sons of Christine Devlin, primarily because they asked me to look into this. That is sort of a loose end I need to tie up. After reading Patsy's codicil, I think I'm equipped with enough info to answer at least a few of their questions. the best person to evaluate that. Also, Susan, I want you to have the letter from Patsy's safe deposit box, the cassette tape, and the financial data she included."

"Tell you what," Susan said. "I'll approve your trip to Dallas, but you'll have to wait until next Friday. That way, I can get an agent in place to go with you, and I can get more research done this week on the Savolios. The FBI must approach this situation just right, Jim, so you will have to do exactly as I say. Capisce?"

"Since when do you speak Italian?"

"Since I am now knee-deep in the ugly world of Nicky Savolio."

Susan arrived midday on Sunday, just in time for a lunch of cold boiled shrimp, a crab salad, and the requisite Bloody Mary. She was dressed in shorts and a tee shirt, with worn sneakers and her hair in a ponytail. She looked like a teenager. She carried a large briefcase full of information about the Savolio crime family and their "business" dealings over the years. Like other crime families, most of the money came from gambling, prostitution, loan sharking, and money laundering through commercial real estate properties, including those schemes created by the men now known as Louis Devlin and Johnny Amato. While many of the various properties owned by the Savolios appeared to be completely legitimate enterprises, Susan pointed out how vast sums of money could be made through illegal kickbacks during the purchasing and construction periods, and through discounts and cost-cutting measures provided by a few cooperating trade unions.

While I was anxious to get to Dallas and meet Christine Devlin's children, I had a full schedule of surgery and patients and prided myself in never having had to cancel my work schedule voluntarily. It so happened, years back, that I was mugged in the parking lot of the University Medical Center and had a concussion and lost a few days of my life. People planned weeks or even months ahead for surgical procedures and lined up family and friends to mitigate the inconvenience, so to disrupt their schedule for my own convenience, well, I just did not believe in doing that, if possible.

One of the first items on my agenda on Monday afternoon after surgeries were completed was to have a discussion with my somewhat new but valuable administrative assistant, Maya Stern, niece of Patsy Simmons.

"Why didn't you say anything about that, Maya?"

"Well, Dr. Brady, I saw no reason to discuss family matters with you. I'm concentrating on doing a good job for you, and, well, Aunt Patsy is, or rather was, a personal matter. Plus, she had cautioned me about keeping a social distance from you. She wanted to limit my proximity as well as yours from her job and the people she was involved with, for our own safety. I hope you'll continue to let me work for you."

"Maya, there is no question about that. Having learned of your recent inheritance, I didn't know if you would want to continue working."

"Dr. Brady, that inheritance from Aunt Patsy is my security blanket, my retirement fund, if you will. I have yet to decide whether I want to live in her house or sell it and invest the proceeds. I have a nice townhouse and I'm comfortable there. I can make that decision later. I'll do my best to keep up her property until I decide what to do. In the meantime, it will be business as usual for me, if that's okay with you."

"Absolutely, Maya. I am honored to have you on board."

When Mary Louise realized I was really making a trip to Dallas, she intended to accompany me to see J. J. and her only grandchild. There was no stopping her. So, after a grueling week at work, we set out Friday morning for Dallas. We were chaperoned by Agent Gerald Tipton. He and his partner, Steven Sonnenberg, had been staying at our home that week. Mary Louise had tried to do the nice host thing and feed them at least one meal per day, but the agents were never around except to sleep. One was always on duty at our home, or at my office, or with Mary Louise, depending upon our activities. The three-hour drive to Dallas was the first time we had a chance to converse with Agent Tipton except to say good morning or good night.

Agent Gerald Tipton was over six feet tall, clean-shaven, and in his mid-thirties. He hailed from the Boston area.

"How did you manage to get assigned to Austin?" Mary Louise asked.

"No offense, but at the outset, I thought it was a demotion. I mean, Texas? For a kid from Beantown, an assignment in Texas is like being banished to Siberia. I mean, the Red Sox. The Patriots. The Celtics. The Bruins. They were my life."

"And then?"

"And after a few years, I started to appreciate how nice the people were. And sports? Man, I have never seen such rabid sports fans. Especially the high schoolers. They have stadiums here that rival college stadiums in Massachusetts. Now I'm addicted to the University of Texas, the Dallas Cowboys, the Texas Rangers, and the Dallas Mavericks. And if that's not enough, I have the Texans, the Rockets, the Astros, and the Spurs as backup teams to root for. I still love and follow my Boston teams, but Texas is a place I now love to call home."

"And how do you like working with our dear friend Susan Beeson?"

He was quiet for a moment. "She grows on you. I mean, I was a little put off when I learned that I was going to have to leave my home for my next FBI assignment, and that the ASAC was new to the FBI. After a couple of years working for her, though, I've realized she is as tough as they come, and her insight into criminal behavior is uncanny. I am honored to be working with her. You folks have known her a long time?"

"Yes. We became friends after her dad fell out of a deer blind and fractured his hip, ultimately needing a hip replacement. He was the Houston police chief, and Susan was a detective. She eventually was promoted from detective lieutenant to assistant police chief, then police chief. We thought she would end her career in that position, but she surprised us by taking the ASAC position with the Austin FBI. We've been friends for over twenty years," I said.

I had spoken to Robert Johnson Jr., Christine's oldest son, telling him I had some information per their request that I investigate La Cava's financials. I told him during our conversation that I wanted to meet with him and his brothers in person, as it would be more secure.

Agent Tipton had decided that I would be dropped off at the corporate offices of Oak Cliff Development, and that he would then escort Mary Louise to J. J. and Kathryn's home in Highland Park. He said he thought I had a better chance of fending off trouble than my wife, but I think he really thought that if push came to shove, Mary Louise was more worth saving than I was. And in my heart of hearts, I could not disagree.

Oak Cliff Developers was in a midrise building in the southern part of Dallas. The area known as Oak Cliff once had a reputation for rowdiness and trouble, but in more recent years, gentrification had taken place, and it was now considered simply an older, established neighborhood.

A security officer sat behind a desk in a marbled lobby with high ceilings. The lobby itself was small, with a bank of four elevators near the entrance to the building.

"Help you?" the security man asked.

"I'm going up to see Robert Johnson at Oak Cliff Developers."

With that he stood and came around the desk. "May I see some ID, please?"

I gave him my Texas driver's license. He took it back to his desk and copied it on a small copier on his desk and returned it.

"Do you have an appointment, sir?"

"Yes."

"Please wait," he said, and he picked up a desk phone and spoke to someone whom I assumed was in Johnson's office. After a moment, he said, "Suite 700," and returned to his seat.

The building was dated, but the elevator car was new and somewhat opulent for its home. It was also speedy, and it quickly deposited me directly into another small lobby. There was a large built-in desk adjacent to the entry, where sat a young woman with headphones speaking softly into the mouthpiece. Engraved on the desk in front and in large letters was "Oak Cliff Developers."

"May I help you, sir?" she asked.

The woman appeared to be in her thirties, with large blond Texas hair. She had on thick eye shadow and mascara and bright-red lipstick, and she wore a silky white blouse with a plunging neckline.

"I'm Dr. Brady, here to see Robert Johnson."

She perused a computer monitor, apparently found the appointment, and stood. I had underestimated the depth of her plunging neckline. She had on a tight black skirt and spiked black heels, and she walked with tiny steps as though her skirt restricted the length of her steps. She was a caricature of a secretary that resembled the one on the old Carol Burnett shows. I followed her, careful to walk slowly so as not to run over the woman. She showed me into a conference room down the hall. Refreshments were set up, with sodas, water, and a coffee urn. There were even pastries set about in boxes.

"Please be seated," she said, "and help yourself."

I watched her shuffle in slow motion out of the room.

I poured myself some coffee, chose a cheese Danish, and sat down in a swivel chair. I entertained myself, swiveling while waiting. I was about to go after a bear claw when a trio of individuals entered the room.

"Dr. Brady, I'm Robert Johnson," said the leader of the pack. I stood and we shook hands. Robert was a few inches taller than me and looked to be in his early forties. He had a receding hair line—male pattern baldness inherited through the mother—wore glasses, and had on a white dress shirt with a tie that was loose at the neck.

"This is my brother Alan," he said. Alan was shorter than Robert and heavier, with a paunch he attempted to hide under a Tommy Bahama shirt.

"And this is Sam." Sam looked to be a hybrid of his brothers, in between their heights, levels of fitness, and formality of attire.

"Please, have a seat, Dr. Brady," Robert said, as he and his brothers sat at the conference table.

"Thank you for coming all this way. We know we were asking a lot of you when we asked if you could look into the finances of the La Cava project, so we wouldn't be surprised if you felt obligated to tell us in person that it was an impossible quest."

"Then you may be pleased to know some headway has been made in uncovering the La Cava financial situation and, perhaps, the reason for your mother's murder. The investigations continue, but it appears possible the reason for your mother's murder had to do with information your stepfather Louis may have shared with her about his business dealings at La Cava.

"The FBI is in fact involved in investigating the project and they have concluded that financial malfeasance is taking place through Louis's involvement with old friends and business associates from Kansas City, as you suspected. I am privy to this information because the ASAC out of Austin is the former Houston chief of police and an old friend of mine. I cannot tell you what is going to happen over the coming weeks, but I hope your house is in order here, and that you can sustain viability of your other commercial properties. You should have a conversation with Mr. Devlin about separating this business from the goings-on at La Cava. It sounds like that is already in effect, but in an informal way.

"The other reason I came up is to see the three of you in person. I'm no law enforcement professional, but I, at least, have no reason to believe your mother was involved in the problems at La Cava in any way. In fact, I believe that Louis was hoping to keep her safe by not divulging to her the steps he had taken and continues to take to fund La Cava."

All three siblings were crying at that point in time, and I was more certain than ever that these three men had nothing to do with the financial shenanigans of their stepfather.

"Alright. I don't feel I can tell you any more about the investigation at this point, but I hope you and your families will be able to continue on with the business, unscathed by La Cava. I am so sorry for your loss."

We all stood and shook hands. Having successfully presented the information I was allowed to communicate, I had nearly forgotten one thing. "Is there anything any of you would like to ask or say before I go?"

"Yes," Alan said. "When you find the bastard that killed my mother, please give me five minutes alone with him before you stick him in a jail cell. I want him to remember me for the rest of his life."

CHAPTER 35

THE SHOOTING

I took a Lyft over to Highland Park and met up with Mary Louise and Agent Tipton at J. J. and Kathryn's home. Both J. J. and Kathryn were still at work, it being late Friday morning and all. The housekeeper/nanny had let Mary Louise in and had prepared finger sandwiches for lunch. J. J. Jr. was in Mary Louise's lap, having a noontime bottle. He was having difficulty keeping his eyes open. Still, I squeezed his little hand, and he returned the favor.

"Did it go well?" she asked.

"Yes." I quietly told her an abbreviated version of the information I'd given to the three Johnson men, confirming what she already knew we were allowed to reveal.

"Murders, potential financial ruin, a crime family. That seems like so much to deal with, Jim Bob."

"I agree. I just hope they can successfully extricate their business from that of La Cava's. What a mess."

"Sad. My boy here is sleepy, and it is time to put him down for a nap. I might lie down with him to make sure he's safe and not afraid."

"I would expect nothing less. I need to make some calls. See you in a bit."

After eating, Agent Tipton returned to his position in my SUV. I called the office and checked in with Maya and Belinda. I still could not believe Maya was Patsy Simmons's niece. Belinda had made rounds on the inpatients, and all was well.

I called Susan Beeson on her cell. "Well, I have met the Johnsons, Christine's three adult children, and I'm certain they'll cooperate with you in every way."

"That is good news, and it's a good thing you're in Dallas. All hell has broken loose here. After studying those financial records that Patsy Simmons provided to you, I got subpoenas for the La Cava project's finances, and served subpoenas and warrants on Devlin, Amato, Stewart, and Winters, as well as Nicky Savolio and his associates in Kansas City. Everyone in the higher echelon of his business has, of course, lawyered up, but I think we might get them this time."

"We just left this morning. How can all that happen in a few hours?"

"We started the process-serving yesterday but waited until you were far away before we served Louis Devlin, his daughter Lisa, and his two sons-in-law. We were unable to serve Charles Fixatore because we couldn't find him. He has no local address, and he is the one loose end that worries me. He is called the Fixer for good reason. When are you coming home?"

"Probably tomorrow, possibly Sunday. Do you think we're in any danger?"

"Absolutely. When he finds out that you provided the documents that can put his boss away, he will come after you with abandon. You need to give me some time to flush him out."

"We can probably stay over until Sunday, but I have to get back in the afternoon to prepare for the Monday surgical cases."

I shared the conversation with Mary Louise, and she decided staying over until Sunday was a good idea. She discussed it with Agent Tipton, who immediately phoned ASAC Beeson for clearance. She supported the idea of us staying an extra night in Dallas to let the dust settle in the Marble Falls area.

On Saturday, Bill Hicks, J. J.'s father-in-law, took me to play golf at Highland Trails Golf Club, a men-only golf club and touted as Dallas's most exclusive fraternity house. When I entered the locker room, I encountered many sports and political figures, all sitting around having breakfast, and mostly in the buff.

"Eyes front, Jim Bob," Bill said, as we entered. "A lot of guys like to sit around in the nude; why, I do not know. The only requirement here for a dress code is that you must have a towel around your waist in the dining room."

We changed our shoes at Bill's locker but otherwise remained clothed. He greeted friends and introduced me to most of them, again, all in the nude. I finally adjusted to the situation and kept unwavering eye contact with those I met. It had been a while since I was in college, but I did not remember my fraternity brothers running around the halls with nothing on but their skivvies . . . or less.

The golf course was nothing short of spectacular and had to be one of the best courses in the state. Rock Creek meandered through the tree-lined fairways, giving the course just the right combination of water and bunkers. The shrine to Mickey Mantle, a longtime member, was inspiring. The course was difficult, and even though we did not play the back tees, I was unable to break 90. The lightning-fast bent grass greens got the best of me. But what an experience!

After the round, back in the locker room to change shoes for lunch, I met an entirely different crew of older men wearing no clothes. "Eyes front" is a term I will never forget.

Mary Louise was thrilled to spend the day with our grandson. They were napping when we returned from golf. I showered and took a siesta myself. It was nice to have a change of pace, away from the office and the operating room, and away from the worries of La Cava Golf Club and Estates. I briefly wondered how Susan was holding up, then fatigue from playing Highland Trails overtook my conscious thought processes and I was shortly in dreamland.

J. J. opted to grill steaks for dinner. He invited his in-laws, but they declined in favor of a social function that required their attendance. Kathryn joined us for dinner, and it was a most pleasant evening, made so especially due to the absence of her mother. I managed to get along with Mrs. Hicks when it was necessary, but she was born and raised in Highland Park, she lived in Highland Park, and to her, no other place on earth mattered. I often wanted to offer, free of charge, the removal of the stick someone had inserted up her posterior years ago, but I always quieted myself just in the nick of time. I was especially thankful that Kathryn took after her father and not her mother.

Sunday morning came too soon. Tears were shed, mostly by Mary Louise, goodbyes said with promises to see each other soon, and she and I and Agent Tipton were off.

"I miss him so much already," said Mary Louise.

"J. J. Jr.?"

"Yes. I wished we lived closer."

"We're only three hours away. That's close enough for me," I said.

"But it would be nice just to be able to drop by and see him every day, even for a few minutes."

"And then it would be babysitting chores and who knows what else. It wouldn't be fun after a while."

"Says you, not me. I love our grandson."

"I love him too, Mary Louise, just from afar."

That conversation produced a quiet ride back to Granite Falls.

There was some discussion with Agent Tipton about the logistics of our return. He wanted Mary Louise and I to stay together. I needed to go to the office and review the cases for the next day, Monday. One of us needed to go to the vet's office and pick up Tip. We finally agreed that I was safer at the Hill Country Medical Center than at home. So, I drove us all to the house. Agent Tipton's plan was to drive Mary Louise in either her car or his governmental sedan to retrieve Tip, drop them back off at home and secure them inside with the alarm set, and return to the clinic to follow me home. He also insisted on calling Lt. Randall Mims, apprising him of the situation with the Devlin group, and to be on the lookout for any sort of trouble at the Brady home until he returned with me safely in hand. He also called Susan Beeson and told her of the plan, and she put herself on alert for a call from Mary Louise for any sort of problem that was brewing at home.

I returned to the clinic undisturbed, at least as far as I knew. I entered the office building from the main hospital entrance, greeted the security guard on duty, and informed him of my intent to go to my office and review the charts and X-rays for Monday cases. I also hinted to him of the trouble brewing in town between the FBI and out-of-town undesirables.

"Are you armed?" I asked him.

"Yes, sir," he said, then he stood and showed me his holstered Colt .45 automatic, a favorite among law enforcement and military personnel. "And I know how to use it, Dr. Brady. You're safe with me here."

I walked through the tiled hallways, always with the slight medicinal smell, to the clinic building elevators, and rode up to the third floor. The place was deserted. I stopped by the kitchen and made a fresh cup of coffee with the Keurig system we had recently purchased. I unlocked my private office, sat and reviewed the contents of the desktop, and signed documents and dictated the required notes and reports. Once that chore was done, I perused the patients' charts for the next day. We had seven cases to do: three knee replacements, two virgin and one redo hip replacement, and an ankle replacement. That would be a full day's work. I started to get tired thinking about it.

We had converted an unused office into a radiology suite with radiology boxes on three walls so we could spread the films out and look at them in groups rather than struggle with looking at the films one at a time on a single X-ray box. I was standing there reviewing the films of the redo hip replacement, deciding whether bone grafting would be necessary, when I heard a distant scream, then what sounded like the pop a gunshot would make. I shut off the view boxes, turned off the overhead light, and quietly shut the door. I stepped back to my office, shut off the light in there as well, and closed and locked the door. I'd had no reason to fear for my safety in my office, so I was bare . . . unarmed.

I stood by my office door and listened for abnormal sounds. I heard the elevator "ping" in the distance and waited. We had tiled the floors when the building was first built, but we did not appreciate the echo of noise that would be produced by so many doctors and ancillary staff. We had decided to carpet it the prior year, and it was a good decision unless one found oneself hiding in one's office trying to hear footsteps. I held my breath and listened. I saw and heard my office door handle rattle, then heard a foot kick against the door.

"Brady, if you're in there, you might as well come out now, because any way you cut it, I'm going to kill you."

I was silent, then heard a foot kick the door again. I waited for what seemed like an eternity, quietly unlocked the door, and looked around outside. No one was visible. I gently shut the door and headed for the stairwell. There were two, one on each end of the floor. I avoided the one adjacent to the elevator bank, figuring that the stranger would take the elevator because it was fastest, at least on a Sunday. My office was on the other end, nearest the back stairwell. I opened the door as quietly as possible. I stepped into the stairwell, took off my boots, and closed the door silently. I padded down the two stairwells to the elevator bank of the clinic building. I had parked on the hospital entry side, in an unlabeled parking spot. I had avoided using my personalized spot, which was near the door I was about to exit from. As quietly as possible, I opened the door and peeked through it. There was a man standing near my parking spot, smoking. I let the door close gently, then took the other route into the hallway that led into the hospital lobby.

I smelled the blood before I saw it. The security guard was lying in a pool of it, shot in the chest. He had his Colt .45 in his right hand, but I doubted he had a chance to fire it. I had only heard one shot. There were no other people around. I wondered if the person who screamed had called 911, but I could not wait to find that out. I slipped on my boots and started walking toward my SUV. I heard my name shouted and I started running. I hit the OPEN button on the remote and jumped into the driver's seat. I could see the man after me stop, realize he would have to chase me in his car, and divert his run at me for his vehicle. I started the engine and tore out of the parking lot.

I knew of only one place that I might be safe, and I headed out on Highway 71. I saw a car in my rearview mirror and sped up. I made the turn onto FM 2147 on two wheels and floored the accelerator. The Horseshoe Bay Police Department was committed to keeping the speed limit to 45 mph, so when my speedometer hit 75 mph, I hoped they were out in force to at least lend me a hand. But no police cars were in sight.

The driver behind me caught up somehow, extended his left arm out the driver's window, and fired a couple of rounds at my back windshield. The tempered glass broke but did not shatter. I continued east, saw my destination in the distance, and drove onto the shoulder. I hit the entry parking lot at 70 mph, avoided a few cars, then slammed on the brake with both feet, stopped the car on a dime, and jumped out, leaving the truck door open, and ran for the entry of my destination.

My assailant, who I assumed was the Fixer, was right behind me and jumped out of his vehicle only a few seconds after I did. I pulled the entry door open and let it slam against the wall of the building, jumped into the packed room, and dove under the first table I saw.

"He's trying to kill me!" I yelled as I fell.

Imagine the Fixer's surprise when he ran into a room with thirty-odd officers from law enforcement, all suddenly standing and drawing their weapons. He made the mistake of brandishing, then raising his weapon and pointing it at me as all the officers in the room opened fire.

He died in a hail of bullets in the main dining room of the Hole in One diner, the safest place in town at lunchtime on Sunday after church.

CHAPTER 36

HAPPY ENDINGS

Del Anderson, owner and publisher of our local paper, the Highlander, got the exclusive reporting rights on the business dealings of Louis Devlin and his associations with the criminal underworld of his old friend, Nicky Savolio. I couldn't tell what she enjoyed more—having the scoop and the rights of first publication, or having the editors of the Austin American Statesman, the Dallas Morning News, and the Houston Chronicle beg her for bits and pieces of the real story. Probably the latter. And what small-town editor/publisher/owner wouldn't?

Devlin tried to play the innocent man and blamed all his financial troubles on the Savolio family and its shell corporations masking as real investors and their intrusion into his legitimate businesses, unbeknownst to him. However, that position eventually went by the wayside, as both Bill Stewart and Kirk Winters, his two sons-in-law, turned state's evidence and became witnesses for the FBI in the cases against Devlin, Savolio, and their associates. Louis Devlin was in fact a part of the scheme to defraud the legitimate investors, his overall plan being to make a fortune for himself and his criminal associates and leave the legitimate investors of La Cava high and dry.

That brought up the issue of three murders: Christine Devlin, Patsy Simmons, and Greta Amato. Charles the Fixer was killed at the Hole in One and obviously could not testify. However, the gun recovered at the scene contained bullets that matched the one that killed the security guard at HCMC and the one used to kill Christine Devlin. DNA also recovered at the scene of Patsy Simmons's murder matched DNA samples from the Fixer. There was no DNA recovered in the drowning of Greta Amato, so the FBI could not prove he had killed her, but it was presumed by all that he had done so.

Devlin swore on multiple occasions that he had nothing to do with the deaths of the three women. He repeatedly testified that the murders were the doing of the Fixer at the behest of Nicky Savolio in order to keep Devlin in line. He had been suspicious that Christine Devlin and Patsy Simmons knew too much, which is why he sent the Fixer down to Texas in the first place. The murder of Greta Amato could not be proven, so that matter was left to suspicions only. However, the day Mary Louise and I saw Devlin and Johnny Amato fighting on the green at La Cava hole eighteen might have implied that Amato was none too happy about his wife being drowned and took that moment on the golf course to carry out his frustrations.

Both Devlin and Amato pled guilty to financial crimes, as did Nicky Savolio, but all denied culpability in the three murders. Since the Fixer was dead, the origin of the order to murder the three women could not be proven. And since the charges of financial crimes and fraud carried much lighter sentences than murder, the feds estimated that the miscreants could be out of prison and back in business in five to ten years with time off for good behavior.

All assets of those charged in the La Cava Golf Club and Estates case were frozen. It took months to sort through the financial maze, but with the help of Bill Stewart and Kirk Winters, the legitimate investors were returned most of their money. Collectively, they decided to take their funds and purchase the golf club. Dr. Buck Owens and his investor group led that charge, and felt that with already 100 members, they could grow that into twice that many, which would be more than adequate with their entry fees and dues to run the club at a profit. What the locals knew, that perhaps out-of-towners did not know, is that you do not necessarily have to have a housing development adjacent to a golf course for the course to be successful. In a small area like Horseshoe Bay and Marble Falls, there are many opportunities for a beautiful residence either on the water or with a water view. For some, driving a golf cart to the course might be essential, whereas for some, living on the water and driving five or ten minutes to the course was preferential. The La Cava Golf Club would probably make it on its own merit. The residential portion was not essential.

Therefore, the real estate development portion of the project was a quagmire. There were realistically only 100 buildable acres at a reasonable price to make a profit. Since 100 acres sat on granite, and 100 acres had granite outcroppings and was designated as common area, the various accountants and lawyers hired felt that it could take years to profit from only the 100 acres of an "easy build." While most of the infrastructure was in place, there was not a single contract to build a house at the time the arrests took place. Perhaps Texas investors knew a little more about building on rocks, as no one was willing to take over that project, even for a few cents on the dollar.

Fortunately for my family, the Brady name was kept out of all court proceedings. Since Lisa Stewart had opened the books to me, and possibly to other potential investors, and since her husband and her sister's husband had turned state's evidence, attorneys for the defendants presumed she was responsible for leaking the information that sealed her father's fate. I never saw her again in my office. Too much water under the bridge, I presumed. She seemed to be such a nice young woman, it was hard for me to believe she was involved in her father's shenanigans. Last I heard, both she and her husband and her sister and her family had moved back to Dallas. How the sons-in-law were doing after turning state's evidence, I did not know. Maybe they got together with Christine's three children in Dallas and have gone on to bigger and better things. Or at least honest things.

For Mary Louise and me, life returned to normal. We started making a few more trips to see our grandson. Occasionally, I stayed home and played golf, but most times I accompanied her. She mentioned, one evening at home, sitting on the terrace watching Lake LBJ, that we should buy a second small home in Dallas so we could watch J. J. Jr. grow up.

"A second house. We haven't talked about a second house since we moved to the Hill Country. But in Dallas? I would be more excited if they lived in Colorado Springs or Palm Desert, where there is golf."

"There isn't golf in Dallas?" she asked.

"Well, yes, but not like Colorado or California."

"I'm sure Bill Hicks would be happy to get you into Highland Trails Golf Club."

"Oh, I'm sure, but I would have to practice strolling around in the nude. 'Eyes front' is the motto."

"Men walk around in the buff? At the golf club? Why on earth?"

"Even at mealtime, although a towel around the waist is required in the dining room."

She thought for a moment. "Wonder what kind of views we could find in Dallas."

"Probably have to be from the balcony of a midrise."

We looked at each other.

"Rosewood?" she said.

"Cheers!"

READ ON FOR A SNEAK PEEK
OF ACT OF TREACHERY

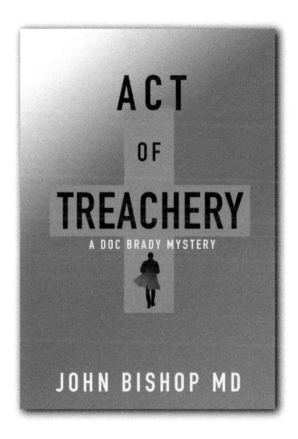

I hope you have enjoyed *Act of Aggression,* the ninth book in
the Doc Brady Mystery series. I'm pleased to present you with
a sneak peek of *Act of Treachery,* the tenth book.

Please visit **JohnBishopAuthor.com** to learn more.

CHAPTER 1

SHERIFF JOAN WILCOX

Burnet County Sheriff Joan Wilcox had become a family friend to both Mary Louise, my loyal and understanding wife, and me after the Louis Devlin matter had been resolved. Devlin, originally from Kansas City, had changed his name after a stint in prison in a failed attempt to "go straight" and leave his underworld roots behind. Unfortunately, they say your past catches up with you eventually, and how true that had been for Devlin. He had attempted to defraud a group of local investors involved in the construction of the new La Cava Golf Club and Estates. And, according to Del Anderson, owner of the Highlander, the local paper in Horseshoe Bay, Texas, his criminal partners were led by the notorious Nicky Savolio, Devlin's boyhood chum from the old Italian Kansas City neighborhood they both grew up in.

The feds and the media had invaded our little piece of Eden in the Texas Hill Country for months while the FBI and other government agencies tried to unravel Devlin's scheme to put at least $100 million in his and his criminal associates' pockets. Private sources said that Devlin took his chances and aligned himself with the Savolio family rather than turn state's evidence, thinking that a prison term was better than a death sentence from the Kansas City people. As it turned out, he got shanked while serving a fifteen-year term in Leavenworth for financial crimes, and he bled to death before the guards could come to his assistance.

While my day job consisted of performing the duties of an orthopedic surgeon specializing in hip and knee problems at the Hill Country Medical Center, I have repeatedly found myself embroiled in precarious situations in which I had no business. My foray into the Devlin business almost got me killed, and were it not for a herd of police officers and sheriff's deputies in the Hole in One diner having Sunday brunch, I would have gone to meet my Maker prematurely. Which would serve me right, some would probably say, as payback for Dr. James Robert Brady's recurrent involvement in matters of mystery and sometimes murder. Stick to your job, stick to what you know, stay out of trouble, people would say, including on occasion, Mary Louise, my long-suffering wife and partner of over thirty years. But she knew I had a penchant for trying to solve the unsolvable and was supportive up to a point. When my life was put in danger, however, she drew the line, which is why I had been so good and unpredictably uncurious for the past year or more. But does a leopard change its spots? Hardly.

And so it was that I found myself seated in Sheriff Joan Wilcox's office, sipping a fresh cup of strong coffee that Sharon Baldwin, deputy and factotum to the sheriff, had made. Deputy Baldwin was a full-figured woman with light-brown skin. She specialized in massive designs for her beautifully braided hair, with multiple adornments. That day she had managed to weave her thick plaits through a pair of handcuffs which, despite how it sounded, was actually a statement in nouveau art.

Sharon was quite the contrast to her diminutive boss, who probably weighed no more than 110 pounds soaking wet, and whose pale complexion with freckles suggested an Irish heritage and a habit of minimal sun exposure. That morning she had on a white dress shirt and a blazer, with her badge clipped onto the outside of the jacket pocket.

"You're dressed for a meeting?" I asked.

"Yes, oh great perceptive one. A meeting with the town council."

"Have you been bad again, Joan? Have you been showing up the boys in your investigations?"

"Nothing like that. They're worried about these last two murders, that we might have a serial killer in our midst."

There had been three murders in the past few months, all characterized by blows to the head with an instrument that resembled a hatchet, according to the coroner and chief of Hill Country Medical Center pathology, Dr. Jerry Reed.

"Do you have any clues?"

"Nothing, really. We've found three bodies, two female and one male, each behind a different convenience store in different areas of two counties, one in Burnet and two in Llano. The Llano County sheriff and I have spoken on several occasions and have included the chiefs of police of Marble Falls, Horseshoe Bay, Granite Falls, Granite Shoals, and Kingsland in the discussions, but to no avail. The only common factor in the three murders was a bag of groceries found at each crime scene, as though each victim was attacked after exiting the store."

"Each attack occurred in the evening I assume?"

"Yes. Each was estimated to have occurred between 10 p.m. and one in the morning."

"That's pretty late for grocery shopping, don't you think, Joan?"

"Yes, but if you think about it, different folks have different shopping patterns. Could be late-shift people just getting off work, or employees stopping by at the store on the way to work. We found nothing to relate the victims in any way."

"So, why am I here, in danger of missing my tee time?"

I tried to reserve Friday afternoons and Saturday mornings for golf games with my bandit friends. Sometimes an emergency would arise on Thursday, and I would have to take care of it on

Friday, but I had slowed my schedule down a bit to try and preserve my quality time, also known as my mental health time.

"When Sharon called your office to schedule this meeting, she was told that you had to be on the road by 11 a.m. so as not to miss your tee time. It's 10:30, and we're almost done."

"Good. I appreciate that. The thing is, I don't know why you called me. I am an orthopedic surgeon and try not to get in harm's way these days. I try and stick to my own business, stay out of trouble."

"That might be true, but you will never stay out of harm's way and mind your own business. I called Mary Louise yesterday and told her I was asking you to meet with me about these cases. I thought if you reviewed them, you might give a fresh perspective on the killings."

"This is a first for me, having a law enforcement representative contact me for assistance. Normally I would have to beg for scraps of information and plead for permission to get involved in such matters."

"I came to know Assistant Special Agent in Charge Susan Beeson well during the Devlin investigation, and she showed me how useful you could be in certain situations and investigations. And I felt I owed you a debt of gratitude for your support during my re-election campaign. And so here we are."

Susan Beeson was one of our oldest friends. She had been Houston's chief of police, following in her father's footsteps, when she accepted the position of ASAC of the FBI, Austin bureau. She and I had been paired through eight or nine crimes of different sorts over the years. She even had a badge made for me during a Houston investigation some years back. I kept it framed in my office. It was much safer there than in my possession. I had been shot at a few times, mugged, concussed, and run off the I-10 freeway in Houston. I could understand Mary Louise's concern for my safety. When I carried that badge, it for me was a license to steal. Without the badge, reality set in and I was a little more cautious about where I stepped, because going "bare" reminded me of my limitations.

In addition, Joan Wilcox had been elected a couple of years back as the first female sheriff of Burnet County. Her predecessor had been a real horse's ass, part of the good-old-boy network that had prevailed in Central Texas for many years. For her re-election, Mary Louise and I had held a few fundraisers in her honor, and getting the doctors and nurses at the massive Hill Country Medical Center behind her candidacy had turned the tide in her favor.

Joan opened one of her desk drawers and pulled out a sheaf of papers held together by a large clip. "Here you go, Jim Bob."

She handed me the stack of paperwork. I stood and shook her hand.

"Thanks for this," I said. "I'll get back to you if and when I find something."

She stood. "No, thank YOU. I hope to speak with you soon."

On the way out, I stopped by Deputy Baldwin's desk. "That is some do you have today. Who would have ever thought? Handcuffs and hair. Sheer genius."

"Oh, Dr. Brady, you are so nice about my hair. Most people think I am crazy."

"Everyone must have a passion, Sharon. Your hair art may be unconventional, but your passion and talent are clear, nonetheless. I will see you when I see you, Officer."

"Dr. Brady, you did not lose my business card, did you?"

"No, Sharon, I have several now, so I am in good shape. Thanks much."

She winked at me as I exited the door.

ABOUT THE AUTHOR

Dr. John Bishop has led a triple life. This orthopedic surgeon and keyboard musician has combined two of his talents into a third, as the author of the beloved Doc Brady mystery series. Beyond applying his medical expertise at a relatable and comprehensible level, Dr. Bishop, through his fictional counterpart Doc Brady, also infuses his books with his love of not only Houston and Galveston, Texas, but especially with his love for his adored wife. Bishop's talented Doc Brady is confident yet humble; brilliant, yet a genuinely nice and funny guy who happens to have a knack for solving medical mysteries. Above all, he is the doctor who will cure you of your blues and boredom. Step into his world with the first five books of the series, and you'll be clamoring for more.